POWDER SMOKE

A Jim Stringer Novel

ANDREW MARTIN

corsair

CORSAIR

First published in the UK in 2021 by Corsair
This paperback edition published in 2022

1 3 5 7 9 10 8 6 4 2

A CIP catalogue record for this book
is available from the British Library.

PB ISBN: 978-1-4721-5484-2

Printed and bound in Great Britain by Clays Ltd, Elcograf S.p.A.

Papers used by Corsair are from well-managed forests
and other responsible sources.

Corsair
An imprint of
Little, Brown Book Group
Carmelite House
50 Victoria Embankment
London EC4Y 0DZ

An Hachette UK Company
www.hachette.co.uk

www.littlebrown.co.uk

POWDER SMOKE

Cast of characters

(Un-named or purely incidental characters not included.)

Jim Stringer – a detective inspector with the London & North Eastern Railway police, based at York.

Lydia Stringer – Jim's wife.

Bernadette Stringer – their daughter.

Harry Stringer – their son.

Superintendent Saul Weatherill (also known as 'the Chief') – Jim's boss.

Jack 'Kid' Durrant – a sharpshooter, writer of Western tales and aspiring film star.

Cynthia Lorne – a film star.

Tom Brooks – her husband, a director and producer of films.

Walter Bassett – an American connoisseur of the Old West; also a sub-postmaster at York.

Mary Ainsworth – a balloonist of York.

Cliff Hemingway – night sergeant in the York LNER Police Office.

Wright – elderly Chief Clerk of the York LNER Police.

Stephen Spencer – a young constable with the York LNER Police.

Colonel Maynard – head of the LNER Police, based in London.

Lowry – desk sergeant of the York City Police.

Ibbotson – a constable with the London, Midland & Scottish Railway Police.

Backhouse – a farmer's son, and driver of a car for hire at Bolton Abbey.

Mr Marshall – a gamekeeper at Bolton Abbey.

Superintendent Monk – an officer with the Leeds City Police.

Paul Goodall – driver of a car for hire at Bolton Abbey.

Jerry Miller – a film-maker, business partner of Tom Brooks.

Kevin – a young American film editor.

Fred Bannister – a publisher.

The Green brothers – two criminals (probably), resident in Leeds.

Mrs Ellis – keeper of a tea rooms at Knaresborough.

Miles Howell – a constable with the LNER Railway Police, based at Pickering.

Sidney – a car mechanic.

Vernon Bibby – formerly a 'lad porter' with the LNER.

Ezra Clifton – an elderly freelance carter based at Pickering.

1

YORK STATION, ABOUT HALF-PAST SIX ON THE EVENING OF SUNDAY, 6 DECEMBER 1925

In the Parlour Bar of the Second-Class Refreshment Room, Detective Inspector Jim Stringer was filling in his detective diary.

Jim had taken his diary into the Parlour Bar at six o'clock with the intention of having a pint of brown ale; it was now gone half-past and he'd had two. There was nobody else but Jim in the Parlour Bar, which was widely ignored in favour of the adjacent room, lately billed as a 'snack bar'. There weren't even any people in the framed photos around the walls, which showed the station as it had been before the North Eastern Railway became the London & North Eastern Railway and before the footbridge had been put in. There were studies of the newspaper stall and bookshop with the shutters down. On the main 'Up' and 'Down' platforms were a couple of luggage barrows, but no human beings.

When it came to the diary, Jim's practice was to make a quick note when what was called an 'occurrence' occurred, then flesh it out later. The previous month – November – had been quiet, and Jim suspected this might be the new trend. While men in the wider world were being laid off from work, the London & North Eastern Railway was boosting what it called police 'manpower', the accountants having twigged that the more police you had, the more money you saved. Why? Because policemen protected not only 'assets' but also 'revenue'. The Police Office on the main 'Up' platform accommodated a dozen more constables than this time last year. Some came from down south, and Jim had a job to remember their names. They soaked up a lot of the investigating Jim used to do and now, as a relatively senior member of a very bureaucratic organization, he found much of his time given over to paperwork.

The number of crimes was certainly falling, but whether on account of 'manpower', Jim couldn't say. The station was better lit, and modern trains often had open seating, whereas the old-fashioned bad lads had favoured the secrecy of compartments. Jim, too, preferred compartments. He also favoured gaslight over electricity and slow, stopping trains to 'streamlined' expresses – and maybe this was to be expected of any railway copper of twenty years' service and a somewhat romantic bent.

He'd come to the most recent occurrence. Twice in the past week a fellow called Barraclough had been found to be occupying a first-class seat on a Leeds train while in possession of a third-class ticket. This was not an offence unless Barraclough had 'fraudulent intent'; unless he knew what he was doing, in other words, and it seemed to Jim that Barraclough must have known, since until recently he had been working for the LNER, and in the passenger department of the York District at that. Yet he was a highly respectable-seeming gent who'd apologized both times for his 'mistake' and shifted smartly into third class when the 'error' was pointed out to him. The second time, his name and address had been taken, and the question for Jim was whether Barraclough should receive a summons to the magistrates' court in order – very likely – to be fined 40 shillings under the Regulation of Railways Act, 1889. Jim put a question mark next to Barraclough's name.

The next question was whether he should have another pint of brown. Or maybe a half. The one thing in the Parlour Bar that was moving (apart from Jim) was the minute hand of the clock, and it now showed five minutes to seven or, as the London & North Eastern Railway called it, 'six fifty-five'. At seven, Jim was due to meet Lydia at the footbridge, so they could walk together to a charitable function at the Railway Institute: an ill-conceived event, it seemed to Jim, kicking off at seven and combining card playing and dancing.

Jim thumbed back through the pages of the Detective Diary. The year hadn't been completely quiet, and some of the pages back in early October were dense with occurrences. Jim read the words 'double murder', underlined. Amid the detailing of those heavy events, he kept seeing a certain name, always carefully written in full and never abbreviated, that made him feel sad, which in turn made him want to order another drink. The case had flared dramatically, and just as quickly fizzled out for the shortage of leads. It remained unresolved.

Jim pocketed the diary and stepped out into the station lobby.

To the left lay the station exit and carriage drive – which was more like a motor car drive these days. To the right were the ticket gates for the platforms. Over opposite lay the booking hall, but the Christmas tree blocked Jim's view of it. In North Eastern days, the tree had been just that: a tree, with paper streamers, but now there was a Christmas 'display'. Whereas the old tree had been dark at night, this one was illuminated with electric lights that went off and on – which they were *supposed* to do, but it seemed like a faulty circuit or whatever was the term.

Alongside the tree was something resembling a boat. It had been knocked up from spare timber in the Carriage Works and was clad in railway seating material, probably Rexine. It was meant to be a giant shoe, because the theme of the display was 'The Old Woman Who Lived in a Shoe', but you wouldn't necessarily know from looking at it. The Old Woman herself was a mannequin from

Brown's department store in a Victorian dress and a grey wig. The children she didn't know what to do with were so many baby dolls propped up to stare glassily from the edge of the shoe. In other words, this display would have been a candidate for any chamber of horrors going. In front of the shoe were red fire buckets, into which the public were invited to throw coppers in aid of the Old Comrades Association to help war widows and orphans.

This was all part of the new-fangledness of the new company, along with public telephones on every platform except number 14. The wireless room in the Station Hotel was part of the newness. So were the very fast trains that sometimes – especially at night – ran right through York with electric light blazing in the carriages, and the washed-out faces of passengers not giving the station so much as a glance.

Jim watched the tree lights flash three times. Then he turned and walked towards the ticket gates, where the ticket collector on duty was a woman: Margaret Long. Margaret was a kind of leftover from the War, when many women had worked in the station.

'You're looking very smart, Jim.'

He was wearing his four-guinea suit, made to measure in blue worsted.

'So are you, Margaret.'

She touched her peaked cap and coloured up rather. Margaret quite fancied Jim, as Jim's wife Lydia – who knew Margaret from wartime canteening on the station – often said. Lydia would also suggest that Jim quite fancied Margaret, which was also true.

'Off somewhere nice, Jim?'

'Don't know.'

'You don't know?'

'It's a dance and whist drive at the Institute.'

'A dance *and* whist drive? I suppose they have the cards first, then the dancing.'

'No. They both kick off at seven.'

'Then I suppose they'll be in different rooms.'

'They're both in the reading room.'

'Dancing *and* whist . . . in the *reading room*?'

'My aim is to play whist badly, get knocked out, then go to the bar.'

'Where you can get knocked out all over again, Jim Stringer! What's it in aid of, anyhow?'

'York Station Mutual Aid.'

'Well . . . Lydia likes all that sort of thing, doesn't she?'

Now that was a clear case of damning with faint praise. Jim said, 'She knows some of the ladies who are laying on the supper.' Those ladies were involved somehow in the York Women's Co-Operative Guild, for which Lydia worked.

Margaret Long said, 'Is the supper *after* the dancing and whist?'

'During.'

'And what time does it all wind up?'

'Half eight.'

'You're having me on, Jim Stringer.'

But he had merely described the programme as he understood it.

He could see Lydia waiting by the footbridge. 'Better go.'

But as Jim approached Lydia, she turned and began climbing the steps of the footbridge. She hadn't seen him yet, and she was going to the other side of the station – from the 'Up' to the 'Down'. That wasn't so irregular: their arrangement was always 'the footbridge' – could mean either side. The 'Down' side had the draw of a small newspaper and tea kiosk near the foot of the steps. Jim followed Lydia over the footbridge. In her cloche hat, shortish skirt and grey calfskin boots she looked very fashionable – and young. Not forty, at any rate. Lydia was slightly bow-legged, which Jim thought was great, but he knew not to mention it because he had done once . . .

She still hadn't seen him. Her bootsteps echoed under the great vault of the station roof. The gas lights along the platforms seemed – in Jim's imagination – to be illuminating cold, empty streets, and the clock over the main 'Up' stood in for the moon. There was one train in – over on the platform known as Scarborough Corner, waiting patiently for no-one. And there was a rake of apparently dead carriages on Platform 10, one of the bays near the kiosk. Jim knew – but didn't really think about it – that those carriages would eventually be collected by a biggish engine, and a train to Liverpool would be formed. You'd be able to have dinner on that train; it was a semi-express.

Lydia stepped off the footbridge, and turned right, into the Ladies. Jim waited for her outside the kiosk, which was shuttered and closed, it being Sunday. One minute to seven by the big clock. An engine was backing onto the Liverpool carriages. Lydia was taking her time in the Ladies, but then again, she'd come direct from work – from the offices of the Women's Co-Operative Guild, which were above the main Co-Op on Railway Street. She'd need a bit of a spruce-up for the party. She often went in on Sundays. Just now she'd be in front of the mirror, applying a little kohl to deepen the darkness of her eyes, which were already very dark.

The clock said three after seven. The station was regaining a little life: a flurry of people coming over the footbridge, approaching with a quick clatter, as if blown along beyond the ticket gate by the bad weather. Passengers for Liverpool, no doubt, or Manchester or Leeds, where that train would also be calling. Lydia stepped out of the Ladies. She looked lost for a moment; then she saw Jim.

'I thought you were going to get Mary to press those trousers?' she said. (Mary came to their house three days

8

a week to clean and iron, but Jim never felt able to ask her to clean or iron anything.) Lydia said, 'Undo your bottom waistcoat button, Jim,' and did it for him.

'Margaret said I looked smart,' said Jim.

'Yes, she would do.'

Lydia kissed Jim. 'Your tie's nice, though – or it would be if it was straight.'

As she was straightening his tie, Jim was aware of a man coming fast over the footbridge. His wide-brimmed grey hat was pulled down low, and he was more elegant and purposeful than the rest of the passengers: a cut above.

Lydia had bought the tie for Jim last week. It was dark blue with little white spots. She was forever taking Jim in hand, so she bought most of his clothes, including the coat he was wearing, which was black and double-breasted with even blacker velvet lapels (or 'revers', as Lydia called them). Jim thought it rather old-fashioned; made him feel as if he was off to an expensive funeral. Despite being a socialist, Lydia appeared to want to dress him like Mr Baldwin.

The man in the wide-brimmed hat was descending the steps. It was a cold night, but the grey muffler over most of his face was over-egging it. He was heading for the Liverpool train, gripping two bags: a biggish blue-and-black carpet bag and a small leather bag, like a doctor's. He passed Jim and Lydia, walking fast.

'Let's go, Jim,' said Lydia. 'There'll be hell on if we miss

Harriet Howard's welcome speech.' Harriet Howard was somebody involved in charitable work. 'Oh, no – hang on a mo.' She was heading back towards the Ladies. 'Left my powder by the sink,' she called back.

The clock said seven after seven. The clockface was so big you could always tell the time to the minute, and Jim had the feeling these minutes were becoming important. He had seen that blue-and-black carpet bag before, he thought.

The platform guard – a young chap, Jim knew him by sight – was waiting to give the Liverpool train the 'right away', but not quite imminently, because Jim could see either the fireman or the driver on the platform up ahead – probably the fireman, since he was quite young, whereas drivers tended to be quite old. This fireman was looking under the boiler frame of the loco for some reason. But there didn't seem anything amiss: his manner wasn't agitated, and now he climbed back up to the footplate.

But now another man climbed down – from the carriage before the engine – and closed the door behind him. It was the muffled-up man, still muffled up. He set his two bags down on the platform, and his black-gloved left hand, held down by his side, was somehow too long. He was looking at Jim. The third man on the platform, the guard, was some way to Jim's left, about in line with the middle of the train.

The guard didn't seem to be aware of either Jim or the

muffled-up man. He was absorbed in a little book: his guard's manual, possibly. His whistle was in his lips, and the hand that held the book also held the green flag. The fireman – obviously the more active of the footplate pair (or the one who did all the work) – was leaning from the footplate and looking towards the guard for the 'right away'. The fireman called out to him, an echoing shout, not too polite. The guard barely looked up as he blew the whistle and gave the flag a single wave. He was evidently more interested in learning how to be a competent platform guard than actually being one.

Jim could hear Lydia's returning steps behind him. The engine was surely about to make its first lurching chuff. But the muffled-up man was now pointing at Jim – pointing with the revolver that was in his black-gloved left hand. His right hand seemed to stroke the top of the gun; he had moved back the hammer. He had Jim in point-blank range. When he squeezed the trigger, the world would be as black as his glove and Jim would be dead. So Jim ought to be coming up with important thoughts, but the only thing in his mind was an image of a large, pink balloon, sailing through a summer sky.

2

FLASHBACK TO
THE LAST SATURDAY IN AUGUST

The Gala

The famous balloon was high above the showground of the York Summer Gala, as though to signal its location, but everybody *knew* its location. The Gala had been held in the gardens of Bootham Hospital on the last Saturday in August for half a century, the war years excepted.

The balloon had come into view as Jim turned into Exhibition Square. He had walked from York Station to Exhibition Square many times. The walk took ten minutes – at least, it always had done, but today it seemed longer. Jim put it down to the heat and the fact that every time he put on a spurt of speed, his right leg hurt. His right thigh had been crocked on the Western Front, and it was obviously going to stay crocked. The nightmares were going to continue as well. The main mistake people made about the war, it seemed to Jim, was to say it was over. His suit coat prickled through his shirt. At the Gala, he was going to meet the Chief, who wanted to take him to a shooting show.

Jim crossed in front of the Theatre Royal. A clanking, crowded tram was doing the same. When the balloon was new, Jim recalled, it had been red-and- white-striped, like an inflated Punch & Judy booth, but now it had faded to dirty pink. Dangling from it was a middle-aged lady – a balloonist, naturally. She was well-known, forever cropping up in the *Yorkshire Evening Press*: York's very own aviatrix, Mary Ainsworth. Jim was certain Mary Ainsworth must be smiling gracefully as she floated over the Gala, because that was what she was always doing when pictured in *The Press*. She wore a dun-coloured, one-piece trouser suit, and the kind of round hat worn by people who get fired from cannons. Hanging down beside her was an untidy-looking length of rope which let the gas out of the balloon. She would pull on this when she wanted to descend, but she wouldn't be doing that until the Gala ended, and when the York Gala ended, summer would end with it.

Half the town was in the hospital grounds, it appeared. Somewhere in that throng an organ machine blared, a mechanical version of a song Jim's daughter Bernadette often sang: 'If You Were the Only Girl In The World'. (In her own mind Bernadette undoubtedly *was* the only girl in the world.) Steam engines steamed, petrol engines smoked; every other person, it seemed to Jim, was eating a toffee apple, and continued blithely doing so even as rifles repeatedly cracked – so there must be a shooting gallery within the crowd, but that wasn't the kind of gunplay Jim had been summoned to see.

Over the heads of the crowd, a great red and gold gondola reared up every few seconds: called a 'fairy boat', it was more like a fairy *barge*, with a crude Union Jack painted on the hull. Screams accompanied its swinging. There was a smallish big wheel on which more sedate Yorkists sat. It came to Jim that the lightbulbs on the wheel were all switched on, but lost in the glare of the afternoon. Suddenly there was a single loud gunshot, and for a moment the Gala crowd was stilled, but this was not what was known in the Police Office as an occurrence. The wheel kept turning, the fairy boat kept swinging.

The only consequence was a drift of people to the far side of the garden, towards the great grey mansion of the Bootham Mental Hospital itself, presiding so incongruously over the festivities held in aid of it. Jim joined the drift.

The shooting show was housed in something like a boxy circus tent, but it was made of wood as well as canvas, and somehow incorporated two kinds of wagon of the kind hauled by traction engines. Overall, it resembled a giant, coloured sideboard. It was basically yellow – the colour of the Wild West, Jim supposed – and there was a doorway in the middle covered by a green velvet curtain. The figure of a Red Indian had been painted at one end, a cowboy at the other, and the painted cowboy stood next to a painted cactus. In front of the tent was a wooden stage about the size of a country railway station platform. Here placards read, 'Shooting Show', 'See Kid Durrant, Number One Crackshot', 'Red Indian Torture', 'Human Naked Target' and 'This Show Not Suitable for Small Children'.

Jim was well-acquainted with cowboys and Indians. Like any boy he had read cowboy comics and, like any father, had read cowboy comics to his son. He and Lydia had taken Harry to see Buffalo Bill's Congress of Rough Riders at Scarborough in July 1904. Harry was only eighteen months old, but already talking and coming out with his famous 'unexpected words', one of which was uttered at the end of the show when Buffalo Bill removed his wide-brimmed hat and made a low bow. Harry, from his vantage point in Lydia's arms, said, 'Bald.' Lydia had given Jim one of her wide-eyed, marvelling looks, as if to say, 'Here is a boy who will get on.' And so it would prove, because Harry was now articled to a firm of solicitors in Leeds.

These days Jim would read the occasional Western novel, especially if it involved a 'railroad', and he and Lydia encountered many cowboys and Indians in their picture-going, mainly at the Electric Theatre in Fossgate. So Jim knew the painted Indian, by the ferocity of his scowl and the relative smallness of his headdress (just two feathers), to be a Brave, and the cowboy, by the whiteness of his ten-gallon hat and wide leather trousers, to be a good cowboy.

The Chief was right at the front of the crowd. He had more or less ordered Jim to the Gala. Jim had grown more resistant to the Chief of late, but he would indulge him in this year of 1925 because the Chief had attained the age of superannuation and was scheduled to be leaving the force at the end of the year. That, at any rate, was how Jim had couched the matter to Lydia.

'Don't kid yourself, Jim,' she had said. 'You indulge him, and that's that.' In half an hour's time she would be at the Gala herself, to see – or endure – the Railway Queen Pageant, in which Bernadette would be competing.

The back of the Chief's neck was scarred and dinty, like the bowler hat above it. Jim knew if he didn't walk away he'd spend the rest of the day drinking with the Chief, but instead he tapped him on the shoulder. The Chief turned around with a smile of somewhat bitter triumph: Jim Stringer would play along once again.

'How do,' he said. 'Amazing show, is this.' He'd seen it in some other town already, and he'd been going on about it in the Police Office for weeks.

'How long does it last?'

'What sort of question is that? I'm not keeping you from anything, I hope?'

Jim maintained his enquiring gaze, until finally the Chief said, 'About twenty minutes.'

'Good. I'm meeting the wife in half an hour.'

Lydia did not care for being referred to as 'the wife' – she had a *name*, she would point out – but it was expected that Jim would call her 'the wife' when speaking to the Chief, who didn't really go in for names; seemed embarrassed by them. His own, Saul Weatherill, was little used, and he was happy to be called 'the Chief', although he was a Superintendent these days. If he called Jim anything, it was usually 'lad', even though Jim would be forty next birthday.

Two men stepped onto the wooden stage, approximations of the painted figures. A white cowboy stood on the left, holding a length of rope; a scowling, bare-chested redskin on the right, only he was not so much red as orange, the colour of the make-up he was plastered in. The cowboy began twirling his rope; the Indian was staring at the crowd with folded arms, fastening his gaze on particular individuals until they looked away or laughed. It was amazing the Indian himself didn't crack a smile. After a while, he put his hand up, like a policeman stopping traffic. When Indians did that in films, the caption came up reading 'How!' which possibly meant 'Hello', but this Indian said, in a slow, booming voice, '*This* is the Wild West show!' The cowboy, still twirling his rope, said 'Yee-haw!', and that was how it went on for the next ten minutes, with only those two lines spoken. But they did the job, because the crowd was getting bigger all the time.

The cowboy wore a gun belt with two holsters, a revolver in each. Jim had thought they were fakes, but the cowboy pulled out the right-hand one and fired it into the sky, causing Jim to glance up in case he'd hit Mary Ainsworth or – just as bad from her point of view – her balloon. But she was well out of range, sailing peacefully over the loony bin. The shot was the cue for somebody inside the tent to pull back the middle curtain, and the cowboy and the Indian began saying, 'Step inside please, for the Wild West show.' They were friendlier now; their Yorkshire accents were evident and it was obvious they were pals.

Inside the tent (it had cost a bob to get in) Jim sat next to the Chief. There was no stage set to speak of, just a few trunks here and there, as if the company hadn't yet unpacked. One of them was open, revealing a knife rack with half a dozen long knives fanned out. A barrel had rifle butts sticking out of it like umbrellas in an umbrella stand. There was a contraption that resembled a propped-up coffin lid, and one lonely-looking wooden chair. Down each side of the stage was a big sheet of steel or maybe lead, dented with many bullet marks, but these were not, Jim believed, bullet *holes*, for this was a backstop, meant to stop the bullets flying through the walls of the tent and out into York. The interior was hot; smelt of trampled grass, gunpowder and the little cigar the Chief was now lighting. The Chief's cigars were a brand called Babies, and he kept them in a bent black tin. Lydia had a word for the Chief's Babies: acrid.

A younger cowboy stepped onto the stage, all in black, so possibly a bad cowboy, but not necessarily. A white cowboy was always good, but a black one might be good *or* bad. Anyhow, it was the black ones that meant business.

This cowboy seemed bashful. 'Howdy, folks,' he said quietly. 'My name's Durrant, and they call me Kid Durrant, and this here ...' – and he extended his arm in greeting towards a blonde woman entering from the other side. She wore a very short dress that ended in tassels above her knees, and white leather boots with pointed toes, and that was about it. Her appearance brought a round of applause, so Kid Durrant had to repeat his introduction. 'This here is the lovely Miss Dorothy Hill, and she is very partial to the smoking of a pipe, a habit she picked up out Colorado way, where the ladies ain't quite so genteel as they are on this side of the pond. Now, Miss Dorothy, she gets through a goodly number of pipes, and we're going to show you folks why.'

Miss Dorothy was fishing about in one of the trunks, which required her to bend over and show her frilly knickers. Kid Durrant was selecting a rifle from the barrel. 'Eighteen-ninety Winchester,' the Chief whispered to Jim. 'Two-point-two.'

The Chief loved guns. He'd been thirty years in the Colours, and his only regret in life, he'd once told Jim, was being too old for Fourteen-Eighteen. He presided over the Railway Institute Rifle Leagues and encouraged gun use among his officers. The 'armoury cupboard' in the Police Office was the Chief's own desk, which held a selection of loaded revolvers.

Kid Durrant had taken his rifle to the left side of the stage; Miss Dorothy carried a handful of clay pipes from the trunk over to the right. She put the first pipe in her mouth and turned side-on to Durrant.

'Ladies and gentlemen,' announced Durrant, 'no blanks or soft bullets are used in this show. Our ammunition is the genuine article, and a stray bullet could prove fatal to the lovely Miss Dorothy. Experienced shootist though I am, any sudden noise might cause me to flinch, with who knows what consequences. Therefore, I would ask that you remain silent during the discharge of the guns. You will have the chance to show your appreciation at regular intervals, and I thank you in advance for that.'

Jim had been wondering about this young fellow's nationality, and now reached a verdict: some of his *words* were American, but Durrant was Yorkshire through and through – possibly from Barnsley or Sheffield way. Jim also thought he might have done a spell down a pit: he had that sort of wiriness – and little flecks of black in his pale

20

face, which complemented the blackness of his thick hair. He had a way of shoving a handful of hair from his very blue eyes, drawing attention to both. He was a handsome lad, all right. Bernadette and her friends would call him '*divino*', or 'the bee's knees'.

In a rapid volley of sharp cracks, Kid Durrant shot five clay pipes out of the mouth of Miss Dorothy, and that was the rifle empty (and Jim practically deafened). The Chief, Jim knew, loved watching the cartridges leap from the rifle, because that was further violence. The Kid took another Winchester from the barrel and did the same to another five clay pipes.

The shooting over, Miss Dorothy, showing no surprise at being still alive, took the centre of the stage. 'Now just what does a gal have to do,' she said, 'to get a quiet smoke in these parts?' Her accent was better than Kid Durrant's, and Jim believed she might have been from as far west as Liverpool, for there was a touch of Scouse in it. 'I tell you,' she was saying, 'I'm tuckered out. Reckon I'll go and lean against that board over there.'

Jim did not believe that would prove very restful, and neither did the Chief. 'Earns her money, this lass,' he whispered.

'But first,' Miss Dorothy was saying, 'I'm fairly swelter-ing in this dress. Would any kind gentleman be willing to come forward to assist me in the removal of it?'

Half the men on the front row stood up, while the

remainder made do with applauding. A fat, confident man was making to climb the steps onto the stage. He had a waxed moustache and triangular beard like Buffalo Bill, but his face wasn't triangular. He was baby-faced, like whichever was the American one in Laurel and Hardy. His tie was what Jim believed was called a ribbon tie: a skimpy affair tied in a bow.

'Back to your seat, Walter Bassett,' said Miss Dorothy. 'I specified a *gentleman*.'

He said something like 'Aw, shucks,' and sat down again to general laughter. But he must have been in on the joke – some stooge or hanger-on. And he'd sounded genuinely American.

Miss Dorothy had selected the meekest-looking of the blokes who'd come forward. She held up her tumbling blonde hair while he – face crimson – unhooked the back of her dress, which fell down to reveal another dress, even smaller than the first, about the size of the baggy jumpers Bernadette went in for. This was as far as she'd go in the direction of being a 'naked target'. From the side of the stage Kid Durrant was looking on, arms folded, with a kind of half-pitying smile. The implication was that he could remove Miss Dorothy Hill's dress any time he pleased. As Miss Dorothy walked over to the board, Durrant stepped back centre stage, and Jim wondered if he was going be the knife chucker. But no: he was only going to make an announcement. 'And now, from the far frontier of the United States, please welcome Black Cloud!'

The 'redskin' who'd been scowling at the crowd from the front stage collected an armful of knives from the trunk while Miss Dorothy, leaning on the board with her arms at her sides, pretended to doze. She opened her eyes as the first knife thudded home; perhaps it had landed a bit closer than she or Black Cloud had intended. Even the Chief winced. Jim stared down at his right boot until a dozen knives had been thrown, and applause broke out.

Kid Durrant stepped forward again with another rifle. This time, Miss Dorothy held a sackful of what turned out to be glass balls, the size of snooker balls. She pitched one into the air; Durrant shattered it with a bullet. He broke another five, changed rifles, and broke another three.

Then a strange thing happened: he missed one. A pale, angelic woman in the front row stood up and blew a kiss towards Durrant, which brought some applause. Jim was perplexed. Did she know Durrant? Must do. A blown kiss would be over-familiar otherwise. Either way, the gesture must be a sort of consolation for missing, or an encouragement to carry on.

The woman sat down again. Next to her sat a handsome man – debonair, you might say, with a fine head of grey hair, which matched his grey suit. With his wide-brimmed grey hat on his lap he had London written all over him. He did not look best pleased at what his companion had just done. Certainly, he had not applauded. Now he was leaning towards her and saying things that did not seem to be making her smile – and Jim wanted to see her smile, because a moment earlier she had been so good at it.

Durrant smashed a further twenty-or-so balls, then he missed another. Jim looked along the row at the beautiful woman. She was rising to her feet again as her companion, the debonair man, looked down at his knees. The woman was blowing further kisses.

'You should miss a few more, son!' somebody called out as she sat down.

Jim wondered if this was all part of the act, but the way Durrant had smiled and coloured up – that had not been fake. This time the debonair man did smile as the woman re-joined him, but without conviction, and only, Jim felt, because he knew people were looking at him.

As the balls continued to shatter Jim looked at his watch. Twenty-five past three. The Beauty Pageant – and Bernadette's ordeal – would be starting imminently.

After the last ball was shot, Miss Dorothy took a bow, and Black Cloud came on with a broom to sweep up the cartridges and smashed glass.

'And now ...' said Durrant, addressing the audience while loading a revolver.

'Now *what*?' thought Jim. Durrant spoke slowly as well as quietly, and it seemed to Jim he was rather short of patter. The Chief smiled an evil smile and held out one of his Babies. Some instinct of self-preservation told Jim – an occasional smoker – to refuse, but he took the cigar anyway, and the Chief already had a lit match to hand.

'And now,' Durrant said again, 'would any of the smokers among you gentlemen care to step forward?' He was looking directly at Jim, and it was not an amiable look.

'He'll shoot it out of your mouth,' said the Chief, indicating the little cigar. So the Chief had known what was coming and set Jim up.

'Get lost,' muttered Jim, and he stomped his cigar out on the grass. The fat American in the audience, Walter Bassett, stood up for the second time and Durrant slowly removed his gaze from Jim. Durrant smiled a slow smile. 'I guess we have *one* brave man on the front row here.' Bassett, wheezing somewhat, was climbing the steps to the stage – and this time wasn't sent back. He took a carton of cigars from his shirt, put one in his mouth, turned meekly side-on. Durrant looked at the revolver he held as though he'd never seen it before.

'Colt 45,' whispered the Chief.

That, Jim knew, was a powerful piece: 'The Gun that Won the West'.

'Is he supposed to fire that in here?' said Jim.

'He does just what he likes,' said the Chief.

With hardly a glance at the fat man, Durrant loosed a bullet, which left the cigar still in Walter Bassett's mouth, but half the size. Bassett examined the stump before walking off the stage.

'This is a twenty-cent cigar, Kid,' he said.

'It *was*,' muttered Durrant.

The Chief was applauding; then he rose to his feet while lighting another one of his Babies, an act that earned applause – and he climbed onto the stage. Durrant did not at first acknowledge him, but eventually glanced sidelong – as though reluctantly – at him. 'What is your name, sir?'

'Saul Weatherill.'

'And your profession?'

'Police superintendent.'

Durrant smiled, muttered something about 'special treatment for cops'. The Chief wore an unfamiliar, silly smile. He was shy about being on the stage.

Durrant had set down the revolver and picked up a rifle. 'You might want to quit taking draws on that,' he said, indicating the Chief's cigar: 'it gets a little smaller every time.'

This raised an uneasy laugh.

Durrant waved the rifle towards the target area. 'A little further back, please.' Then he turned his back on the Chief as though he'd become sick of the sight of him, and rested his gun over his shoulder like a huntsman returning from a long day in the field. He jerked the trigger with his thumb and Jim saw the cigar spinning through the air, but couldn't make out where it landed – the risk of fire seemed one of many in this tent.

But the crowd was applauding and the Chief was smiling his normal, twisted smile again.

As the audience filed out, the Chief stayed on the stage, obviously wanting to talk guns, but Durrant was in a conflab with the beautiful woman in the front row, while the debonair grey-haired man hung about looking spare. The Chief had to make do with Black Cloud, who evidently knew guns as well as knives. 'I'm partial to t' thirty-two,' Jim heard Black Cloud saying. 'It fires t' same rounds as t' Winchester.' Vocally, he had completely ceased to be a Red Indian.

The Railway Queen

Outside, Lydia was waiting. 'What was that like?'

'Loud.'

'Who did the shooting?'

'A character called Kid Durrant.'

'And what did he shoot at?'

'A pretty woman, mainly.'

'I thought so.'

'He also shot the Chief's cigar out of his mouth.'

'I've wanted to do that for years. Where is he?'

'Who?'

'The Chief.'

'Talking to a Red Indian, so-called.'

'Have we got rid of him for the day?'

'I reckon not.'

'Come on, Jim,' Lydia said. 'Let's go and see if Bernadette is to be Queen of the Goods Siding.' The day had grown hotter, and the smell of the Gala had come on a bit: less in the way of petrol fumes, more of frying sausages and drink. The Fairy Boat seemed to Jim to be swinging more wildly, but still the screams that came from it were happy screams.

The Railway Queen competition was held on the lawn directly in front of the hospital. It made use of some wide stone steps leading up to the terrace, and all the girls were sitting on them looking like a lot of Ancient Greeks, for they all wore white toga-like dresses, cinched around the middle with silk sashes, and had paper petals about their heads. Jim wondered how many other girls aside from his daughter had been reduced to tears by the making of the crowns, but now they were all smiling in the same sort of painted-on smile. There were no seats for the spectators; they would just muster behind a rope, which was good – meant the proceedings wouldn't last long. Jim and Lydia had spotted Bernadette on the extreme right.

'We have orders not to wave,' said Lydia, after Jim had waved and Bernadette had scowled back.

'She's the prettiest one by a mile,' said Jim.

'That's irrelevant,' said Lydia. 'They like to pick a deserving case.'

Bernadette was certainly not a deserving case.

'Last year's winner was the daughter of a carriage and wagon cleaner,' said Lydia. 'She was called Mabel.'

It was characteristic of his wife that she'd bothered to find out. For all her Labourism, Lydia was socially ambitious. The most important thing – more important, Jim suspected, even than the Co-Operative movement's number-one aim of securing World Peace – was that she and her family should 'get on'. In theory she was against beauty pageants, but they were an opportunity for getting on. So Lydia had paid her friend Lillian Parker ten shillings to assist in the making of Bernadette's competition dress, which was supposed to be made by the competitor herself; they had all been required to submit an essay on the theme 'Queen for a Day', describing their preparations. 'The making of the paper crowns was the most fun,' Bernadette had written. In their essay the girls were also asked to say what they would do to improve the London & North Eastern Railway if they were Queen for a Day, the winner's suggestion to be forwarded to the board in London. Bernadette had deigned to consult Jim on this point. 'You should tell them to put ticket inspectors on the Scarborough trains,' he'd said.

She'd sighed theatrically. 'Why?'

'Because that's where the most ticket fraud occurs.

Call it "fare evasion" – they'll like that. The Passenger Department think it's a main-line problem, but for some reason there's more fare evasion on York–Scarborough services than York–Doncaster or York–Durham. It would be interesting to know why.'

'No, it wouldn't,' Bernadette had said.

In the end, she'd proposed building a London & North Eastern Railway theatre in the West End of London, or 'London's West End' as she'd called it in her essay. Bernadette wanted to be an actress. She had performed with amateur drama companies in York, including the Railway Players, who had a little theatre in one of the obscure back rooms of the Railway Institute. Bernadette believed that she – if not necessarily anyone else involved in railway am-dram – deserved a bigger stage.

As at the shooting show, Jim concentrated on his right boot while the girls paraded on the lawn, skirting the floral borders and doing their best to look floral themselves. Jim fancied a pint. After a bit, he said, 'She's the only brunette.'

Lydia – very dark herself – appeared not to hear. Her tactic of evasion was to look at the sky – in practice, a matter of looking at Mary Ainsworth. 'Doesn't she ever want to do a wee?' she demanded. Lydia ought to admire Mary Ainsworth, since she was a woman in a man's world, and indeed she *had* admired her, to the extent of inviting her to give a talk to the York Co-Operative Women. But

Mary Ainsworth had pulled out of the engagement at the last minute, having had a better offer: an invitation to take part in a radio broadcast. 'I trust you will appreciate,' she had written to Lydia, 'that this is a once-in-a-lifetime opportunity, and I hope very much that I will be able to accommodate you at a later date.' But that would not be happening. 'What *she* doesn't appreciate,' Lydia had told Jim, 'was that our invitation was *also* a once-in-a-lifetime opportunity.'

Jim recognised Oughtred, the Passenger Manager, among the judges, and the head of 'Public Relations', who was new, and whose name temporarily escaped Jim. They sat along a trestle table and, even though they were all in summer rig, it did look like an outdoor board meeting. A few feet away another dozen people held musical instruments, being a small brass band. The judges made notes and pointed at the girls as they paraded – walking back and forth in a sort of military criss-cross – to the accompaniment, for some reason, of 'A Bicycle Made for Two'.

The spokesman of the judges was a little bloke Jim had never clapped eyes on before – secretary to one of the high-ups, possibly. He wore an orthopaedic boot. But any sympathy he might have earned from Jim and Lydia on this account was dissipated when he announced that the London & North Eastern Railway Queen of 1925, who would be going forward to compete in the National Railway Employees' Gala in Manchester, was Helen ...

somebody or other. Her surname was lost in a sudden burst of hurdy-gurdy music from the fair: another traction engine had started up. The girl herself came forward and received a bouquet from Oughtred, the most senior man present. She took it all in her stride, as though she'd known all along she would win.

The girls were now released, and Bernadette came towards Lydia and Jim, who were braced for tears or furious recriminations. But Bernadette continued smiling the strained smile, as if the beauty pageant were not really over, and now Jim saw the reason: the beautiful woman from the shooting show – the one who'd blown kisses at Durrant – was standing close by. Next to her was the debonair chap Jim had down as a Londoner. Bernadette had been directing her smile at them, and they were smiling back. When Bernadette came up, Jim said, 'Hard luck, love. You were easily the prettiest.'

'It's probably a fix,' said Lydia.

'Oh, well,' said Bernadette – and Jim had never heard her use that phrase before.

The beautiful woman touched Lydia on the elbow. 'Is this your daughter?' she said. 'She's absolutely gorgeous.'

Bernadette herself answered, using one of the expressions she reserved for people she thought more sophisticated than her immediate family. 'It's awfully kind of you to say so ... But – aren't you ... Cynthia Lorne?'

She *was*, it turned out. Jim ought to have known: her

superb smile was offset by sad eyes, and all women in films had sad eyes. Her companion was Thomas ('Most people call me Tom') Brooks, and he too was in pictures – a producer. Lydia was giving Jim one of her wide-eyed, incredulous looks, because here really was a chance for Bernadette to get on. Cynthia Lorne was very famous, although Jim couldn't quite recollect the name of any film he'd seen her in.

The five began sauntering back towards the fair, the ladies going on ahead. Jim had fallen in with Brooks, who was about of an age with him, and a good-looking-enough fellow, Jim supposed, to be in films himself. His grey flannel suit was summer-weight and had that suppleness of expensive cloth. You didn't feel hot to look at him. He was very clean-shaven, in a way that made Jim doubt his own moustache. (A number of people doubted his moustache, principally Bernadette.) Brooks's hair was prematurely grey, but he had an abundance of it, and he carried – rather than wore – his wide-brimmed hat so as to show it off. His eyes were very blue, as were Cynthia Lorne's, and you could see how this blueness might have been the basis of a kind of pact between them. She, with her bobbed blonde hair, wore a simple pleated skirt and grey jumper and the two of them made a flowing, silvery pair – as though they were simultaneously at the York Gala and in a film. Up ahead, Bernadette was getting down to business. 'I'd love to be in films,' she said. 'I want to go to drama school.'

'I've told her it's an impossible dream, really,' Lydia was saying to Cynthia Lorne, by which she meant: *Please give the girl some advice on how to accomplish this.*

'You must try for the Royal Academy, my dear,' said Cynthia Lorne. 'You'll need two test pieces. A Shakespeare and a modern.'

'I know,' said Bernadette, at which point Jim lost track of their conversation, because Tom Brooks had asked him, 'What do you do, Mr Stringer?' When Jim told him, Brooks said how fascinating it must be but looked slightly bored. He took two cigarettes from a silver case, handing one to Jim, and lit them with a lighter that made a big, expensive-looking flame.

'I was careful not to advertise my cigarette habit in the shooting show,' he said. 'You were in there, I think?'

Jim explained that he had been present at the urging of the Chief. 'He has a gun fixation, my governor.'

'I still carry a Webley,' said Brooks.

'Any particular reason?'

'It's a souvenir, I suppose.'

'Of what?'

'Oh, happy times on the Western Front,' Brooks said, with a sad smile.

The Webley meant he'd been an officer, as if that weren't already obvious. Jim speculated on the whereabouts of the piece. It did not seem to be spoiling the line of Brooks's suit just then. They began talking about the war – turned out they'd both been in the Somme battle – but not for long. War talk would undo any happiness a sunny Saturday might offer.

'Do you know the crackshot?', Jim said. 'Kid Durrant?'

'We both do,' said Brooks, indicating Cynthia Lorne up ahead. 'Well, you'll have gathered that *she* knows him.' He was presumably referring to the blown kisses. 'I've been talking to him about a film role. A cowboy picture, you know. Trouble is, I'm not sure he can act and – more important – can he ride a horse? But we'll probably do something. My wife says he's magnetic.'

They were coming up to the gates of the hospital grounds, the boundary of the Gala. And now the Chief was wavering through the hot crowds, cigar in hand. He must have visited the beer tent. You could tell when the Chief was drunk because his thin lips would form the beginnings of a snarl whenever you said anything to him, and you'd think he was going to hit you. He wasn't quite at that stage.

He brought his beer-reek right up to Jim and said, 'Where are you off?'

It was Lydia who answered. '*We* are going into town for tea.'

'Or,' said Jim, 'for a drink.'

'But we're not going to a *pub*, are we Jim?' said Lydia, and Jim knew that the film people were looking on with interest because, being artistic, they were all students of character and Jim's character was very different from his wife's.

'We're going to the Station Hotel,' said Jim. He was happy to make that concession, having just then heard, amid the roar of the Gala, the York Minster bells chiming four. The Minster bells were supposed to remind you of God, but they usually reminded Jim of licensing hours. The pubs were not yet open, but hotels were licensed separately.

'Suits us,' said Tom Brooks. 'We're putting up there.'

Jim felt obliged to ask, 'You coming, Chief?'

'I'm off back in there,' he said, indicating the Gala crowd – and from that direction Jim heard the stunted sales pitch: 'This is the Wild West Show!' Durrant was about to do his stuff again.

'Where will I find you in the hotel?' asked the Chief.

'The Oak Room,' said Lydia, and where she'd got that from, Jim didn't know. He was often in the Station Hotel, but never in any Oak Room. He seemed to recollect that it might be the library.

The gates of the hospital grounds gave onto that distinguished street called Bootham. Jim sensed something missing – some quintessential summer thing – and then it came to him. Dust. The street had been macadamed over a month earlier, and it was as if all the motorists of York had come along to test it out, so the traffic was blocked up, the throbbing engines contributing to the heat of the

36

day. A single horse, with wagonette behind, was trapped in the block.

Brooks had gone quiet. Remembering the cowboy film he'd watched at the Electric Theatre two weeks ago, Jim asked, 'Have you seen *The Ranch Hand*?' realizing too late it was a silly question. It was as though Tom Brooks had asked *him*, 'Have you seen York Station?' But it was an even sillier question than Jim knew, because Brooks said, 'That's one of ours, actually.'

'Ours?'

'Piccadilly Pictures.'

In that case, Jim had better compliment it. 'I thought it was interesting. The story was told sort of backwards, in a series of reminiscences.'

'Flashbacks,' said Brooks, blowing smoke. 'My own reminiscences of that shoot are rather painful.'

'Why?'

'Oh, the usual, only more so. Problems with the financing, problems with the star – a temperamental young man. And, in fact, not as young as he should be.'

Brooks did not seem to approve of his own picture, and Jim hadn't really approved of it either. He had preferred the supporting 'short', a Buster Keaton flick. Keaton was Jim's favourite.

'I'll tell you something Jim,' Brooks was saying with a sigh. 'The drama you see on the screen is usually nothing compared to the drama taking place off it.'

The Oak Room

If not quite a library, The Oak Room of the Station Hotel was certainly a reading room, and it reminded Jim of some Calcutta clubs he'd inhabited while investigating corruption on the East Indian Railway. There was that generosity of scale you got in colonial circumstances: the wide-spaced tables with bamboo chairs, expensive magazines strewn about, in particular the *Field*. As so often in Calcutta, there were flowers in the fireplace for a blaze of colour, a real blaze being surplus to requirements. Beyond the wide windows, the lawn of the hotel garden seemed quite dead from heat, yet still a gardener was walking a petrol-driven lawnmower across it, making a sleepy drone that drew Jim's attention to the fact that two sets of French windows were open. There was not a cloud in the sky, only Mary Ainsworth, clearly visible from here, albeit smaller than before. Her balloon seemed to resemble a badly drawn sun, in a vista that included the riverbank trees and the tower of the Minster.

If the hotel was quiet – a matter of expensive shoe leather on thick carpet – the Oak Room was quieter still. It was in order to talk and order drinks, but a certain decorum was dictated. As Jim settled down at a table with Tom Brooks, Cynthia Lorne, Lydia and Bernadette, he wondered what would happen when the Chief pitched up.

When the waiter approached, Jim determined to order the drinks. It was the least he could do, in view of the advice

Cynthia Lorne was continuing to give Bernadette about her application to the Royal Academy of Dramatic Arts, evidently the only drama school worth bothering with. 'And if you don't get in, dear,' Cynthia Lorne had just told her, 'which I am sure you will, you must simply try again the next year.' Cynthia announced as a highly impressive fact that a big star called Lillian Dean (whom Jim had never heard of) had got in only after two failed attempts.

As it turned out, Brooks insisted harder than Jim on standing drinks: champagne for everyone except Brooks himself, who ordered a mineral water.

The waiter brought the glasses before he brought the drink, and when he set one down in front of Lydia she did not hand it back to him, as she usually did. In theory Lydia was teetotal, but she would have half a glass occasionally, sometimes with strange results. There was no question of Bernadette handing *her* glass back, and Jim fretted that Bernadette might have inherited his own taste for drink. He and Lydia had discovered that she would drink at the Saturday dances she frequented. Lydia had been collecting her from one of these when, feeling thirsty, she'd decided to have some of the 'fruit cup' on offer, whereupon she was asked, 'With or without?'

'With or without what?' she'd asked.

'Gin,' she was brazenly told.

As the drink was being poured, Cynthia Lorne was saying to Lydia and Bernadette, 'We're here to see the

Kid – Jack Durrant. Tom and I would like to put him in pictures, wouldn't we, darling?'

Brooks just lit a cigarette, the smoke adding to his elegant greyness. But Cynthia Lorne's superb smile did not falter. 'Tom is not a man to express enthusiasm. But he thinks Jack has the makings of a big star, don't you, dear?'

'He looks the part, of course,' Brooks said eventually. 'Not sure about his voice, though.'

Jim said, 'But that doesn't matter in films, does it?'

'It will do soon,' said Brooks. 'And we'll have to get a new name for him. Durrant's no good.'

'Why not?'

'It's too northern. And it rhymes with currant.'

'What would he be called ideally?' said Jim, who'd been inspired to ask the question by the arrival of his drink.

'Good question,' said Brooks, although he didn't seem minded to answer it.

'It's a *very* good question,' Cynthia Lorne put in. 'He's written stories under the name Ned Keach. He's a wonderful writer, you know. We thought Ned Keach could be his film name as well.'

But Brooks was looking towards the window.

Jim turned to see. A man was walking on the lawn, which you were not supposed to do: the Chief, and he had two men trailing across the grass behind him. Immediately behind came the shambling figure of the fat man, Walter Bassett, carrying a big carpet bag of black and blue checks

40

and a leather doctor's bag. A dozen yards behind him, surly and languishing somewhat, came Jack 'Kid' Durrant, who carried a wide-brimmed grey hat – a very similar hat to Brooks's. The gardener with the lawnmower had stopped mowing to stare at the Chief, who hadn't noticed. Now the gardener cut the motor, presumably in hopes that the sudden silence would alert the Chief to his crime, but the only effect was to make audible (thanks to the opened French windows) Walter Bassett. 'We're figuring on partnering up,' he was shouting to the Chief: 'me and the Kid. He's been on the powder-smoke circuit for five years ... Looking to get into movies now. I aim to help him in any way I can.'

The Chief stood at the threshold of the Oak Room. Walter, panting somewhat, came and set down the bags beside him and said, 'Where's your buddy, Saul?'

The Chief nodded at Jim. New chairs were brought from empty tables, and so the party of five became a party of eight, with a ninth chair for the carpet bag and the doctor's bag. Jim believed he knew what they held. The most significant thing about the new seating arrangement was that Jack Durrant had sat himself down next to Cynthia Lorne.

'We were just talking about you,' Tom Brooks said to Durrant, rather rudely. 'We were talking about your name, and how it's going to have to be changed.'

'Sure,' said Durrant, as if Brooks wasn't worth more than a single word.

'We've been giving this a little thought,' said Walter

Bassett, 'and the Kid has a suggestion.' He looked at Durrant, inviting him to speak.

But Durrant said, '*You* say, Walt.'

Walter said, 'The Kid writes Western stories, as I think you know.'

'We do,' said Cynthia Lorne. 'We think they're absolutely wonderful.'

Brooks was carefully putting out his cigarette.

'He's been writing them as Ned Keach,' said Bassett, 'which seems to have a nice ring to it. What do you reckon, Tom?'

Brooks shrugged.

Cynthia Lorne said, 'I think Ned Keach is just lovely.'

There was clearly a big push on the name front, but Walter now changed tack: 'The Kid's latest tale is damn fine. It's set in Nevada. The Kid tells me he'd like to live in Nevada.'

'That right, Jack?' said Cynthia Lorne, and she touched Durrant on his bony knee.

'I like the sound of the place,' said Durrant. 'They call it the Silver State.' He looked tough but spoke softly, which must be part of his appeal. He was a working-class lad all right, but his Yorkshire accent wasn't too broad – a touch of refinement there. He was a superior type all round, and he was certainly hypnotising Cynthia Lorne.

'I've told the boy,' Walter said: 'lot of rattlesnakes in Nevada.'

'There's a lot of rattlesnakes in *London*, from what I hear,' muttered Durrant, and this was aimed at Brooks.

Cynthia Lorne said, 'Do you fancy playing Billy the Kid, Jack? Tom has the rights to an interesting story about him.'

'I might just write my own Billy the Kid tale,' said Durrant.

Cynthia Lorne said, 'How about it, Tom? Jack as Billy the Kid?'

Brooks looked back at his wife, his expression blank.

'Or we have our gold mine scenario, don't we dear? We should tell the Kid about that.'

At length, Brooks said, 'If I'm going to do another cowboy and Indian picture, I'm going to have a *lot* of cowboys and Indians. Maybe we could round up a few redskins from Buffalo Bill's old company? What was that chap? Sitting Bull?'

'Hate to break it to you, Tom,' said Walter, 'but Sitting Bull's dead.'

'Really? Of what?'

'Lead poisoning.'

'I'm sorry?'

'Shot,' Durrant put in.

'By whom?'

'The law,' said Durrant, and he looked first at Jim, then at the Chief – a pretty cool gaze in both cases. The Chief was lighting one of his horrible little cigars, but he'd picked up Durrant's hostility. As he shook out his match, he flashed a wink at Jim.

'"Lead poisoning"', said Tom Brooks. 'We really must get that into a script.'

Here Bernadette, who'd been paying close attention, risked a question. 'Do you call them scripts? The subtitles, I mean?'

'We do, Bernadette,' said Brooks, 'and you'd be horrified to know the amount of money we sometimes pay for them.'

Lydia said, 'The films have never done the Indians justice.'

'You got that right,' muttered Durrant.

Silence for a space. It occurred to Jim that Brooks and Durrant could have been father and son, were it not for the difference in class. They might be in a film together. Durrant would be the wild young gunslinger; Brooks would be the sheriff who finally – with a certain amount of regret – is obliged to shoot him dead. They were both the cowboy type: tall and thin, with a world-weary manner. Perhaps this was the quality that had caught Cynthia Lorne's eye; or maybe she'd *caused* the weariness.

Jim stood and turned towards the windows. There was a marbling of pink in the sky, and no Mary Ainsworth. With an excuse to the party, Jim quit the Oak Room and turned along the corridor that led to the palatial Gents. Mary Ainsworth might have let Lydia down that time, but Jim always thought of her as a good fairy presiding over the city. Nothing really terrible could happen while she was in flight, but now that she had landed, Jim was thinking of those bags on the seat in the Oak Room. He knew they held guns.

On his way back, Jim diverted into the main bar for a quick brown beer. He did not want to be entirely sober for whatever was going to happen next; nor did he want Lydia or Bernadette around when the guns were brought out of the bags.

In the Oak Room, the French windows were now closed. Lydia was placing one of her shawls over Bernadette's shoulders preparatory to departure, but they were still fretting about the drama school test pieces. Lydia said, 'I think something by Shaw. He's our favourite, isn't he, Bernadette?'

'Not exactly.'

Cynthia Lorne was about to respond when Durrant leant towards her, whispering. He took his watch from his pocket and, with Brooks observing, showed her the time. Then Brooks, in turn, leant towards Lydia. 'You like Shaw, Lydia?'

'Yes,' she said, and Jim knew that wouldn't be the end of the matter, since Lydia had emptied her glass of its two inches of champagne.

'I like plays to be about something,' said Lydia, 'and Shaw's are. He is perhaps a bit long-winded sometimes.

I would say that his plays are all about half an hour too long, except *Caesar and Cleopatra*.'

'So that's your particular favourite?'

'No, that's an *hour* too long. But he's always eloquent. On the women question especially. He has a lot to say about that.'

'So does Mother,' said Bernadette.

'Please explain, Lydia,' said Brooks.

That's twice he's called my wife by her first name, thought Jim.

Lydia began giving Brooks a rather breathless account of her work for the Co-Operative Women's Guild, and Brooks let her run on. Jim believed his apparent interest in Lydia was in retaliation for Cynthia Lorne's interest in Durrant – those two were continuing their confidential conversation. When Brooks was sure Lydia had finished he said, 'You sound to me like a socialist.'

'I'm not sure I want to *sound* like one,' Lydia said. 'Certainly I *am* one.'

The Chief and Walter Bassett had got the carpet bag open, so the thing Jim had not wanted to happen was under way. The bag held rifles – the 2.2s, which, Walter was explaining, were 'take-downs': the stock could be detached from the barrels, which was how they'd fitted into the bag. Walter was showing how one of the rifles could be reassembled.

Cynthia Lorne had finished her conference with

Durrant. She suddenly looked very pale, but with no diminution of her beauty. Jim thought of a stone angel in a graveyard. She was apparently making to leave, as were Bernadette and Lydia.

Indicating the rifles, Jim asked the Chief, 'What are you going to do with these?'

'We're going to shoot them, lad.'

'Where?'

'Now you have a little think about it.'

'The range?'

'Got it in one.'

A waiter – a new one – had approached. He said, 'The manager asks that you put those guns away.'

'Cundle?' said the Chief.

'Mr Cundle, yes.'

Cundle, the hotel manager, was a very precise Scot, with a small bald head and such perfect enunciation that he sounded like a machine. The Chief had had many run-ins with him over the years, and had developed a certain respect for him.

'Tell Mr Cundle we'll be leaving presently,' he said, 'and we'd like a dozen bottles of brown beer to take with us. He's to send the bill to me at the Police Office. I'm Saul Weatherill.'

'Yes,' said the waiter, 'Mr Cundle knows who you are.' And he turned on his heel.

'Cheeky young sod,' said the Chief, cheerfully enough.

The Range

The Railway Institute Rifle Range could be reached by walking through the station. That's how the Chief reached it, anyhow.

He led the way out of the hotel through what was known as the Railway Entrance, and onto the main 'Up' platform, where he diverted for a moment into the Police Office to ask Cliff Hemingway, the night sergeant, if any occurrences had occurred. Jim waited outside with the others. Tom Brooks looked as though he wanted to be elsewhere, but he had presumably come along to keep tabs on Durrant. As long as Durrant was shooting rifles in the range, he wasn't sloping off with Cynthia Lorne. Walter Bassett was carrying the two bags. Jim reckoned the doctor's bag must hold revolvers, and if the guns in either bag were loaded, Bassett was committing a criminal offence by bringing them into the station. Also tagging along was a lad from the hotel, deputized by Cundle to carry the crate of beer.

The Chief came out of the Police Office.

'Owt doing?' Jim asked.

'Nowt,' said the Chief.

As he led the little troop along the main 'Up', a train was coming from the opposite direction. It would not be stopping. It was a run-through, bound for Scarborough: a nice big Gresley K3 hauling half a dozen smart teak coaches full of trippers impatient for cocktails and dinner at the seaside. Some kids were messing about on a luggage barrow close to the edge of the platform. Shouting over the roar of the oncoming engine, the Chief shooed them back from the edge – his good deed for the day, although one of the kids (who'd looked a tough customer a minute beforehand) was left in tears: the Chief had sworn at him. Jim pulled the barrow back from the platform edge and shoved it over towards the station signal box. Jim loved the station and liked to keep it smart. The driver of the K3 gave a pop on his whistle by way of thanks, and Jim stopped to admire the engine as it thundered past. It was the steam he was admiring, really. It always did different things when it rose up from the chimney. Sometimes it split into two when it hit the station roof; sometimes it rolled backwards and squashed itself under the footbridge. What had Bernadette called engine steam when she was about eight years old? Train clouds – not rain clouds but *train* clouds.

Jim found himself in step with a silent Durrant, who wouldn't give him so much as a glance. Durrant was aware of his own importance: he was about to show off his gun-play again. So Jim pushed on until he was in step with the Chief. They diverted left, onto little-used Platform 5b, from where they did something that wouldn't be allowed to the general public: they stepped down onto the four-foot, crossing the tracks of what was known as Old Station Sidings. Jim signalled to those behind that it was all right.

'Durrant's not over-keen on policemen,' Jim said to the Chief.

'There's a reason for that.'

'Been lagged, 'as he?'

'Six months in Wakefield.'

'What for? Couldn't be a shooting scrape if he only got six months.'

'Having wines and spirits away from Pond Street goods yard.'

Pond Street was a goods depot in Sheffield, on London, Midland & Scottish Railway territory. The Chief was thick with the LMS Police high-ups, and it was evidently through them that he'd first heard of Durrant – an example of an ex-convict made good sort of thing.

'Where does Walter Bassett come in?' said Jim. 'Is he with the shooting show?'

The Chief shook his head. 'He's a sub-postmaster.'

'Give over!'

'I'm *telling* you. He runs the post office on Lawrence Street.'

Jim thought: a little dusty shop with a leaning post box outside. 'But I *know* that post office. It's run by an old lady. She's called Ethel – has a big cat that sleeps on the counter.'

'She's dead,' said the Chief, with some satisfaction, 'and so is the cat, probably. For the past six months it's been run by Walter Bassett. He also sells books on the premises.'

'What sort of books?'

It was Walter himself, suddenly close behind, who answered: 'Tales of the Old West. Ranging from dime novels, for which I charge a shilling, up to some titles falling not too far short of actual literature.'

On the Old Station Sidings, a couple of tank engines had been dying for years, with three broken guards' vans to keep them company. One had a stove that still worked, and some tramps of the town would doss down there on cold nights, thereby contravening Section Four of the Vagrancy Act, 1824. Jim and the Chief would turn a blind eye. Beyond the sidings lay the Institute, which was lively enough most nights, but the other buildings in this corner of the Railway Lands were abandoned or getting on that way. They were passing a turntable that hadn't turned in ten years, and had grass growing on it. Then came some kind of crumbling smithy with a disproportionately high chimney. Its whitewashed walls were soot-blackened, and Jim always found it sinister, as through it were a little crematorium. The hot sky was turning a dirty greenish shade.

They came to the rifle range, which had not been *built* as a range, but was an old boiler repair shop converted by the Chief and some of his followers in the Rifle Leagues. The Chief unlocked the door, which took a while. It was chilly inside, despite of the heat of the day – gloomy too, in spite of whitewashed walls. There was a smell of cordite

51

which, together with the wall of sandbags behind the targets, caused Jim to start thinking war thoughts.

The door had admitted them to the section where the guns were fired. A low barrier came between this and the main area of the hall, through which the bullets would fly. The low barrier was known as the gun rest, and was formed of railway sleepers. You knelt at it to fire, and there were more sandbags to serve as kneelers. Two rows of gaslights suspended from the ceiling ran the length of the range, each row corresponding to a target. To the right of the targets was a little bulletproof shelter made of boiler plates. During competitions, a bloke would be stationed in there, whose job it was to replace the targets. They were on wires, and he'd turn a wheel to winch them into the protection of the shelter, where he'd attach new ones, like somebody putting washing on a line.

The Chief was walking the length of the left-hand row, lighting the gas. Coming back, he lit the right-hand row. He did this reverently, like a priest lighting the candles at the start of a church service. The other men had remained behind the gun rest.

Walter Bassett, the sub-postmaster (Jim still couldn't quite believe it) had laid out the 2.2 rifles on top of the barrier, and was now speedily loading them. Durrant waited, leaning with hands in pockets by the back wall.

Tom Brooks had walked up to him. 'Do you really want to move to the States, Jack?'

'Too right,' said Durrant, without looking at Brooks. 'Why Nevada?'

Durrant shrugged, so Brooks tried again: 'What's the attraction?'

'The heat . . . and the cold.'

Walter Bassett, who'd been listening as well as loading, said, 'Anyone who likes extreme heat and extreme cold and nothing in-between is going to love Nevada. It also has an excellent legal system, by which I mean that most things are legal. I don't like to say *what* things, on account of this young boy.'

He meant the boy from the hotel who'd carried in the beer. 'Be gone, boy,' said Walter.

'Can't I see the shooting?'

'No, son, you're liable to be deafened – and the Kid doesn't give free shows.'

Durrant, half smiling, waved the boy away. 'Cloud the dust, son.'

'"Cloud the dust"', said Brooks. 'I like it.'

But it was evident that Durrant didn't like *him*, and his attempt at conversation had come to nothing. Jim saw little prospect of Durrant being given a start in films by Tom Brooks, even though Walter Bassett was evidently set on bringing this about. Bassett's role was to try to smooth things over, filling up holes in the conversation with his pleasant American voice, which Jim liked listening to. He asked him, 'You from Nevada yourself, Walter?'

53

'No sir. I'm from California, and was never east of the Sierra Madres 'til I came here.'

But why he had come here must remain a mystery, since Jim didn't think it would be polite to ask.

The Chief was handing out bottles of beer (he didn't run to glasses, of course), and it seemed he had a couple of other crates in the range, besides the one brought from the hotel. He was also offering around little wisps of white cotton – ear defenders. The guns would be noisier here than in the shooting show, on account of the brick walls. Jim did not intend shooting. He would hang back, drink a couple of bottles of beer, then slope off. He was curious, though. It was odds-on something bad was in the offing.

Brooks, Jim noticed, was the only man to refuse a beer.

The Chief invited Walter to shoot first – a reward for all his hard work. Walter took one of the Winchesters and fired five times. To Jim each shot seemed louder than the last. 'I'm not exactly a dead-eye these days, you know,' said Walter, rising from the kneeling position of the rifle shootist. 'I'm reading my Westerns in Clear Type.'

The Chief picked up a second Winchester and handed it to Walter for another go, and this time Durrant stepped forward to give quiet advice – too quiet for Jim to hear, except for the opening words, spoken in a kindly tone. 'Look here, old timer . . .'

The kid from the hotel was still hanging around. Jim frowned a question at the Chief, who just shrugged.

Perhaps he saw in this youth a candidate for the Rifle Leagues. He would be eligible, since anyone who worked in the hotel was technically a railway employee.

Tom Brooks shot next, evidently with fair-to-middling results. After his turn, he came up to Jim. 'I suppose this is what's called a shooting party.'

'You enjoying it?' said Jim.

'Not overly.' Brooks gave a glance at his watch. He then fell to staring at Durrant, who was still leaning against the back wall.

'Quiet sort, isn't he?' said Jim, as the Chief took up the firing position.

'He saves his mouth for breathing,' said Brooks. 'He told me that himself. Mind you, he's talkative enough when it comes to the ladies.'

Jim risked a provocative question. 'You're thinking of his partner in the shooting show? Miss Dorothy?'

'No,' said Brooks.

The Chief was evidently shooting pretty well – at least, at first.

'But too bad about that last one,' said Walter.

The Chief called over to Jim. 'Your turn, lad.'

But Jim shook his head. He was no shootist. One or two Germans had reason to be grateful for that in the war, not that they ever knew it. 'If you're not shooting,' said the Chief, 'will you just go along to that last light and pull it off?'

The last light on the left-hand side was flickering, and it seemed the Chief was blaming this flicker for his poor final shot. The chain that dangled from the lamp was fitfully illuminated by little flashes of the man-made lightning. Something ghostly about it. Of all the dozen dangling chains, it was the only one swinging.

A voice piped up. 'I'll do it!' The kid from the hotel was already scrambling over the gun rest.

Jim saw that three more or less drunken men held rifles: the Chief, Walter and Durrant. 'You get back here!' he shouted, and the boy turned on his heel, muttering something about 'only trying to help'. 'Now bugger off back to the hotel,' said Jim, trying a slightly milder version of the shock tactics employed by the Chief when dealing with kids. The kid barged through the door, leaving it open in his angry little wake, and the slight draught of warmish summer air caused the chains hanging from *all* the gas lamps to swing. But the one with the broken mantle swung through a wider arc. Jim climbed over the barrier and walked towards it, very conscious of his bootsteps on the stone floor.

'Obliged to you, lad,' called the Chief.

Turning about, Jim saw exactly what he had expected to see: Durrant, standing with rifle raised. His finger was on the trigger. Neither the Chief nor Walter could see what he was about, since they were looking towards Jim – and if Durrant fired, the bullet would go in between them. Only

Tom Brooks could see the whole picture. He gave a shout of warning, but it was lost as Durrant loosed his bullet.

Jim had been determined not to flinch, and he did not flinch.

The Chief turned to Durrant. 'Leave off, will you?' It was a pretty mild reprimand, but a reprimand nonetheless.

Had the Chief anticipated the shot? Had he been testing Jim in his habitual manner by sending him into an exposed position? Jim had decided to treat the Chief's request about the light as if it *had* been a test, and he had been determined to pass it. He wanted to show the so-called cowboy that he, Jim Stringer, had a bit of steel about him. Jim didn't know why he'd been on the end of so many contemptuous looks from that direction – was it because he would not volunteer to be fired on in the shooting show? Or just because he was 'a cop'? Anyhow, he had grown tired of those looks.

Now Durrant himself spoke up, addressing Jim at unaccustomed length. 'You'd shut the light. I thought that gave me the all-clear to fire. I guess I jumped the gun, so to speak. I was shooting down the right channel; you were in the left. You were never in any danger.' He indicated the farthest of the two targets. He had obliterated the dead centre.

Saying nothing, Jim walked back to the firing positions.

With a shake of the head, Tom Brooks handed Jim the half-drunk bottle of beer he'd set down two minutes earlier. 'Kid's nuts,' he said.

It seemed Durrant wasn't done with his speech. 'Sorry if I scared you,' he said. 'But I don't believe I did.' He turned to the Chief. 'Sorry, pops,' and the Chief gave one of his twisted smiles. The incident was closed, but Jim believed he'd caused a small adjustment in the thinking of Jack Durrant.

Cynthia Lorne

Just then the door crashed open.

'Sin!' said Durrant, grinning.

In fact, he'd said 'Cyn', and here was Cynthia Lorne, smiling a silly smile, and trying to make up for having banged open the door by closing it with exaggerated care. Tom Brooks went to take her aside, but in that bare, bright hall there was no 'aside'. She did not seem to want to look at her husband – she was trying to look *around* him, like a child playing peek-a-boo, and the person she wanted to see was Durrant. She said, 'Kid! I have the toolbelt.'

'You sure do,' said Durrant.

She wore, half over and half under her expensive baggy jumper, a gunbelt with two holsters but no pistols in the holsters. She also wore a headband, with a single feather in the side of it. Brooks, with his hand on her shoulder, turned her quite roughly towards him. 'I thought you were going to turn in early?'

'I was, Tom!' she said. 'I was, and I did! And I had a lovely refreshing sleep!'

She'd certainly had a lovely refreshing something: her silvery flame had been reignited. She broke away from Brooks, and for the moment seemed like an actress in the spotlight who had forgotten her lines. With a sweep of her arm from her waist to her head she said, 'I hardly know whether I'm a cowboy or an Indian.' She looked in turn at Jim, the Chief, Walter, Durrant – but not Brooks. 'Good evening, gentlemen,' she said, and then laughed. 'I was hoping you would let a girl join in the gunplay. But as you can see, I'm a little short of guns!' She indicated the empty holsters, smiling hugely. To Jim the appeal of this person lay in a series of paradoxes: she was very small, but her beauty gave her great presence. She was plainly intoxicated, but with no loss of gracefulness. On her, the gun belt looked absurd, but it also complemented what Bernadette would have called the modern 'look', emphasizing the hips.

The Chief was looking at Jim in puzzlement. Tom Brooks, having retreated from his wife, was leaning against the wall. As for Durrant, he was grinning boldly back at Cynthia. She brought him alive, and Jim knew this was all quite disastrous. He thought he'd better say something, but had no idea what. In desperation, he said, 'Can I fetch you a glass of water, Miss Lorne?' He had decided on 'Miss' at the last minute. Lorne was her stage name, after all. She was Miss Lorne and Mrs Brooks at the same time.

'Thanks awfully,' she said. 'Do you *have* a glass of water?'

All the other men were watching Jim.

'I could go to the Institute to fetch one. It'll only take a minute.'

'Oh, please don't bother going into an institution on my account,' she said, and looked so warmly at Jim he thought she was on the point of coming over to kiss him. 'You're a really lovely man, Mr Stranger. I've always thought that. I mean always since I met you about three hours ago, was it? And your daughter is a doll, and your wife is also very lovely. And, you know, I think they should *both* go on the stage! In fact you should set up as an impress ... arrino, or something. You know what I mean – like Tom here. Now won't *anyone* give me a gun? I promise not to shoot anybody, but only the targets on the bullseyes!'

Under the heavy gaze of Brooks, Durrant went up to her.

'How do I look, Kid?' she said, suddenly helpless.

'You look nice,' he said. 'Real nice. But perhaps you're a little tired, dear? Look here – would you like to try a little fast draw before we call it a day?'

He flashed a glance at Tom Brooks – asking permission, perhaps, to indulge his wife. Brooks gave a half-nod.

Durrant carried one of the chairs out into the middle of the range. Back at the gun rest he entered into a conference with Walter, who took a pistol out of the doctor's bag – one of the Colts – and said something like, 'You sure about this, Kid?' Seeing it was coming her way, Cynthia Lorne gave a kind of gasp.

'The equalizer!' she said.

Durrant broke it to see if it was loaded; evidently it was. He climbed over the gun rest and beckoned to Cynthia Lorne. She scrambled over the sleepers, giving everybody a glimpse of her suspender belts, and trotted down towards Durrant. 'Now this is a single action piece,' he told her, to demonstrate the hammer of the Colt. So you must remember to do *this* before you squeeze the trigger.'

She put the gun into her right-hand holster.

Durrant said, 'Do you want to go against a falling dime?'

'I rather think I would. But what does it mean?'

'I flip a coin – 'fraid it's going to have to be a shilling. You must clear leather, cock and fire before it lands.'

From behind the gun rest, the Chief gave a snort of contempt. Walter was sitting on the gun rest.

'Can I start with my hand on the gun?' Cynthia enquired.

'You can if you want to cheat,' said Durrant.

'But you know, dear, I think I'm going to *have* to cheat. Let's try anyway. Oh, by the way, what will I be shooting *at*?'

'Just fire in the opposite direction from where these gents are standing,' said Durrant. 'Ready?'

'No! But let's do it!'

Durrant moved to about six feet to the right of her gun hand. He flipped the coin up in the air; it clattered to the floor. Only then did Cynthia draw the gun and cock the hammer; then she turned towards the gun rest. Jim, and every man behind the gun rest, made to duck.

'That wasn't very good, was it?' she said. 'And I haven't even fired. I want to try again!'

This time was a little more creditable, albeit performed over the course of about ten seconds, and finished with a shot at, or towards, a target. From the gun rest Walter applauded. Tom Brooks was looking away, examining cracks in the wall, tracing one with his finger.

'I want to try again *again*,' said Cynthia Lorne. 'This time kindly toss the coin a little higher. Or – wait. Could you stand on a chair when you toss it? Then it'll take longer to fall.'

The third time was better still, the sequence accomplished in perhaps six seconds, and the bullet lodged in the edge of a target.

'And now the most important thing,' said Cynthia Lorne as she raised the gun to her face. She pursed her rouged lips and Jim thought she was going to kiss the piece; instead she blew on the thin stream of smoke trailing from the barrel. To Durrant she said, 'It's very necessary to do that, isn't it?'

'Not really, Cyn. Not since about 1890 when we quit using the black powder cartridges.'

'Oh, but in the flicks. For the close-up at the end – you

know. When the heroine has shot the baddie. When she has *shot him down!*' Jim heard a sigh from the direction of Tom Brooks. 'Will you help me off with this belt, Kid?' There was some difficulty in unbuckling it, which they both greatly enjoyed.

'Now you must make *your* shot,' said Cynthia.

The preparation occurred silently, as in a film. Durrant handed the coin to Cynthia; he put on the belt, lowered the Colt into the right-hand holster, faced the targets. Cynthia flipped the coin, and Durrant cleared leather, cocked and fired – did three things, that is to say, but it looked like one. There was a new, ragged hole in the centre of the target, and Jim believed Durrant had beaten the coin, although it was hard to say because the noise of the gun had masked that of the shilling hitting the floor. Durrant seemed pleased with the shot, anyhow, for he gave Cynthia Lorne a wink.

'You're no slouch with the equalizer, pardner,' she said, in a pretty good American accent. 'Now blow the smoke' – and Durrant obliged.

'Give me the gun,' said Cynthia. She turned towards the gun rest again.

'Darling,' she said, 'would you like a try?'

Brooks pulled on his cigarette and eyed her for a while. Then he dropped his cigarette and crushed it with his boot heel. He climbed fast over the gun rest and, as his wife held the Colt out for him, he withdrew another pistol from his suit-coat pocket – the Webley he'd mentioned before, Jim assumed, but it was an unusual Webley: very short-barrelled, a true pocket revolver, as favoured by men who didn't want their suit outline spoiled. He fired three angry shots at one of the targets, and there was something a bit queer about his firing action, but as far as Jim could tell the results were pretty good. Pocketing the pistol again, he took his wife back to the gun rest, which she obediently clambered over. They approached the exit, pausing only for Brooks to light another cigarette in the doorway. 'Good*night*, gentlemen,' he called over his shoulder.

Only Walter replied, in a sad, echoing voice. 'So long, Tom!'

Durrant was holding the Colt and smiling shyly down at his boots, even though his career in films was surely over before it had begun.

There was the distant rumble of a late train, for Brooks had not closed the door behind him.

'Okey-dokey,' said Walter, in an attempt to pretend all this had been harmless gunplay. 'Three rounds left in the piece.' He was looking at Durrant's Colt. 'You know the drill, gents: draw, cock and fire. Anyone fancy trying to beat the falling dime?' But the dime had been a shilling, and there were no takers.

A mysterious seething sound arose, like gas escaping – but it couldn't be that, for it came from outside. Beyond the open doorway heavy summer rain was falling. Jim stepped out into it to watch the departure of Brooks and Cynthia Lorne. Brooks had a gun; he was angry with his wife. Jim didn't really think violence was in the offing, but he realized he wanted to protect Cynthia Lorne.

Neither of them belonged in this place, which was perhaps why she now took his hand – or he hers. They were about to turn the corner when they raised their clasped hands, and this was for Cynthia Lorne to perform a dancer's twirl. But they quickly let each other go and veered apart again. Then they were gone, and Jim was watching the rain.

3

YORK STATION,
EIGHT MINUTES PAST SEVEN ON
THE EVENING OF SUNDAY, 6 DECEMBER

In the war, Jim had been fired at by many anonymous enemies, but here was a single individual proposing to kill him. It was as though the war, aggrieved at Jim's having survived, had sent out a special agent to finish the job. But if Jim defeated the special agent, the war might finally end.

Jim believed he knew the identity of the man holding the gun in his black-gloved hand, but he couldn't be *absolutely* sure. A clear five seconds had gone by since the gun had been raised towards Jim and the hammer thumbed back. And the train had not yet departed, even though the right-away had been given. Jim might have been tempted to think time had stopped, but Lydia had not stopped. Jim could hear her footsteps coming up from behind as she said something like, 'What are you staring at, Jim?' But her words were drowned out because the locomotive of the Liverpool train had commenced to scream – for which there was a very simple explanation. Some delay, perhaps connected to the mechanical problem the fireman had been investigating beforehand, had caused the steam pressure to lift the safety valve, so the screaming was accompanied by a geyser of steam rocketing up to the station roof.

Lydia was alongside Jim, speaking inaudibly. She had to be got out of the way, so Jim opened the nearest carriage door. 'Get in!' he roared. She couldn't hear him, but she knew what he meant, and now she'd seen the man with the gun. An orange flame floated from the barrel, and it was as if the firing of the gun rather than the blowing of a whistle had started the train, for it was now moving.

Jim pushed Lydia into the train. As he climbed in, he fell on top of her. He stood up immediately, which caused him some pain. Lydia stood more slowly.

Jim said, 'Are you all right?'

She nodded.

'Are *you*?'

Jim had forgotten about the Detective Special. Well, it was such a small piece, fairly buried in his right-hand suit-coat pocket. He verified the presence of the gun by pressing his hand against that pocket. There was blood on that hand – and on the suit coat.

'I'm shot,' he said.

4

FLASHBACK TO
FRIDAY, 2 OCTOBER

Fog

There was already ink on Jim's right hand, and he'd only just started to write his report on what he called 'ticket fraud' but what Mr Oughtred, the York District Passenger Manager, called 'fare evasion'. Jim had written the date – Friday, 2 October – and underlined it twice. It was the second underlining – in retrospect, completely unnecessary – that had brought the fatal smudge. It was always the same: the harder he tried to be neat, the more ink there'd be in the wrong places. He blotted the smudge; the date was still perfectly legible. He looked out through the window of the Police Office.

Fog was in the station, so he couldn't even see the main 'Up'. When he'd walked along that platform on his way to work, the illuminated station signals had stood out like so many blurred jewels: red and green mainly, but with jaundiced yellow on occasion. Now, all was quiet, but the fog detonators had been going off all morning as the trains rolled in and out, reminding Jim of the war, and making him sweat.

Later in the morning, some further entertainment had been laid on for anyone hanging about on the main 'Up'. The Chief had been drilling some constables. Most of the twenty or so attached to the York Police Office hadn't got an earthly when it came to standing to attention, or even 'at ease'. The constables had now dispersed to station patrols, which were always stepped up in fog, it being the next best thing to night time for the criminal classes. The Chief might be out on patrol himself, preventing whichever constable he'd teamed up with from having a smoke in some quiet siding. Alternatively, he might've adjourned to the Parlour Bar of the Second-Class Refreshment Room, or he might be in the disused waiting room over on Platform 14, which he used as a kind of annex to the Police Office.

Platform 14 was the outermost one. You had to go through an arch in the station wall to reach it. The goods yards lay beyond 14, and more trains on its line gave it the go-by – being freights or non-stop expresses – than actually called there. The Chief held private consultations in that waiting room, on occasion with the bad lads of York, whose company he preferred to any other copper's except Jim. And if any constable of the Police Office was asked by Wright, the Chief Clerk, to step over to Platform 14, they knew they were in for a rating from the Chief. Sometimes of an afternoon the Chief would even have a nap on Platform 14, stretched out on the long bench, with the horsehair bursting through the holes in the leather, and his celluloid collar undone. But he never did that in the morning, and it was still only half ten.

The telephone on the Chief's desk was ringing. It was one of two telephones in the office and Wright – the only other man on the premises just then – was talking on the other. 'Can't help you with that,' he was saying. 'It's a matter for the city police.'

So Jim walked through to the Chief's office, but as he reached for the receiver the telephone fell silent. It was really just an alcove, this office, but, besides having his own phone, the Chief also had his own fireplace, and it had a very pretty hearth, with white and green tiles depicting climbing vines. The Chief never lit the fire, and the grate was full of the stubs of his horrible little cigars, and sometimes a whole one, because every so often the Chief would discover a rogue Baby in the carton – one that didn't draw – and chuck it away in disgust. Who would be sitting here in the New Year when the Chief had departed? That was up in the air. It wouldn't be Jim, anyhow. York was the headquarters of both a police district and a police region, and you needed to be a super-intendent to run a region. The smart money was on some bloke from the London Region, who either was, or soon would be, a super. In any case, the whole affair would be decided from London – by Colonel Maynard, LNER Chief of Police.

Wright had got shot of his own caller. 'Where's the Chief?' Jim said.

'I've no notion,' said Wright, who was now perched on the edge of his desk in order to swing his feet, which he liked doing. Wright was a very grey man in the early or even middle sixties, but with surplus energy, owing to having always been bone idle. He indicated one of two cocoa tins that stood on the mantlepiece. 'I put five bob in there yesterday,' he said. A label pasted to it read, 'The Chief'. The men of the Police Office were supposed to pay into it for the Chief's retirement present. They'd not been in any hurry to do so, and for weeks there'd been little advance on the ten bob Jim had put in to get the ball rolling. (As well as being in charge of the fund he would be buying the present and making the speech at the Chief's leaving do.)

'You might just have enough for a clock now,' said Wright. 'Only the Chief doesn't want a clock. He told me that yesterday. He said another word before "clock" an' all. I told him, "That'll cost you a tanner in *there*, Chief."' The second tin on the mantlepiece was labelled 'Swear Box'. 'He didn't pay in, though,' Wright continued, 'and what he told me to do after I'd asked him should by rights have cost him another tanner.' Wright was still swinging his bloody legs.

'You could buy him a pipe rack, you know ... only he hardly ever smokes a pipe. Tell you what, though: *I* wouldn't mind a nice pipe rack when *I* go.'

The Chief's phone was ringing again. In hopes of escaping Wright, Jim went to answer it again. The call was from the Railway Exchange in Manchester: LMS territory. The caller was put on – a strong Mancunian accent, but a confident one. This, and the caller's brusque 'Is Saul about?' told Jim it was a senior copper on the line.

'Not just at present. Can I take a message?' Looking down in search of a pencil and scrap of paper, Jim saw that the gun drawer was open.

'Tell him it's about the cowboy,' said the senior man.

'Jack Durrant?'

'That's him,' said the senior man, surprised – and annoyed – at Jim's being in the know. 'Who's speaking?' he demanded. When Jim told him he said, 'Well, this is Superintendent Sowerby at Manchester. You can tell your governor that Durrant's very likely done a double murder.'

Jim looked at the photograph on the Chief's desk. In the absence of any wife or child, it showed the York Railway Institute tug-of-war team winning a tug-of-war contest against some other Railway Institute in about 1906.

A double murder. It was the kind of event that having been in the war taught you to expect. He'd seen the signs of trouble around Durrant and not wanted to see them. He took down a number and said he'd have the Chief call Sowerby the moment he came in.

The tug-of-war picture had a defect – too much light had got in at one side – and that was the impression Jim had had back in August, in the Station Hotel and at the firing range. Several matters had been too clearly revealed, as if by a series of lightning flashes. He returned to his own desk and sat in silence, or tried to.

'What's up?' said Wright.

'Nowt much.'

'Come on – out with it.'

'Apparently, a lad called Jack Durrant's done for two people.' Jim stood, and put on his topcoat.

'Jack Durrant?' said Wright. 'Who's he when he's at home?'

'A cowboy.'

'Eh?'

'Tell you about it later, Wrighty.'

Jim crossed the footbridge. While the fog had been somewhat dispersed by train movements in the station proper, it had made itself at home on Platform 14. The abandoned waiting room was locked; only the Chief had a key. Jim put his face to the door glass, making out the empty fireplace, the dead aspidistra in the pot it shared with the Chief's cigar stubs, the clock that had stopped at quarter past four. The framed poster over the fireplace had been produced by a dead company: the North Eastern Railway, predecessor of the London & North Eastern. It showed a gloomy, blue-green landscape of rocks and hills, relieved by a pool of light in the foreground. In this, fairies danced above a legend reading, 'The Magic of the Yorkshire Dales'. Every one of those fairies looked like Cynthia Lorne.

Jim re-crossed the footbridge. A London train had just come in. Businessmen flowed away from it, carrying their heavy bags of documents towards the station lobby and the taxi rank beyond. They were not here for York itself, so much as for a continuation of London. Jim merged in with them but diverted into the Parlour Bar of the Second-Class Refreshment Room. No sign of the Chief or anybody else in there. Jim managed to resist the thought of a pint.

Then he was minded to do something he'd been meaning to get around to for weeks. He turned left and walked out of the station. The misty air of York was impregnated with a burnt-chocolate smell – this being a 'making day' at the cocoa works. Cutting through the arch in the Bar Walls brought him face to face with what was now the LNER Head Office, having once been the NER Head Office: all the lights in there were lit against the darkness of the day. He followed a rattling tram as it crossed Lendal Bridge, looking quite intrepid as it headed off into the fog, which had entirely obliterated the Minster. Down in the water below, two coal barges were chained together. The rest of the river, he must take for granted.

On Museum Street he was tempted by Thomas's Hotel: he might just have a half pint, and not of brown, but only mild. That would be an enjoyable thing to do, and you ought to do enjoyable things while you still had the chance. Tom Brooks and Cynthia Lorne no longer had the chance, having been shot to death by Durrant – well, who else could Durrant have worked himself up to shooting?

In Thomas's Jim ordered a pint of mild. The place was cold and the fire smoked, as did the three other men in the public bar, who all looked thoroughly miserable. Somebody ought to remind them they were still, to some extent, alive. Having ordered a pint, Jim told himself he'd better leave an inch or two in the bottom of the glass, but in the event he drank it all off. It was only mild, after all.

Back outside, he crossed Museum Street to enter the warm, sleepy embrace of York Library. He climbed the wide stone steps up to the reference section. At the counter, beneath a sign reading 'SILENCE IS REQUESTED', he murmured his enquiry to a woman who seemed to disapprove of him, perhaps having smelt the beer on his breath – or because he had asked to see back numbers of a rather 'fast' publication: the film magazine *Picture Show*.

They had it, anyhow, and Jim took a bundle over to a table. Bernadette would sometimes read *Picture Show*, but Jim had never looked at it in detail. It was really a series of gossip columns, punctuated by fuzzy photographs of film stars, some of them – billed as 'Art Supplements' – filling a whole page. There were also many advertisements for beauty treatments, and Jim had been reading things like 'Superfluous Hair', 'Does Tennis Freckle You?' and 'How Do They Get Such Beautiful Skins?' for ten minutes before he came to a mention of Cynthia Lorne. It was in a column headed, 'Do You Know?'

'*Do you know*,' Jim read, 'that Cynthia Lorne is much smaller than she appears on screen, and is just as pretty?'

He turned to another number, where – under 'This Week's Films' – he found a mention of the picture by Tom Brooks that Jim had seen, *The Ranch Hand*.

Western Drama about a lowly ranch hand who corrects the vices and follies of the ranch owner and his family. There's plenty of romantic interest and a few (a very few) thrills, but the story peters out at the halfway mark, and Dan Kelly, as our pious hero, is irritating to the extent that, when at long last he rides off into the sunset, this viewer was entertaining the desperate hope that he would finally do something wrong, to wit, fall off his horse.

Jim wondered whether this was a particularly peevish reviewer, but no, the other write-ups were pretty good. In the same edition, he came upon Cynthia Lorne again:

this time a small picture, under the heading, 'From the Back Row: Comments on Cinematic Things in General'.

In *The Black Circle*, the latest of Piccadilly Pictures' Cynthia Lorne vehicles, Miss Lorne is certainly delightfully easy to look at, and the way she wears her clothes is a joy. But as in her previous release, *A Mistaken Marriage*, her natural charm and vivacity – so frequently demonstrated in her early Canonbury films – is forfeited. She looks most uncomfortable as she portrays another in her run of heavy sirens. The audience seemed similarly discomfited at the screening attended by your correspondent, the lovely Mrs Lorne evoking nervous laughter rather than sympathy for her romantic travails.

Behind Jim, somebody had made a noisy entrance into the Reference Room. It was a boy, red-faced and dripping from the fog, carrying a pile of newspapers, wrapped in old ones and tied with string. These would be the day's first edition of the *Yorkshire Evening Press*, which in spite of its name was really *York's* daily newspaper. As such, it was the sacred text of York Library. Jim went and stopped the boy as he was leaving. 'Can I have a look at one of those?'

'Ask her,' said the boy. The woman who'd disapproved of Jim was cutting the string on the parcel.

'A copy will be placed on that table in due course,' she

said, pointing to the other end of the room. 'If you want to read one sooner, you can always go out and buy one.'

Jim produced his warrant card, which he never liked doing. 'I'd like to see one now, if you don't mind.'

She didn't go so far as to hand a paper over, but just cut the string and left Jim to it. The fate that had been foretold in the sad eyes of Cynthia Lorne was set down in the hasty print of the 'Stop Press'. 'Body of film actress, Cynthia Lorne, discovered on Wednesday in Wharfe River at Bolton Abbey, nr. Skipton. Murder investigation to commence.'

Jim hated the sight of those words.

No mention of Tom Brooks. Perhaps he wasn't thought *worth* mentioning. Or the body hadn't been identified. What had taken the three of them to Bolton Abbey? Some sort of holiday, presumably. Even in autumn, it was a pleasure ground, and Jim had been there once, mainly for the sake of the train ride from Skipton to Bolton Abbey Station. There was the ruined Abbey itself, the woods and river walks, and a big, posh hotel, the Devonshire Arms – the whole Bolton Abbey estate being owned by the Dukes of Devonshire, in spite of being one of the most Yorkshire places imaginable. Another question was why the trio were still going about together, having had such a falling-out at York in late August.

Jim returned to his table, and another edition of *Picture Show* – this one dating from July 1924. It contained an interview with Brooks, who was pictured leaning against a car and smoking a cigarette, Cynthia Lorne alongside him. Judging by the grandeur of the street, they were somewhere in the middle of London. The article was headed, 'HIS WIFE AND STAR', with the subhead, 'Cynthia Lorne, as Seen Through the Eyes of Her Producer Husband, Tom Brooks'. It was written by 'Our London Correspondent':

It is said that it is practically impossible to get an interview with Tom Brooks, the well-known producer. He is not at all inclined to talk about himself. He is quite enthusiastic, however, to talk about his beautiful wife, Cynthia Lorne; so one day when I endeavoured to get a word with him, I assured him most sincerely that I wanted to hear about her, and that I would not talk about anyone else.

One of Tom Brooks's first remarks was rather astonishing until he went on to explain it. 'I am afraid I have not been quite fair to Cynthia. I have always been so desirous that the public should not get the idea that any favouritism was shown to her because she was my wife that I am afraid I have gone too far the other way, and rather played down her abilities in our publicity material, but I would like to state here and now that she is one of the greatest and most versatile actresses of the screen ...'

His theme was that while 'Miss Lorne' had made her name in 'the lightest of light comedies' she was now demonstrating versatility by taking on roles of a more dramatic nature. She was also invaluable to Brooks as an adviser on artistic and business matters. Several scenes in their latest film, *The Black Circle*, had been – in effect – conceived and directed by Miss Lorne, who was always on the lookout for talented young actors and actresses to join the 'informal company' of players Piccadilly Pictures had built up, there being 'no scintilla of jealousy' in the make-up of her personality. Brooks went on to talk about 'the real Cynthia'.

> She is very observant and has a delightful sense of humour. She is very clever at mimicking, with a fondness for reproducing the accents and phraseology of our friends, much to their astonishment. She is an extremely active person, a positive demon on the tennis court, and I'm afraid she disapproves most strongly of my smoking habit, and my propensity to lie in of a morning!

It was all, Jim felt, not quite true, and when it came to her physical health it might be the opposite of the truth, because Cynthia Lorne had liked a drink, to say the least.

Jim was turning pages. He did not believe Cynthia Lorne and Tom Brooks would get an obituary in any future edition of *Picture Show*, because the magazine did not seem to *carry* obituaries. The worst that could happen in its world was a bad review, and it seemed Tom Brooks and Piccadilly Pictures had been coming in for a few of those, which was surely Brooks's fault. Perhaps he wasn't very good at his job. Cynthia Lorne was good at hers, though, and her job was to make people fall in love with her.

Jim realized that he had fallen in love with her, ever since she had pirouetted in the rain on leaving the shooting range. He had dreamed about her. He had seen her latest film, *The Mistaken Marriage*, twice at the Electric Theatre, once with Lydia, once on his own. He had taken the train to Scarborough – again alone – to see *The Black Circle*, having read in the *Press* that it was on there at the Futurist Cinema. Jim had never previously been to a cinema on his own, and had certainly not travelled any distance to see a film. He had not mentioned his solo trips to Lydia; she would have surmised that he could only have gone to watch Cynthia Lorne, and she would have been correct.

Jim collected up the copies of *Picture Show* and returned them to the woman at the counter, who ignored him. As he descended the library steps, he felt ashamed of himself. Film fans were not a very dignified lot; he had been reminded of that in his reading just now. They could send their letters – 'fan mail' it was called – to the stars, care of *Picture Show*. They were mainly women, and their principal target was Rudolph Valentino, who had seemed to be on the cover of every other edition. Jim was a forty-year-old man. He was married and in love with his wife; it just so happened that Lydia had a rival in the shape of a dead woman.

The fog was still lying thick on Museum Street. People would suddenly appear and disappear. The yellow lantern above the entrance to Thomas's Hotel illuminated little more than the door, but as a man walked through that door he was briefly spotlit: a wiry old criminal (judging by his appearance) with bowler hat too small, dark coat too long. It was the Chief. Jim crossed the road and followed him in. The main bar lay to the left, but the Chief turned right, heading for the billiards room, which held one table, a small fireplace and a hatch for the serving of drinks. The Chief was banging a coin on the counter and calling 'Service!' when Jim tapped him on the shoulder. He swivelled round with fist raised.

'You nearly copped it there, lad. I thought it might be one of Bobby Hunter's pals.' The Chief had a cut over his right eye. Bobby Hunter was one of the regular bad lads of York Station.

'Hunter? Met him in the fog, did you, Chief?'

'Met him, and ran him in. He's in the copper shop nick.' There were no holding cells at the station, so prisoners had to be taken to the City Police Station on Lower Friargate, usually by cab.

'Offence?'

'Unlawful Possession ... and assault,' the Chief added, indicating his eye.

'What did he have? A picklock?'

'A crow.' (The Chief meant a crowbar.) 'In the Fruit Dock.'

'But he wouldn't be going after fruit, would he?'

The Chief shrugged. 'You seen the price of oranges these days? He had two sacks wrapped round his middle. I asked him to hand over the crow. He chucked it at me head and legged it. I was with Spencer, who chased him down.'

Stephen Spencer was barely twenty. He was about the most athletic of the constables, also the brightest. He'd been to a grammar school somewhere down south, and his old man had been an officer killed in the last week of the war. Spencer was coming up for his exam to join the detective branch, and there was no doubt of the outcome. Jim didn't much care for Spencer.

A small bloke had appeared at the small hatch. The Chief ordered two pints of brown and requested the billiard balls. 'Where've you been, lad?' he asked Jim.

'In the library.'

'The bloody *library*? What the bloody hell were you doing there?'

'Reading a magazine.'

The Chief shook his head.

Jim said, 'Did you get onto Sowerby?'

The Chief nodded.

Jim said, 'Cynthia Lorne's been shot dead up at Bolton Abbey. It was in the *Press*. Sowerby reckons Durrant did it, I know.'

'It's not a matter of what he reckons,' said the Chief. 'Durrant *did* it, and that's flat. It's a bloody shame, 'n' all. Had a brilliant future as a shootist, that lad.'

'Sowerby said two had been killed. The other's Tom Brooks, right? But he's not mentioned in the *Press*.'

'Body hasn't turned up yet. It's only a matter of time.'

'How do they know?'

'He's disappeared for starters. The pair of them were booked into the pub up there, the Devonshire.'

'Was Durrant booked in as well?'

'Aye.'

'Then what's happened to him?'

'He's scarpered, en't he? He was seen going away on the train on the day they think it happened. Or he was seen at Bolton Abbey Station, anyhow.'

The pints and the billiard balls arrived. Three was all you needed, which never seemed enough to Jim, who could play snooker after a fashion but was hopeless at billiards. The Chief would rather play billiards on his own than with Jim, and this he now commenced to do.

'Who's running the investigation?' said Jim.

'Monk. He's all right.'

Jim had heard of this character – a super with the Leeds City force. 'Monk,' he said. 'That's rum. To have a bloke called Monk investigating a killing that happened near an abbey.'

'You're going soft, lad.' The Chief fired his cue ball at the red ball, causing the cue ball to go into a pocket: 'in-off', this was called. It would be a mistake in snooker, but it got you points in billiards.

Jim said, 'It's not a railway police matter, then?'

The Chief had lit one of his cigars. He eyed Jim as he shook out the match. 'It could be,' he said. 'In part. The Midland boys have one of their lot involved. Fellow called Ibbotson. Sergeant at Skipton. He looks after the Bolton Abbey branch.' The Chief laid his cigar down on the edge of the billiard table before taking his next shot. You weren't supposed to do that, because the lighted end could burn the wood. He took his shot, apparently with a satisfactory result. He picked up the cigar and eyed Jim again. 'After I spoke to Sowerby, I got on to Monk; told him I had a man with some experience of the personalities involved in this matter – in particular, knowledge of the wanted man. He's a bit shorthanded at present, and he's happy for you to assist.'

'Good,' said Jim, and he decided not to enlarge on that. He didn't say he wanted to avenge the murder of Cynthia

Lorne, because a detective inspector was supposed to be more objective than that. Instead he said, 'First thing will be to go and see his best pal Walter Bassett.'

The Chief nodded. 'And tomorrow, you'll get up to Bolton Abbey.'

'Right. I'll consult the timetable.' (Jim liked consulting timetables.) 'It's generally quicker via Harrogate – rather than Leeds.'

'Is it now,' said the Chief, who had no interest in the times of trains. 'Ibbotson will be waiting for you.'

'Know anything about him?'

'Apparently, he's an idiot.'

'In what way?'

'You'll see.'

The Chief took another shot, and almost smiled at the result; he was apparently doing rather well against himself. He paced around the table, weighing all the angles three balls could create. 'She was shot in the back, you know? Twice.'

Jim said nothing to that.

The Chief took his next shot and said, 'Nice.' It was certainly a sarcastic comment, either on his own shot, or the shooting of Cynthia Lorne.

'What calibre?'

'They can't say for sure. There was some distortion, but probably a forty-five. Think on, lad,' said the Chief. 'Durrant's dangerous, and he's at large out there.' He waved his cue at a foggy window. 'You wouldn't go up against his revolver in the shooting show, but you're in the firing line now. When we get back to the office, we're going to get you a nice little pistol from the gun drawer.'

What with his recent scrap in the goods yard, the billiards and beer, and putting Jim Stringer in the way of danger, the Chief was enjoying himself. How he would get on in retirement, Jim could not imagine.

The Detective Special

When Jim and the Chief got back to the station, they had a bit of bother with four big blokes from Hull who'd been cutting up rough in the Parlour Bar, having been refused further drinks on account of being drunk. They'd been making out that, naturally, they were drunk, their train back to Hull having been delayed owing to fog. It was the railway company's *fault* they were drunk, so to speak. And then the usual thing: they'd all done their bit in the War, so were entitled to a few drinks now and again. Then they'd started taking books from the bookstall and pitching them on to the tracks of the main 'Down', so bringing Wilful Damage into the picture. It was necessary to send a constable to Lower Friargate, requesting the City force to dispatch its police van, the York railway force – in common with all railway police – not possessing any such vehicle of its own. When the bad lads were off their hands, the Chief took Jim into his office, where he yanked open the gun drawer. There were half a dozen pieces in there.

'The wife doesn't like me having a gun in the house,' said Jim.

The Chief eyed Jim narrowly. 'They could be your famous last words. If Durrant comes after you with his Colt, it's not going to be like the funfair, you know. You won't have the option on whether he fires at you.'

It'd be a while, Jim realized, before he could live down his refusal to get up on stage at the shooting show.

'Have you thought that it might be *Brooks* who comes after me?'

The Chief was shaking his head. 'Why will you not *have* it? Durrant's the killer!'

'That night in the range,' said Jim, 'I thought he acted pretty white.'

'He took a pot shot at you, for Christ's sake.'

'But it was a kind of test. And then he apologized.'

The Chief made no reply. He was laying out the guns.

'I don't want to faff about with any hammer-cocking,' said Jim.

'How about this?' said the Chief, picking up the smallest piece. 'I only got this in last week. You're a detective – supposedly – and this is a Colt Detective Special, all the way from America. Double action, and it's chambered for a thirty-eight, which'll give you something decent to go against Durrant and his forty-five. Swing out, six-shot chamber, lovely little two-inch barrel, walnut square butt, half-moon sight. It's an *extremely* pretty gun. Put it in your pocket and you'll hardly know it's there, and – more important in your case – nor will your bloody wife.'

'At the range, Brooks had a short-barrelled gun. He said it was a Webley.'

'Aye. A British Bulldog, that was – and the early lot *were* made by Webley. Nice little double-action piece; five-round chamber.'

'Calibre?'

'Came in various – thirty-eight or forty-five.'

The Detective Special did seem to more or less disappear into Jim's suit-coat pocket when he tried it for size.

'All right,' said Jim. 'Sold.'

The piece was already loaded, but the Chief was fishing in his other drawer, where he kept his ammunition (and his cigars). He handed Jim a tin of 38s.

'I'm not going into a bloody war, you know.'

'You might be, lad,' said the Chief, obviously enjoying the thought.

Walter Bassett

Jim carried the Detective Special in his pocket as he walked to Lawrence Street, which was just outwith the

City Walls on the east side of town. It was about five o'clock as he stood contemplating the little post office. The window was brightly lit in the fog, and the strangeness of the set-up was advertised by this illumination.

The premises were in the middle of an ordinary terrace. The pillar box out front was too close to the shop door, and it leaned badly. Alongside the shop door was another, extra door, thinner than all the others in the terrace, and Jim supposed this must lead to Walter Bassett's living quarters. The sign over the window read, 'Post Office, Provisions, Book Store'. '*Store*', not 'shop'. Posted onto the window was an advert for Woodbines and a notice: 'Radio Licences Available Here'. Behind the glass was a book-shelf with the book covers facing outwards. Jim had heard of one title: *Riders of the Purple Sage* by Zane Grey – that was a famous book.

The shop interior smelt of dust and ripe bananas. About half of it was given over to bookshelves. The actual post office counter was closed. You knew that because the parcel scales were covered with a cloth, and because Bassett was sitting at another counter for the sale of sweets, cigarettes, a few dusty food tins and four ripe bananas. Bassett had on a worn black suit, a waistcoat in the same condition and a skimpy (therefore somehow American-looking) tie. He was smoking a pipe and reading a book. Fragments of tobacco littered book and counter. Seeing Jim, he stood up. 'Mr Stringer!' he said. 'To what do I owe the honour, sir?'

He spoke like an actor, Jim thought, as they shook hands. The book Bassett had set down was *A History of the Pony Express: 1860–61*. The book store was obviously where Bassett had his fun. Rough, hand-drawn signs were pasted up over the shelves: 'Colonel Cody (Buffalo Bill) and Related', 'Doc Holliday and Wyatt Earp', 'Film Books' and 'Boys' Papers (For Boys of All Ages!)'. Also, 'Loaded Guns Must Be Cached With The Proprietor', and Jim wondered how the General Post Office (surely a pretty straight-laced set-up) let him get away with it all. A lone customer stood amid bookshelves – a little bloke in a damp Macintosh.

Bassett said, 'Have a browse, Jim, while I fix us a coffee.' His easy-going manner suggested he had no notion of what Durrant had done or was suspected of having done. In which case, Jim thought he would leave him in the dark a little longer: he might not speak freely once he'd heard the news. Jim moved over to the bookshelves, where the customer shuffled aside to make room for him. He was flicking through a picture book called *Wild West Weekly Annual*. Bassett had disappeared into a back room. Jim picked up a book from the shelves. He read, 'A high-stakes faro game was drawing most of the money over to a far corner of the Texicano Saloon . . .'

When Bassett returned, he was carrying a tray. In place of a teapot was a battered article Jim presumed to be a *coffee* pot. Jim glanced at the book Bassett had been reading. 'The Pony Express was a kind of post office of the Old West, wasn't it?'

'You got that right,' said Bassett, and Jim wondered whether he'd got that expression from Durrant or vice versa. It must be that Durrant had got it from him, since Walter Bassett genuinely did come from the States, whereas Durrant would just come out with the odd Americanism.

Bassett said, 'The Pony Express is one of my historical interests.'

Jim said, 'What are Durrant's historical interests?'

The stranger at the bookshelves was listening.

Bassett said, 'Doc Holliday is always number one for the Kid.'

'On account of his shooting skills?'

'Doc was no slouch with an equalizer, but it was his all-round style that the Kid appreciates. I mean, he dressed quite fine-ified ...'

'All in black,' put in the stranger. 'I hope this Kid you're on about doesn't have a cough like the Doc's.'

'Jim', said Bassett, 'this is my good friend Al Mason, who appreciates a good horse opera. Al, this is my other good friend, Detective Inspector Jim Stringer.'

Being a small, clerkly type, who'd forgotten to remove his bicycle clips, Al Mason looked more like an Alan than an Al.

'Was Doc Holliday an actual doctor?' asked Jim.

Al Mason shook his head. 'Dentist. The only interesting one that ever lived.'

'Not so fast,' said Bassett. 'William "Doc" Carver was a dentist.'

'Carver?' said Mason.

'Associate of Buffalo Bill's. Toured England with a shooting act in the 1870s. Carver shattered five thousand glass balls out of a total of six thousand, two hundred and twelve thrown up for him over a seven-hour period – but maybe you don't think that's interesting.'

Mason took the picture book over to Walter.

'How much for this?'

'Excellent choice, sir. Yours for a shilling?'

'That's going it a bit,' said Mason.

'What say I throw in a couple of Buffalo Bill tales?'

'Read all those,' said Mason. He paid up anyhow. As he quit the shop, Bassett was re-lighting his pipe. He poured out the coffee and invited Jim to sit next to him. Jim sipped the coffee: it tasted kind of burnt.

Bassett said, 'You look like a man with a good deal on his mind, Jim.'

'When was the last time you saw Durrant?'

'Well, now: he came back here after that night in the shooting range ... and what a night that was. A regular booze-hound, your governor, ain't he? He stayed here the next two or three nights, then he lit out for the Wild West – Bradford, sort of way.'

'Why there?'

'To shoot in some shooting shows.'

'Not seen or heard from him since?'

'I believe I had a postcard last month.'

'Can I see it?'

'Sorry, Jim. Thrown it out.'

Jim did not believe that Walter Bassett would throw out a postcard from Jack Durrant. He explained what was supposed to have occurred at Bolton Abbey and Bassett listened, sucking on his pipe and nodding. For a while after Jim had finished, Bassett kept silence. Then he said, 'Do you credit that tale, Jim?'

'I take it you don't?'

Bassett was shaking his head. 'You say Brooks is unaccounted for. Who's to say he wasn't the shooter?'

'You think Brooks shot his own wife?'

'Well,' said Bassett. 'He wouldn't be the first, would he?' He kept his pipe in his mouth as he spoke, and his words made little flames leap from the bowl. All of a sudden he was a more serious proposition: a harder man. 'That filly could get any man's mad up, wouldn't you say? A somewhat flighty creature. Flirtatious, too.'

'Do you think there was anything between her and Durrant?'

Bassett chose not to answer that question. Instead he said, 'I'll tell you why I don't think the Kid was responsible . . . You ever hear of the Code of the West?'

'Not exactly.'

'You drink your whisky with your gun hand, you keep your word and so on. But it's mainly about who you can and can't shoot. You don't shoot an unarmed opponent; a man doesn't shoot a woman, and he doesn't shoot anybody *at all* in the back. So there's three reasons why the Kid didn't shoot Cynthia Lorne.'

'I see.'

'*Do* you, Jim? I think I told you the Kid wrote Western tales? Well, the Code figures in most of them; he was a great believer in it, I can assure you. A typical pay-off in the Kid's tales has the two main characters in a stand-off or showdown – a duello.'

'Pistols at ten paces?'

'That kind of thing. A shooting match on equal terms, as required by the Code.'

'Are his stories any good?'

'They need a little editing before they can be submitted, and I'm happy to look them over. His dialogue's a little overdone but, hell, you could say that about Zane Grey, who's sold millions. Thing about the Kid ... he has an imagination. His stories are heartfelt and they contain real people. They're not just shoot-'em-ups, Jim.'

'Have they been printed? Published, I mean?'

'A couple of times, yes,' said Walter, and he stepped out from behind the counter. At the bookshelves, he picked up a paper-bound volume. The cover showed a desperate-looking character riding a horse while shooting two revolvers. The book was called *Smoking Colts, No. 6 (Stories by the New Young Western Writers)*. It contained about twenty short stories. 'The Kid has one in here,' said Bassett, flicking through the book until he came to a tale called 'One to Ten', billed as having been written by Ned Keach. Jim had heard the name before: Cynthia Lorne had mentioned it in the hotel.

Jim said, 'A pen name?'

'Well,' said Bassett, 'he was always looking for the perfect Western alias, whether for stage, screen or print. He likes "Ned Keach", but he's played around with others. In the Old West, Jim, nicknames were usually given on the ironic principle. Laughing Sam Carey was never known to crack a smile. Any "Curly" was generally bald. A few months back, the Kid and I were discussing this very point. I said, "If we applied the principle to you, Kid, you could be Rowdy."'

'Because he doesn't say much? He keeps his mouth for breathing?'

'Just so, Jim – just so. See, the Kid's a dark horse. Much more than just a crackshot. See for yourself.'

As Walter smoked, Jim read the beginning of 'One to Ten':

When Bill Doughty awoke, the dawn – cold and red – was taking possession of Broken Wagon Valley.

His saddle partner, Jake Hogan, was strapping on his cartridge-studded gun belt. Hogan had made coffee for himself and now the coffee kettle lay on its side, and the campfire had died. Hogan had had his drink and got warm, and that was all that mattered to him. 'What's the lay, boss?' Bill enquired of Hogan, and he cursed himself inwardly for being so craven as to call this evil-brained jumped-up cowpuncher 'boss'.

'Listen,' said Hogan, 'and you'll know.'

Doughty listened. At first, there was no sound but the racing river far below. Then Doughty heard a distant thunder, which became by degrees the rumble of horses' hooves. He reached for his own gun belt.

Jim got the idea: it was a tale about a decent young man fallen in with a villainous older one. He flipped back to the opening page, where he read, '*Smoking Colts* is published by Armistead & Bannister Limited, 7(A) Prowse Place, Camden, London NW.'

'Can I take this away?'

'Certainly, Jim,' said Bassett, and he indicated the price: 9d. The gloves were coming off, all right.

'Tell me about Durrant,' said Jim, handing over a bob.

Walter Bassett, it turned out, had first met Durrant a month or so before the York Gala. He'd seen him in the same shooting show in the little town of Knaresborough, which was about 20 miles from York, in late July. Brooks and Cynthia Lorne had been present – it was *their* first meeting with Durrant as well.

'How did they first hear about him?'

'Not sure. He's quite often been written up in the papers, and they were looking for a cowboy actor. They wanted to make a test film of him.'

'And did they?'

'I reckon so.'

'When?'

'Not sure. Not long after the York show, I think.'

'But you never saw it?'

'Nope. But I believe I know what it was called.'

'What?'

'*Powder Smoke.*'

After the Knaresborough encounter, Bassett had become a kind of camp follower of the Shooting Show, seeing it on three subsequent Sundays when his post office was closed. He knew Durrant had 'done a little jail time', and he knew what for. 'He made no bones about that, and, take note – no violence was involved. The Kid's gunplay is strictly for showbiz. He's no killer, Jim. Even in his stories, the hero shoots to wing, not to kill.'

'So nobody dies?'

'That would be putting it a *little* strongly . . . Incidentally, shall I tell you why the Kid was hard on you that night in August? He told me when we were walking to the range. You looked somewhat like the lawman who arrested him.

He was pretty ratty all that day, and he wasn't thinking straight. He knew he shouldn't have opened up with the gun when you were near the targets, but you'll recall that he apologized.'

'Sort of,' said Jim.

'The Kid's a tough customer – a ten-minute egg. But he plays fair.'

'You obviously think a lot of him.'

'Me and the Kid get on like a prairie fire.'

'Any idea why they went to Bolton Abbey?'

'I don't know anything about that trip.'

Jim said, 'There was obviously bad blood between Brooks and Durrant. I'm surprised the association continued after the Gala.'

Bassett gave a shrug. 'I think the bad blood ran several ways.'

'Brooks had not come to any financial arrangement with Durrant?'

'Nothing that I knew of, but the Kid's a hot property. Brooks wasn't the only film man interested in him.'

He was sticking to the present tense where his protégé was concerned.

Jim said, 'Where did Durrant sleep when he put up here?'

'In the spare room I have over the shop.' Bassett looked up towards the ceiling.

'Where else would he put up?'

'Sometimes at his ma's place.'

'Where's that?'

'Downtown Sheffield. But the Kid is itinerant. He travels about with the fairs.'

'Does he just work that one shooting show?'

'He's connected to three or four.'

'You met his mother?'

'Nope.'

'What about the father?'

'He's just as dead as dead can be.'

'Are you surprised by all this?'

'Well … I thought there might be some kind of fuss eventually.'

'Because Cynthia was sweet on Durrant?'

This time Bassett gave an answer, of sorts. 'Maybe she *was* sweet on him. Or maybe he just stood for something she wanted.'

'Like what?'

Freedom, escape – from Brooks, who controlled her life in all respects: money, career, emotions. Her looks, too. Brooks made her a blonde, you know.'

'And to deal with the situation, she drank heavily?'

'You got that right – and don't we all? But it wasn't just the drink. When Cynthia went to the ladies' room, she powdered her nose, but not in the usual way, Jim.'

So it seemed another sort of powder was in the picture – besides that used to propel the bullets. Walter sat back,

100

smoking. A woman in a sou'wester had come in out of the fog. 'I'm after cashing a postal order,' she said.

'Sorry, ma'am', said Walter, indicating the closed post office counter. 'We open again at nine tomorrow.'

'Surely you can open up for a minute? It's a matter of urgency.'

Walter repeated his apology; the woman turned on her heel. As she quit the shop, Walter muttered, 'Get on your horse and be gone.' It struck Jim that Walter was not over-keen on the ladies. He turned back to Jim. 'The way you figure it, the Kid is some indiscriminate trigger flicker. I see a talented, lonely lad who never had an even break. You know where he went to school, Jim? King Edward the Seventh School, Sheffield – what you over here call a grammar school. Entry by examination. King Edward sends about half its boys to university, and the Kid might have been one of them, but his mother needed him earning money. So he worked in a mine for a time, Jim.'

Jim, feeling the need to supply the correct expression, said, 'He went down the pit.'

'Exactly, and then the pit closed, which is why he got involved in that freight train robbery. It was to feed his mother, Jim. He's not what your boss calls "a bad lad". You know, he told me the motto of his school, Jim: "*Verbum tuum lucerna pedibus meis.*" "Thy word is a lamp at my feet." And I believe that, for the Kid, it was.'

'You're saying he was a Christian?'

101

'Not exactly, but I don't believe he shot Brooks or Lorne.'

'Were *you* ever married, Walter?'

'Briefly, Jim, back in the States. My own little Calamity Jane ... she's out in Wichita now, which is an old cow town, fittingly enough.' The clock behind the post office counter gave a feeble chime: half-past five. 'I have to close up now, Jim. Anything else I can do for you?'

'Mind if I have a look in the room where Durrant stayed?'

Walter Bassett *did* mind, but he said, 'Sure, Jim,' and they went through to the back room.

If the post office was somewhat scruffy, Walter Bassett's living area was shambolic. The back room was in part a storeroom for post office goods, but also a kitchen, with a dirty blue pot simmering on a gas ring. Beyond a further door was a staircase and a bannister, with what appeared to be Bassett's nightshirt hanging over the rail. The stair carpet had once been blue, but was now grey with dirt – and there were books piled on the stairs. When they reached the landing there were three doors. One stood open, revealing a bedroom and a very disarranged bed. Walter closed that door, but not before Jim had noticed a rifle amid the clutter.

Walter said, 'You don't want to see *my* quarters, right?' He opened another door. 'This is where the Kid stayed, but I sleep here on occasion too.'

'Why?' said Jim.

'There's a couple of mutts that live in a yard out back. Those critters sure can bark. Many's the time I've levelled a gun at them, but so far common decency has prevailed.'

It was a small room, overlooking the street, and largely filled by the bed, which was neatly made. Handwritten papers were stacked on the bed, and there was a folded newspaper. Jim picked up an alarm clock from the bedside table. It was set for nine. Bassett would need to get up before nine for the Post Office, so the last occupant of this room might not have been him. Next to the clock was a little felt-covered box of the kind that usually holds a ring or cufflinks. Jim was expecting cufflinks when he opened it, but what he saw – nested in sawdust – was a polished spent cartridge. Jim looked a question at Bassett.

'From a Colt revolver fired by Buffalo Bill himself, or so the fellow who gave it to the Kid made out. The sawdust in the box is the sawdust in which it was found.'

'Found where?'

'At the showground where BB was performing – don't know which one.'

'Who gave it to the Kid?'

'Some guy he met in the calaboose.'

'Come again?'

'In prison, Jim. When they got out, the guy came to see the Kid shoot, and this was a token of his admiration. A fan, Jim. The Kid has plenty of those.'

Jim picked up the topmost of the handwritten papers; it seemed to be a rough draft of a Western tale. Jim read:

'You want him dead?'

'Aren't you jumping to conclusions?'

'I don't have a lot of time to waste. You advertised for a man who could do work in the Dunn Brothers Line. The Dunns were bounty hunters.'

'They were also carpenters. How do you know I didn't want a carpenter?'

'If you'd wanted a carpenter, you'd have said you wanted a carpenter.'

It fizzled out in doodles of horses.

Jim said, 'Mind if I take these papers away with me?'

'I doubt they'll make much sense, Jim. They're just notes. And wouldn't you need a warrant for that?'

Bassett was quite right. Jim set down the papers. He glanced over at the newspaper. It was the *Yorkshire Herald*, which was available in York but mainly covered Leeds. Jim would look at the *Herald* on occasion. It would be left lying about in the Police Office, and Jim recognized the page that was uppermost here, which was devoted to 'National News'. A small headline read, 'Vital Railway Problems'. The article began, 'During the next few weeks, a number of vital problems affecting the railways of this country will arise for consideration. Although these questions are in themselves technical, they are not to be ignored by trades and the general public.'

Jim had read those words in an idle moment five days ago – on Monday, 28 September – and that was the date at the top of the page. Someone had been reading this paper in this room this week, and they had been a neater-minded person than Walter Bassett.

For the second time, Bassett said, 'Anything else I can do for you?' But it wasn't *quite* the same as before: he'd left off the friendly 'Jim'.

Jim allowed Bassett to show him down the stairs, which was done in near silence. 'Walter,' he said, 'you appreciate the importance of getting in touch with me, if he turns up?'

Bassett said, 'I'm not holding out on you, and I never would do that.'

It was not quite the answer Jim had been looking for. As he walked off into the fog, Jim heard Walter mutter three words. Jim stopped on the pavement to review the sound of the words in his mind, and at length he deciphered them. Walter had said, 'Cloud the dust'. In other words, 'Fuck off.'

Wagon and Horses

As Jim looked back at the post office, its window lights went off, but there remained a glow from across the road:

the Wagon and Horses pub, which was also a hotel. Jim crossed the road, and entered a series of wide, low rooms busy with travellers. He saw the scene before him in a Wild West light: most of the travellers were men, of a more or less rough type. Some wore muddy boots. Well, the cattle market had been held that day on Barbican Road, which was just around the corner. It would take more than fog to stop that.

Jim walked into the saloon, which was so arranged that you could look out of the window while ordering a pint of brown beer. You saw mainly fog, but two streetlamps revealed the dark front of the post office. Jim's beer came: he would watch Bassett's front door in the time it took him to drink it, then he would walk to the city copper shop in Lower Friargate, where he would request that constables be stationed outside the post office for the next week. That request would not be granted – nothing so thoroughgoing, anyhow – but Walter would be observed to some degree if he remained within this locality. As a sub-postmaster, you'd have thought he was pretty rooted to the spot, but Jim believed Walter Bassett's loyalty to the GPO was trumped by another loyalty.

Jim's brown beer was down by an inch when Bassett stepped out of his post office; he looked up and down the street and turned right. He wore a long white dustcoat and a high-crowned bowler. He had not had time to eat whatever had been simmering away on the stove top, and he was walking fast. If Bassett could have run, then Jim believed he would be running. This was an emergency departure. Jim stepped out into Lawrence Street and began pushing through the fog behind Bassett.

Bassett was walking through Walmgate Bar, the gate in the City Walls, and so had entered York proper. He was now on the *street* called Walmgate, and it was possible he had just given a backward glance.

Is he evading me? Jim thought. *Or is he just a man walking through fog?* Bassett turned right. He'd gone into Hurst's Yard, where there were no houses but only shuttered workshops and warehouses. Every building looked like the *back* of a building. Could the fugitive, Durrant, be holed up here? Jim had thought Durrant's romanticism would take him to a spot more redolent of the Old West: a lonely shack or an encampment in woods.

Jim delayed entering Hurst's Yard until Bassett had turned another corner, into Percy's Lane, and it was as hard to see why any 'Percy' would claim ownership of this street as it was to see why 'Hurst' would claim ownership of *his*. Bassett appeared to be approaching the Foss river, which was York's second river, a dirty sluice running between blank-faced buildings, all overshadowed by Leetham's Flour Mill, which resembled a tall, thin castle. A deep grumble of machinery came from within. Bassett was on the towpath opposite the Mill. He was passing a line of moored barges, all covered with dark tarpaulins, and Jim had to be careful about stepping over the chains that held them. Bassett could not just be taking a constitutional. Some of the worst of the York bad lads inhabited the banks of the Foss, and the coppers went here in pairs if at all.

Then Bassett was gone from sight. Jim could hear his reverberating boots, heading back towards Walmgate by one or more of several alleyways wide enough only for one man. Jim entered the alleys. Every so often there'd be a gas lamp pointlessly illuminating a small patch of fog. He came to a yard where a long-coated man was leading a horse into a building already occupied in part by a motor car that, like the barges, was under a tarp. Every bloody thing was under wraps here, in this suspicious part of town.

Jim said, 'Has a bloke come by this way?'

'When?'

'Just now.'

'What sort of bloke?'

'Bloke in a long coat.'

'*I'm* wearing a long coat,' said the man. 'And so are you.'

That was his last word on the matter, because he proceeded to drag a wide wooden door on rollers across the aperture, and when he'd finished, he and his car and his horse were on one side of the door and Jim was on the other. Jim wandered back towards the Layerthorpe, where he saw Bassett coming fast from the right. He was riding a motorbike – a long, low beautiful thing, that made sense of Bassett's dustcoat if not the bowler. The coat flowed out behind him like wings. On the green petrol tank, the words 'Harley Davidson' were written in gold, making it an American machine, Jim believed. He must have a lock-up for it near the Foss. Bassett rode through Walmgate Bar, and he was away.

Jim turned on his heel and walked for ten minutes until he was on Lower Friargate, where he entered the copper shop, encountering Lowry, the desk sergeant, a bloke who knew the law as well as any solicitor. Jim had brought a bad lad to Lowry on many occasions. He would describe the occurrence that had caused him to become acquainted with the lad, and Lowry would immediately come up with the charge to be preferred. Therefore, he was a bit surprised to see Jim unaccompanied.

Jim told him all about Durrant – just the two of them speaking in the grand, echoing lobby of the copper shop, which was somewhat church-like and always cold. Jim concluded by requesting that the beat constables keep an eye on the post office in Lawrence Street, and Lowry said, 'The one run by the Yankee fellow?'

'That's him.'

Lowry made a note. Something would be done, at any rate. Irregular comings and goings at Bassett's place would be looked out for.

'It's my local post office, is that,' said Lowry. And the

two exchanged the jokey little salute by which they traditionally concluded their business.

Back at the railway station, Jim drank a pint in the Parlour Bar before the bike ride home. He felt he was entitled, having left the best part of his earlier pint unconsumed in the Wagon and Horses.

5

A TRAIN RUNNING BETWEEN YORK AND LIVERPOOL. NINE MINUTES PAST SEVEN ON THE EVENING OF SUNDAY, 6 DECEMBER

Jim and Lydia were in the shadowy vestibule at the carriage end, but Jim could see the blood on his hand, and there was a fair amount of it. The door by which they'd boarded was banging against the carriage side as the train gathered speed. You must always close the door behind you. He dragged it shut as the train flew past the last of the York lamps, and in that moment, Lydia saw the blood.

'I think it's just my hand,' said Jim.

'What else might it be?'

He put his hand inside his coat.

'Come round the corner, Jim, into the light. Can you walk all right?'

It was a different world around the corner: like a hotel corridor, with a thick orange carpet, clusters of electric light, a succession of closed doors to one side. In most cases, the blinds on those doors were drawn down. A fat man stood in the corridor, blocking the way, but he was surely harmless. It was the thin men you had to watch out for. He stepped aside as Lydia led Jim past him and into the final compartment.

Lydia came up to Jim and put her arms under his topcoat. She removed her hands, examined them. 'I don't see any blood. Jim, are you all right?' She seemed on the point of tears – and he had only seen her cry once before, when she was passed over for a promotion at work. But Jim was slowly becoming happy. The blood seemed to be on his hand only. Lydia said, 'Let me see.'

She held his hand for a moment in hers. The wound was on the edge of the palm. In the centre of it blood oozed, but the edge was more like a burn, and stung like a burn. 'It's just a graze, Jim,' she said, and she flopped down in a chair. 'It was Durrant, wasn't it? Do you think he's on the train?'

Jim was closing the compartment blinds.

Lydia said, '*I* don't think he's on the train. He'd be trapping himself. He might as well book himself into prison as get on the train, after what he did. He'll have run away at York. Where's this train going, anyway?'

'Liverpool.'

'I don't want to go to flipping Liverpool. I want to go to the party. Do you know how long I spent making paper chains for that "do"?'

Jim was looking at the little sign above the compartment window: 'To Stop the Train, Pull the Chain Downwards. Penalty for Improper Use £5.'

Lydia said, 'Thank heavens Bernadette is in London.'

Bernadette was staying with her exotic friend Aurora, who lived in Bloomsbury and who used to live in York. It was the second time Bernadette had gone to stay with her. The first time had been in November, when Bernadette had gone down for her audition at the Royal Academy of Dramatic Art. Lydia had wanted to accompany her, but she had insisted on going alone. Now, she was staying with Aurora in order to put off learning the result of that audition, which would be landing on the hall floor of the Stringers' cottage any day now.

Lydia saw where Jim was looking. 'Are you going to pull it, then? *Talk* to me, Jim.'

Two weeks ago, he'd have pulled it. That would have set the train guard stomping along the corridors until he found the culprit – since anyone who pulled the emergency chain was assumed to have done so improperly until they proved otherwise. Jim would then have told the guard to find a lineside telephone, by which he would get through to the nearest signal box, whose occupant would have another phone, by which the York Station Police Office could be reached. But *one* week ago, a circular from London – from the office of Colonel Maynard, head of the LNER Police – had been chucked onto Jim's desk. It was the clerk, old man Wright, who'd done the chucking. 'Put that in your pipe and smoke it,' he'd said.

The circular had informed Jim that the mere presence of a dangerous customer on a train was not a sufficient reason to stop a train between stations. Everything was to be done *at* the stations. This had been prompted by the case of a certain Bailey (Jim remembered the name because this fellow would end up at the Old Bailey), an army officer on a train running down the coast from Middlesbrough. He'd had a row with his wife on the platform at Middlesbrough, and he'd knocked out a porter who'd tried to assist the lady. The porter could consider himself lucky, given that Bailey was armed with a swordstick and revolver. Bailey had boarded the train alone and holed himself up in a compartment. A constable at Middlesbrough, who'd witnessed the platform commotion, had jumped on the train. He pulled the emergency chain, which stopped the train on some cliff edge between Redcar and Marske, and Bailey, realizing this had been done on his account, came tearing out of his compartment and started laying about him with the swordstick. The copper had been run through (not fatally) with the swordstick, and two members of 'the travelling public' who'd attempted to come to his aid had been shot dead. Things might have proceeded a bit more smoothly, Maynard suggested, had the train been allowed to make its natural stop, where it might have been delayed without alerting the suspect to the fact that he was being looked for.

Jim told Lydia about the circular.

'Well, it's flipping daft, isn't it? Of course you must stop the train.' She had stood up again and was looking through the window, where the no-man's land between York and Leeds was flying past. Dark, ploughed fields, broken trees.

Jim looked again at the stop chain. He said, 'I think it very likely *was* Durrant with the gun.'

'Of course it was.'

'I'm not certain, though. It might have been Brooks.'

'But Brooks is dead – isn't he?'

Jim was recalling a trip to the country.

6

FLASHBACK TO
SATURDAY, 3 OCTOBER

Ibbotson

After the Friday of fog, Saturday, 3 October was bright and cold. The sun was like a gold dinner plate propped on a dresser – there for display only.

Jim had boarded the Harrogate train at York, having briefed the Chief on his interview with Walter Bassett. It was a pleasant run to Harrogate, in particular the ride over the Nidd viaduct at Knaresborough, which traverses the whole town. The river was blue and glassy, but descended in a smooth, glacial slope when it came to the weir. Pale smoke floated up from the quaint riverside houses. It was at Knaresborough that Durrant had first encountered Brooks and Cynthia Lorne. Knaresborough must have seemed a bizarre place to them, for they were all orientated elsewhere: Brooks and Cynthia Lorne to London, Durrant to the Old West of his imagination.

Last night, being unable to sleep, Jim had come downstairs to the front parlour, where he revived the fire, lit the oil lamp and read 'One to Ten', the story written by Durrant, under the name Ned Keach, in the volume called *Smoking Colts*. He thought it pretty good. After a while, he'd been reading it just to find out what happened next.

It was a morality tale. Bill Doughty was a young man who'd fallen into 'outlawry' having been unfairly dismissed from work as a ranch hand. He'd hooked up with the much more villainous Jake Hogan, and the two of them had got involved in a shoot-out with a sheriff and his posse. Jake Hogan killed the sheriff and was hanged for the murder. Bill Doughty spent a few years in jail, all the while haunted by something one of the sheriff's deputies had said to him in the immediate aftermath of the shoot-out. Referring to the dead sheriff, he'd said, 'He was worth ten of you.' So when he got out of jail, Bill Doughty resolved to make himself a ten-times-better man, and he'd do this by running down ten of the worst outlaws in the state. He dispatched the first nine in pretty short order, and the story mainly concerned his pursuit of the tenth, and worst, villain. It came to a duello, in which Bill Doughty was killed, but so was the bad lad. Accordingly, Doughty died with a smile on his face, having accomplished his mission of self-improvement.

Harrogate Station, as usual, was a cut above. From the train, Jim could see the white tablecloths in the refreshment room – and the station master put in an appearance wearing his silk top hat. At Ilkley, Jim awaited the little Bolton Abbey train. It was a smart crowd on the platform with him, the men tending to sport white spats on their high brown boots, the women to carry muffs.

The train was hauled by a tank engine, but it was a tank of the London, Midland & Scottish Railway, and Jim knew next to nothing about those, except that they were painted maroon, as were the LMS *carriages*, which was not very imaginative of the company. The loco looked old but well-kept, and that went for the carriages too. It was a stately, museum-like train which progressed slowly through the fields. There were four carriages, and the first-class one was the fullest, but Jim was in second. His duty pass was no good on LMS territory, so he'd had to buy a ticket at Ilkley, and the ticket inspector had been delighted to see it. 'Much obliged to you, sir' – this to a second-class passenger of indifferent smartness and sporting a problematic moustache. So that chap was a credit to his employer.

What we have here, Jim thought, is a train in the country, but not really a country train. The true country train was like a country pub: rowdy, muddy and full of barking dogs. Country trains were too hot in summer and too cold in winter, whereas this one had things the right way around: warm on a cold day. Country trains were liable to last-minute cancellations or sudden losses of steam pressure in the engine, but there was no question of this train breaking down. If it did, letters of complaint would be dashed off. That was the kind of crowd Bolton Abbey attracted.

Above the seats in the compartment were photographs of the River Wharfe with smart people wandering along its banks – but in one picture the people looked less relaxed. They appeared concerned at the state of the river, which at that point had shrunk to a width of about 4 feet and looked to be racing fast between rocks. The caption read, 'A little way north of Bolton Abbey, the gentle Wharfe becomes the fearsome Strid.' It was presumed that Cynthia Lorne had gone into the Strid, and this had somehow accounted for the delay in finding her body. Jim took from his pocket the *Yorkshire Post*, which he had bought in York. He'd put off looking at it because he did not want to read the report of Cynthia Lorne's murder – did not want his mind to see the images it would provoke. But the mention of the Strid had produced the images nevertheless.

He skim-read the article. What he resented was that it was so obviously written by somebody who'd never met her.

Film Star Murder Mystery ...

Miss Lorne's body was found in the river Swale on Wednesday, the discovery being made by an assistant gamekeeper. Miss Lorne and her husband, the film producer, Thomas Brooks, had been reported missing some ten days previously. The Leeds Police are searching for a young man, seen in the company of the couple ... They have issued a description ... Any information regarding this man should be given to the Leeds City Police, telephone 7145 LEEDS.

Jim watched the Dales rolling lazily by – observing the peacefulness Cynthia Lorne had been denied. The theme was green and white: green fields, white sheep, outbreaks of white broken stone, signifying quarries or collapsed barns. Nobody was in a hurry to rebuild the collapsed houses or quarry the stone.

They came to Bolton Abbey.

Getting on for fifty people climbed down from the first-class carriage, and about another hundred were already on the platform, which was about four times longer than an ordinary platform at a country station. It had a W. H. Smith's stall and a footbridge, over which a couple of dozen more trippers were streaming. A train must have come in from the other end of the line, from Skipton way. It would very likely have brought Ibbotson, but where was he? Jim watched the crowd while standing among it. There were many happy shouts of greeting, and a great thrum of well-heeled boots on the platform planks. Jim was looking out for a uniformed constable – also for any sign of Durrant or Brooks returning to the scene of the crime. Jim refused to discount Brooks as a suspect in the killing of his own wife.

The platform crowd was thinning out as people moved through to the white gravel of the station yard. Here, a dozen cars with engines running faced the gates leading to the road. People were boarding the cars or haggling with the drivers. Most of the cars were the small black Model-Ts, like so many beetles. A few forlorn-looking horses and wagonettes stood amid the cars. A big, pink-faced man was suddenly next to Jim and grinning. He wore a constable's helmet and a trench coat, not over-clean. This was Ibbotson. He was older than a constable ought to be: probably about Jim's age.

'Last Saturday of the season, really, sir,' he was saying, after the introductions had been made, and Jim had told Ibbotson to call him 'Jim'. 'You might think this a fair crowd, but it's nothing to what they get here in summer.' He touched Jim's arm and said conspiratorially, 'You'll find this hard to credit, sir ... Ten thousand in *a day's* not unusual. They come for the Abbey, you see. That's what they tell themselves, but the real draw is the river walks. Not to mention the tea rooms and the pub!'

They were walking along the platform; Ibbotson really did plod, as constables were supposed to. Jim wasn't sure where they were going.

'What do you say,' said Ibbotson, 'to a pork pie, paradise slice and pot of tea? The three Ps!'

'All right,' said Jim. 'But aren't we off to the river?'

'We most certainly are, sir. But a little tip for you ...' He became conspiratorial again. 'It's two bob to the woods and the water when there's a crowd waiting. But when there's more drivers than customers in the yard, it's half price *or better*!'

Yes, Ibbotson was an idiot.

There was a queue out of the door of the refreshment room. 'Let's get in line, sir,' said Ibbotson. 'It's worth it, you'll see!' While he held the place in the queue, Jim wandered over to the Smith's bookstall to get away from him. He bought from the bespectacled kid behind the counter a copy of *Picture Show* – this week's issue, and of course it would have been printed long before Cynthia Lorne had died. Riffling through the pages, he found her picture. It appeared under the heading, 'The Double Chin':

There is no greater bugbear to the feminine sex than the double chin, which imparts a look of settled middle age to a woman – even though she still be in her twenties. And in this instance, it is prevention which is better than cure. Cynthia Lorne – who is acknowledged to be one of the prettiest girls on stage or screen – avers that neck exercises should be undertaken rigorously each day. It is, she says, one of the secrets of a woman's charm to preserve the youthful outline of her neck.

Jim was feeling sad when he returned to the tea room, where Ibbotson was beaming and waving at him. He'd secured a table by the fire. 'Plum spot, this,' he said. 'I used a little influence!'

The food was pretty good, but hardly the banquet that Ibbotson kept making out.

'Shall we get down to the facts?' Jim said, and he brought out his pocketbook.

Ibbotson leant towards Jim. 'I'm full of facts, me,' he said.

'Yes,' said Jim, 'but I mean the settled facts of the case.'

Ibbotson, producing his own notebook, said, 'What I'm going to tell you ... Superintendent Monk will tell you just the same. He's putting up at the Devonshire Arms, you know?' (Jim did not know that.) 'I'll take you over there after we've been down to the river, and you can have a word with him. Nice man is the Super. Not over-talkative, but nice. He'll show you all the statements.'

Ibbotson then gave the facts in a straightforward manner that caused Jim to revise slightly upwards his opinion of the man.

Tom Brooks, Cynthia Lorne and Jack Durrant had arrived by train at Bolton Abbey station on the afternoon of Thursday, 17 September. In the station yard no motor car had been available, so they had taken a horse and wagonette to the Devonshire Arms. The carter was called Backhouse, son of a local farmer. In his statement he described the three as in good spirits. Miss Lorne spoke the most; her husband the next most and Durrant the least, but Durrant did not seem 'out' with the other two and was smiling most of the time.

Backhouse was an occasional film goer but did not recognize Miss Lorne; nor had he ever seen Durrant in any fairground shooting show. He realized the couple were southerners, and he'd first thought Durrant an American because of some 'queer expressions' he used. Brooks carried a big, blue-and-black-checked carpet bag and had a camera of the modern 'box' type in a case slung over his shoulder. He took occasional snaps on the way to the Devonshire Arms, and Backhouse had asked if he was a photographer. Brooks explained that he was in the film business, and they were 'scouting out locations' for a possible film. This intrigued Backhouse, who asked what sort of film, and it had been mainly Miss Lorne who replied. It was to be a 'cowboy picture'. Indicating Durrant, she said, 'And here's our very own rough rider.' Backhouse had asked Durrant, 'You're an actor then, sir?' and Durrant had replied, 'You got that right,' which had seemed to cause some amusement among the three.

They had not booked ahead, but rooms were available at the Devonshire Arms. Tom and Cynthia checked into a double, Durrant into a single – for only one night in each case. Brooks paid, taking the money (it was noted by the receptionist) from a pocketbook well stuffed with banknotes.

That evening, they had dinner together in the restaurant. Cynthia Lorne had been recognized as a film star as soon as she checked in, and all eyes were on them as they dined. She was seen and heard to laugh a good deal. Afterwards, the three went to the cocktail bar, where Cynthia and Brooks had a row. It was a quiet row, but the word 'London' kept coming up. It appeared he wanted to go back there to get on with making a film, but she wasn't over-keen on the film in question. Durrant was mainly quiet in the bar, as he had been in the restaurant. Harmony was restored – so to speak – when Cynthia began playing the piano and singing, which the other hotel guests evidently found charming. She sang 'Sweet Georgia Brown' and 'Moonlight and Roses' and was applauded after each. The barman noted that Cynthia Lorne had drunk far more than either Brooks or Durrant.

She was not seen at breakfast, and Durrant and Brooks took the meal at separate tables. Brooks was reading a guidebook.

The trio were together again at midday when they requested a picnic basket and two bottles of claret from the head steward. It was noted by the steward that Brooks decanted the various parcels from the basket into the carpet bag, which evidently held other things besides. They told the steward they were off for a ramble along the river. They all seemed in good spirits according to the steward, especially Cynthia Lorne, whom he found – and here Ibbotson quoted the exact words – 'perfectly delightful'.

'He'd probably fallen in love with her,' said Jim.

Ibbotson gave an uncertain smile. 'We've not much to go on about their walk. At Cavendish Pavilion, a lady serving teas thought she recognized Cynthia Lorne.'

'Cavendish Pavilion?' said Jim. 'Can you draw me a map?' He tore a page out of his pocketbook and passed it over to Ibbotson, who clearly thought this an act of vandalism. With reluctance – and the confidential comment, 'I'm no *great* hand at drawing ...' – Ibbotson began his sketch by putting a north arrow in the top right-hand corner and writing 'North' very neatly. The River Wharfe he showed as a line running broadly north to south but kinking out to the east. On the west bank at the south end, he wrote 'The Devonshire Arms Hotel'. Then, progressing north along the west bank of the river, he wrote the following: 'Bolton Abbey (Priory)', 'Memorial Fountain', 'Cavendish Pavilion and Tea Rooms', 'Cavendish Bridge', 'Strid Wood', 'Aqueduct' and finally, up towards the North arrow, 'Barden Bridge'. Jim took the map and added further details while asking further questions.

The distance along the stretch of river depicted was about 4 miles, and the landmarks mentioned were more or less equally spaced.

'Do you think they ever crossed the river?' asked Jim.

'I don't know,' said Ibbotson. 'Folk generally stick to the west bank.'

'What's on the east bank?'

'The Valley of Desolation,' said Ibbotson.

'You're kidding,' said Jim, but he realized that was an impossibility. 'What is it?'

'Just a wood.'

'And where is it?'

It occurred, apparently, where the Cavendish Bridge crossed the river.

'Is the riverbank wooded on both sides all the way?'

'Aye,' said Ibbotson, so Jim drew some little crosses.

'What are they?' said Ibbotson.

'Trees,' said Jim. 'Where does the Wharfe become the Strid?'

'Hard to say.'

'But do say.'

'About there,' said Ibbotson, indicating a point on the river as it ran through Strid Wood.

'And where does the Strid end?'

'That depends.'

'On what?'

'Where you say it ends.'

'Where do *you* say it ends?'

Ibbotson reluctantly indicated another spot on the Wharfe within the wood. The narrow channel called the

Strid was, it seemed, very short. Jim thickened the line of the Wharfe to show where it was the Strid.

'That's wrong,' said Ibbotson.

'Why?'

'You're making the river thicker where it's the Strid. But it's thinner there.'

'Well, I can't make the first line thinner, can I? Were they seen at the Strid?'

'Aye. We have two witnesses who saw them there. They were having a picnic.'

'What time?'

'About two. Mr Marshall, who's the head gamekeeper on the Estate, was the first witness – a very reliable man. The other witness was the Reverend Simon Preston – in other words, a vicar. So I don't think there can be much doubt about *his* evidence either. Later on, at about three, Mr Marshall, who was still in the wood, heard three shots.'

'But he didn't *see* anything at that point?'

'He did not.'

'And what did he think about the shots?'

'Didn't think anything.'

'Why not?'

'There was always shooting going on at that time of year – back end.'

'Who might be shooting?'

'The under-gamekeepers.'

'But none of those was in fact shooting at three o'clock?'

'No.'

There was a little cold tea left in the pot. Jim shared it between himself and Ibbotson. He didn't half fancy a pint of bitter – it was the effect of talking to Ibbotson. Jim said, 'Now, the last person we know of who saw Brooks and Cynthia Lorne alive was that gamekeeper?'

'The *head* gamekeeper, yes. Mr Marshall.'

Jim glanced over to the counter. Sometimes, a tea room did run to a bottle of beer, but all he saw was a frilly cloth and cakes proudly displayed.

'But then, later on, Durrant was seen here at the station?'

'He was.'

'What time and who saw him?'

'About seven. He was seen by the lad who serves on the bookstall. He recognized him because he'd seen him in July doing his shooting act at the Great Yorkshire Show in Harrogate.'

'I was served by that kid just now. What's his name?'

'Eric Fall. Nice lad. We have his statement.'

'He wears specs. What's his eyesight like?'

Constable Ibbotson sat back and looked at Jim. He was frowning, and this had been coming for a while. He hadn't enjoyed being questioned; he was a complacent man, and his complacency had been ruffled. But now he tried the conspiratorial touch again: 'Good enough to see Durrant, anyhow.'

'Did Durrant get on the train?'

'Well ... that's not certain,' said Ibbotson, and it obviously pained him to admit it. 'An Ilkley train came in at 7.11. It's not known if Durrant got on it.'

'But he would have to buy a ticket. The ticket would probably be checked on the train, and he'd need it to get out of whatever station he ended up at. Is it known whether he bought a ticket?'

Ibbotson shook his head. He was fiddling with the teapot lid, peering hopelessly inside for tea that wasn't there.

'Shall we go to the Strid?' said Jim. Ibbotson nodded glumly, and Jim felt guilty for having spoiled his day.

The Strid

On the way to the station yard, they stopped off at the bookstall, where Jim was hoping to question the kid, Eric Fall. But he'd knocked off for the day, and a young woman had taken over. 'Not to worry, sir,' said Ibbotson. 'I took the boy's statement myself yesterday morning. It's all in there.'

In the station yard, only two cars were left, and one horse and wagonette. The drivers of all three were sitting in a shelter made from an old guard's van. Ibbotson went in there to negotiate, and Jim hoped he'd secure a motor.

Jim knew motor cars would eventually be the death of the railways, but he did like riding in them.

It *was* a motor – a Model-T with, apparently, no roof – and it turned out the driver had to start it with a crank. It was a bit embarrassing to be sitting in the thing as he did this, but Ibbotson just pretended it wasn't happening. 'We're in for a champion ride,' he said. 'Little tip, though, sir – pull your muffler up around your face.' Ibbotson, being in uniform, wore no muffler, but had raised the collar of his greatcoat. It seemed he'd got over his annoyance at being questioned.

They turned right out of the yard gate and were running along next to a stream – not the Wharfe river, evidently. They turned left and the Devonshire Arms came in view on the right – a long, low building of white stone. In the hardstanding to one side were a dozen motors, some of them very long. The driver of the Model-T turned around and said, 'See that Studebaker?'

'Aye!' Ibbotson shouted against the wind. Touching Jim's arm, he said, 'American motor. Lot of Americans come to Bolton Abbey … Don't take kindly to being called Yanks, apparently!'

The Abbey came up on the right, dreaming away its days in a bright-green field with a cloud shadow swinging over it. The river lay beyond. The next landmark on the same side was a pair of noticeboards reading 'Cavendish Pavilion' and (the smaller one) 'Ice Cream Sodas'. Ibbotson touched Jim's arm. 'Cup of cocoa would go down rather better on a day like today, don't you reckon, sir?'

Jim was indeed freezing. The driver was watching him in his windscreen mirror.

'You a detective?' he shouted against the wind.

'I am,' said Jim.

'Here about the actress?'

'That's it.'

The driver continued to eye Jim in the shaking mirror.

Jim shouted, 'Would you like to tell me something?'

But then Ibbotson piped up: 'We can fix a time to take down your statement!' The driver's next shout was something indistinct but evasive, and Jim received no more glances from his direction.

On the right, a cottage was coming up. The word 'TEAS' was propped on a board outside it and, as they went by, a man came out of the cottage and picked up the board. Teas were over for the day; but it was only quarter past three. A couple of minutes later, the car was slowing, and the driver swung them into a gap in the trees where three other cars were parked. The world became very quiet when he turned off his motor. They were in a clearing that had some official status, and there was a notice put up by the Abbey estate saying all cars were parked here at the owners' risk. In the direction of the river was a wide gate with a booth near the gate. At the right – or wrong – time of year, you'd have to pay to go through that gate. Ibbotson and Jim went through it for nothing, however.

They descended through a hanging wood. They heard a few other walkers, but the wood was peaceful, the platform crowd having been widely dispersed over the Abbey lands. There were many evergreens, and Jim could see why this landscape might have suggested the Old West. They began to hear the roar of the water. Then came a loud gunshot. Jim's hand went to the pistol in his right pocket. Ibbotson was frowning: 'Bit near, was that,' he said. 'It'll only be a gamekeeper.'

They had come to a pair of narrow tree stumps with a wire strung between them. It was really a small gibbet: a row of little animals hung by their necks. One was certainly a rat, the others a bit more out-of-the-way: stoats, voles, that kind of thing – a sort of *Wind-in-the-Willows* collection.

Ibbotson said, 'That's Mr Marshall's doing. Sign of a well-kept wood is that.'

They began to hear a sound like a rising wind, but the trees were undisturbed. At the bottom of the valley, they encountered a scene of great violence: white water racing along a crevice between red rocks. The rocks were partly covered in moss or lichen, which resembled seaweed – and the rushing water put a kind of sea-smell into the air. This was the Strid. A handful of people stood about, looking at the water, as people might look at a dangerous animal in a zoo, half amused, half respectful. But they moved away when they saw the three chevrons on Ibbotson's coat sleeve. It was clear to Jim that they all knew what had happened here and didn't want to be thought ghoulish.

There were carvings on the rocks: initials, or sometimes a rather dignified name – 'Henry', 'George' – and a date. 'George' was 'May 11th 1909'. Jim was put in mind of gravestones. He picked a fern leaf, tossed it into the water and it was whisked away instantly, or taken down. Gone from sight, anyhow. The water was a yellowy brown shade with dirty froth on top, like beer you'd send back in a pub.

Jim saw a pair of booted feet on the rock beside him. He'd heard no approach, on account of the roaring of the water. The boots belonged to a man in a leather jerkin and a shapeless hat. He carried a rifle. Ibbotson said, 'This is Mr Marshall, the head gamekeeper.'

After the introductions, Jim said to Marshall, 'You saw them here about two?'

'That's it.'

'On this side of the river?'

'Aye.'

'What were they doing?'

'Eating a picnic and drinking wine.'

'How much wine?'

'A fair amount. I saw two empty bottles lying about. The woman was a bit merry.'

'How did you make that out?'

'She was larking about. Kind of dancing around; the other two were sitting on the rocks.'

Jim turned to Ibbotson. 'What was found here after the body turned up?'

'How do you mean?'

'Was the picnic stuff left here?'

'Nothing was found.'

'So it was probably all chucked into the river by whoever did the shooting?'

Ibbotson said, 'That was Durrant, sir. Take my word for it! What he did with the stuff, I really don't know.'

'Anything chucked in here,' said Marshall, 'that's the last you'd see of it.'

Jim, who wished Marshall was the copper instead of Ibbotson, said, 'Why is the river so fast here? Is it just because it narrows?'

'The river en't *narrow* here,' said Marshall. 'It's on its *side*.' He held one enormous hand out flat, then tilted it through 90 degrees. 'Picture a ribbon – the way it gets twisted.'

'At about three o'clock, you heard three shots?'

'Aye. I thought it were my mate, Clem, shooting rabbits.'

'Is he a gamekeeper?'

'After a fashion. He's the river watcher.'

'Did *he* see anything?' (Jim thought he should have done, being the river *watcher*.)

It was Ibbotson who answered. 'He didn't. Now if

you'll excuse me, I'm off to pay a call of nature. All that tea, you know!'

As he went off into the trees, Marshall eyed Jim for a while; then he said, 'You do *get* 'em, don't you?'

A little blue bird landed on the rock between Jim and Marshall. It was as though it had been waiting for Ibbotson to depart before making an appearance.

'Kingfisher,' said Marshall, and there was a tone of surprise, even delight, buried in his deep voice. ' . . . Don't usually to see 'em that close.'

As Ibbotson returned, buttoning up his coat, the kingfisher flew away. Ibbotson said, 'You know what they say about the Strid? You're not a true Yorkshireman if you haven't jumped it.'

Marshall eyed Ibbotson. '*You've* jumped it, have you?'

'I haven't. But you see, I'm not a Yorkshireman at all! I'm from over the border: Rochdale.'

Jim watched the water: the rocks in the rusty-coloured depths resembled big, smooth monstrous heads. The gap between the banks was narrow enough to tempt you to a leap, but if you did land on the other side, you'd be in with a good chance of slipping on the moss and cracking your head open.

'Lot of kids try it,' said Marshall. 'Some die in the attempt.'

Jim asked, 'How many people drown here every year, do you reckon?'

'Three or four, maybe. Hard to say, since about every other body that goes in never comes out.'

'Why not?'

'It's like a wide bottle with a narrow neck. They get taken under the banks and get trapped in little holes – underwater caves, sort of thing.'

'If they do come out, *where* do they come out?'

Marshall jerked his thumb in an downstream direction. 'Anywhere between here and Cavendish. Or if the river's up, they might get as far as Addingham.'

Jim couldn't bear to ask where Cynthia Lorne had washed up.

By half-past six, darkness had fallen, but it was a blue darkness, and scraps of pinkish cloud could still be seen, owing to the bright moon and the great number of stars over the Devonshire Arms.

Monk

Superintendent Monk sat alone in the cocktail bar of the Devonshire Arms, which was lit with a low, amber glow. Around the walls were oil paintings of the Abbey; in all of which it looked more or less haunted. Any spare spaces on the walls were taken up by cases containing stuffed fish.

Monk gave a slight nod when Jim sat down in front of him. He did look like a monk – or at least Jim's idea of one – in that he was fat and bald. He had a very small nose, mouth and eyes, but you wouldn't say he was mean-featured, just a man with *perfunctory* features because they weren't needed for much. He was out of condition – pale and sweating. He sipped whisky and smoked – evidently continuously, since there were two cartons of Woodbines on the table in front of him.

A waiter came up to Jim: 'Cocktail, sir?'

Jim ordered a whisky, hoping it would be large. It didn't seem to be possible to have a brown ale – certainly nobody else in the place was drinking beer. There was a convalescent atmosphere in the bar: mainly old people coughing muted coughs, talking in strained but refined voices, some of them American. Short, highly coloured drinks were being sipped like medicine. People kept being called through to dinner, to which they would proceed slowly, ushered along by the waiters who looked like hospital orderlies in their white coats. When Jim's drink came, Monk pushed one of the cartons of Woodbines towards him.

Jim thought their conversation was about to begin, but then a uniformed constable walked into the bar and, with a nod at Jim and a whispered word into the small ear of Monk, he put a pasteboard folder on the table. Monk pushed this towards Jim, who proceeded to read the witness statements and other documents connected to the case. As he read, he grew conscious of the orange fire blazing away in the hearth behind his back. He was too hot, but this was not the sort of place where you could loosen your collar or take off your suit coat. He was also conscious of the wheezing breaths being taken by Monk. The fellow had a very limited amount of those left, Jim thought.

The matter was evidently much as Ibbotson had described it, but he'd left a couple of things out of account. Firstly, the Showman's Guild membership card belonging to Durrant had been found in the river on the morning of Saturday, 19 September, the day after the picnic. The card was in the file, looking not much the worse for wear. Secondly, Monk had thought it worth mentioning in the file that on that same morning – the 19th – a car had been reported stolen from outside the Devonshire Arms.

When Monk determined that Jim had stopped reading, he said, 'You've been shown about?'

Jim nodded. 'By Ibbotson.'

Monk twitched a smile, possibly.

Jim said, 'Any progress in the hunt for Durrant?'

Monk shook his head.

Jim said, 'The boy, Fall, would not carry conviction in court.'

Monk nodded. 'A good brief would tear him to bits.'

'He wears specs,' said Jim. 'Dark was falling. He gave his statement when he already knew Durrant was suspected. There'd be a natural urge to implicate a known shootist.'

Monk nodded again.

'I met Marshall, the gamekeeper,' said Jim. 'He seemed all right.'

Another nod, then Jim said, 'What about Brooks? I'm not sure why you're not looking for him as well.' Jim held up the Showman's Guild card. 'It could be Durrant at the bottom of the river and Brooks who put him there.'

This time only a half-nod from Monk. He said, 'You've met Brooks. Can he drive a car?'

Jim thought of the photograph in *Picture Show*: Brooks and Cynthia leaning against a car. He told Monk about it. Monk said, 'But there was no indication he could drive it?'

'No.'

'Why don't you nip down to London? Talk to people about Brooks.'

Jim nodded. He was delighted by this suggestion, but the terseness of Monk was infectious.

Monk said, 'Would you say Brooks was a killer?'

'Impossible to say anyone's *not* a killer, in the right circumstances.'

Having said that, Jim realized it was pompous.

After an interlude of smoking, Monk said, 'A crime of passion, then.'

'Or maybe it was set up by Brooks to look like one – a crime of passion committed by the known hothead, Durrant. I mean, Brooks looks the innocent party by telling the car driver on the day before where they were going and what they were about.'

Monk was nodding, but he didn't quite agree because he said, 'My impression is that it was mainly the woman who was doing the telling. Brooks was not quite so talkative.'

'All right. But Brooks knew that if Cynthia Lorne were shot, Durrant would be blamed.'

'Could be,' said Monk. 'If Brooks doesn't pitch up soon – alive or dead – we'll put him in the *Gazette*.'

'Durrant'll be in next week, I take it?'

'Monday.'

Monk was lighting another cigarette, but when a waiter came and asked if he would care for another drink, he shook his head. He said, 'How've you been keeping, Stringer – all right?'

'Yes, thanks.'

'What's going to be happening at your place when Saul goes?'

'That's up in the air.'

'Are you in line for it?'

Jim shook his head. 'I'm only a DI.'

'But you might be made up?'

'Unlikely.'

The constable returned, and escorted Jim through the lobby, where an amazingly good-looking woman sat at the roll-top desk that served as a reception, and a big fire burned in a baronial fireplace. Then Jim was outside on the white gravel, which was periodically stained with oil, as Jim could see by the headlights of a turning car. When it had gone, there were two cars left, one with a roof up, one without. On this cold night, the car with the roof would be the obvious choice, but the driver of the roofless one seemed braced and ready to be selected. It was the fellow who'd driven Jim and Ibbotson five hours ago. Jim was glad to see him. This time, unencumbered by Ibbotson, he would discover what he had to say.

Jim made a point of climbing in beside the driver this time, so as to encourage confidences. The driver made a fast manoeuvre on the gravel, then they were flying along the dark road to the railway station. The driver reached into a little locker on what Jim believed was called the dashboard. He came up with a pair of gloves, passing them over to Jim. He seemed proud of being able to do this while driving.

'Know anything about cars?' he said.

'No,' said Jim. But the driver was trying to open a conversation, so he said, 'Trains – that's my line. I'm with the railway police.'

'Do all the railway coppers know about trains?'

'They do not. My governor hasn't the slightest interest in them.'

'What's *his* interest?'

'Guns.'

'Sounds a hard nut … I don't want to be making a formal statement.'

'Then make an informal one.'

142

They drove on, big dark trees flowing past on either side.

'Some of the best motors are made by an Italian outfit – Fiat. They're generally big expensive cars, but there's a little Fiat: the 509, known as the Spider. Now, there's a lot of drivers hustling for fares to the Abbey. There's what you might call the established lot – the regulars, who are mostly from round here. They ... well, *we*, because I'm one of them ... have our little clubhouse sort of thing, in that old van in the station yard. We get a bit browned off with these chancers coming in from Ilkley, Skipton, Leeds, looking for a slice of the summer trade, and those blokes are not welcome in the clubhouse or the yard. If a stranger turns up and starts taking liberties – undercutting our fares or touting for business on the platform – we might take him in hand.'

'Such as how?'

'He'll be given a warning; he might find the tyres of his car let down. This is all on the QT, right? Off the record?'

'Aye.'

'If he doesn't take the hint, he might find a scratch on the paintwork of his car. If that doesn't do the trick, he might find a scratch on himself. Now, in late summer we had a bloke pitch up in a Fiat Spider: bright red and brand new, so that's what ... a hundred quid's worth? There'd be a lot of takers for his ride to the Abbey, because of the fancy car. The bloke was putting up in Skipton, but he was from East Yorkshire apparently, and some of the fellows in the club knew a bit about him. He was in the motor trade, and he'd worked in a garage in Beverley and had a falling-out with his governor. Being a bad sod, he was liable to have a falling out with anyone. You could see right away he was trouble. Why anyone ever got in his car, I don't know – certainly any woman. He'd try it on with 'em, so we heard, and some of 'em wouldn't mind, believe it or not. He was warned off, but he stuck around. I don't want to go into details, but he was warned off *again*, and this time he knew we weren't kidding. Next thing we know, he's reported his car stolen from outside the Devo Arms.'

'This was on September nineteenth, right – the day after the murder?'

'That's it.'

'You think it was a con? That he was after the insurance money?'

'He was after the insurance, yes. I reckon he also *sold* it, so then he gets paid twice over for a car he couldn't use as he intended.'

'Is that often done?'

'Standard practice.'

'Any idea who he sold it to?'

'Maybe the fellow who did that woman in.'

'Cynthia Lorne. The likeliest suspect is thought to have left by train.'

'The cowboy. But what about the other one? The posh bloke.'

'What's happened to the Fiat man?'

'Haven't an earthly. He hasn't been seen on the Abbey run since the day after the killing.'

'What was his name?'

'Goodall. Paul Goodall.'

'And what was the garage called?'

'Don't know. Beverley's only a little place. There en't that many garages there.'

They were pulling into the station yard. Jim put a big tip on top of the fare. A train for tomorrow was being made up in the sidings. Jim looked on from the lonely platform until the last train of the day came in.

7

THE TRAIN RUNNING BETWEEN YORK AND LIVERPOOL. NEARLY HALF-PAST SEVEN ON THE EVENING OF SUNDAY, 6 DECEMBER

Jim said, 'I think the man who shot me very likely *is* on the train, but I don't think he wants trouble.'

'How do you make that out, Jim? He's just tried to kill you.'

'I think he shot to wing, not to kill. It was a warning.'

'A warning about what?'

'Not to get on the train. He didn't want me on the train because *he* wanted to get on it. I daresay he'll be connecting for a ship at Liverpool. He'll be heading for the States.'

'It's a pretty drastic way of warning someone, isn't it? Firing a gun?'

'I'm not sure he intended to fire it – only to show me he *had* a gun. But then the engine blew off.'

'It did what?'

'Began making that racket. So he realized he could

fire a shot that might not be heard. Or maybe he just panicked.'

'Why was he in York in the first place?'

'If it was Durrant . . . I think he's been hidden in York by Walter Bassett and helped by him. If it was Brooks, I don't know.'

'You saw him better than me. What makes you think it might have been Brooks?'

'Brooks and Durrant have the same build. They have the same kind of very blue eyes, not that I could really see the bloke's eyes. They also had the same kind of hat.'

'Yes,' said Lydia. 'I'll give you that. Cynthia Lorne told me in the hotel that she'd bought them both grey fedoras in York, and she was very annoyed they wouldn't wear them.'

'I don't think they wanted to be associated, so didn't want to look like each other. But there was something else about the man on the platform. In the rifle range that night after the Gala, Brooks took a turn at shooting. It struck me there was something awkward in the way he did it, and I've just clicked as to what: he was left-handed. The man on the platform fired with his left hand.'

Silence in the compartment, save for the rattling of the train.

'I don't think it was Brooks, Jim. I liked Brooks.'

Jim sat down on the middle seat of the three that had their backs to the engine. Lydia sat on his right, next to the window. The armrest was between them. Lydia asked Jim to put his hand on it, and she inspected his hand again. She took out her handkerchief: a small, sky blue thing. Jim laughed.

'Shut up, Jim,' she said, and she wrapped it around his hand. She held her hand protectively over his. Then she got bored of doing that and moved to the seat opposite. 'Are we stuck on this train with a murderer all the way to Liverpool?'

'No. It stops at Leeds and Manchester beforehand. We can get off at Leeds.'

'We can go and see Harry.'

Jim stood up again. 'I've just thought – there's a restaurant car. It'll be busy. You'll be safe there.'

'What about you?'

'I'm going to walk along the train.'

'Why?'

'See what's what.'

'You just said you were going to leave Durrant – or whoever it is – alone.'

'Yes, well – I've got protection.'

He took the Detective Special out of his coat pocket, and showed it to Lydia. Jim said, 'It's called the Detective Special.'

'What's special about it? It looks like a potato gun.'

Jim was looking through the window. The water-logged field flying past had a black shine to it. They were somewhere near Church Fenton, and now the small dark station rolled by, with the gasometer adjacent. Jim knew Church Fenton station pretty well. There'd been an attempted murder there late on in 1918. Jim was just back from 'Mespot' – from Baghdad – where there had been many attempted murders, and many successfully accomplished, all in tremendous heat. That there should be equivalent violence in the mud and rain of Church Fenton proved either the variety or – more likely – the consistency of human nature.

Lydia said, 'I've just thought. We don't even have tickets.'

'I do,' said Jim, and he showed her his duty pass.

'Oh, yes. I always forget about that. You're like a magician, Jim – producing all this stuff from your pockets.'

Jim slid back the compartment door; nobody was in the corridor.

The windows on the outside world showed two horses standing under blankets. They were approaching Garforth. Jim looked back into the compartment, where Lydia sat with folded arms. 'Come on,' he said. Jim took her hand; he also held the gun as they walked fast along the corridor of the next carriage. Then they were into the brightness of the dining car – and Jim was sure some of the diners must have glimpsed the gun before he could stuff it back in his coat pocket.

'Everyone's staring at us, Jim,' said Lydia.

The restaurant car was *too* bright and smelt of frying

fish. It was about two-thirds full, and none of the diners was the gunman as far as Jim could see. Jim and Lydia found a free table.

'How long 'til we get to Leeds?' said Lydia.

'About fifteen minutes.'

'They'll have a First Aid box in the kitchen, Jim. Shall we see if they've got something to put on your hand?'

'Not worth it,' said Jim.

The blood on the wound no longer oozed; there was only the stinging – now more like a tingle.

Lydia said, 'I suppose I could get a bowl of soup.'

'We're not here to eat.'

'Speak for yourself.'

It was a *new* restaurant car – all Rexine and chrome rather than wood and brass, and it would have an electric cooker. But if the carriage was new, the waiter was not. He handed them menus. 'The fish,' he said flatly, 'is haddock, not cod.'

Lydia was looking at the menu; Jim was looking along the gangway of the restaurant car.

Lydia said, 'Maybe I'll have time for a nice roll of bread.'

The waiter was back already; he'd never really gone away. He wanted to get this Sunday over with – try his luck in another week.

'My wife's eating,' said Jim, and he quit the table.

On reaching the end of the dining car he looked back; Lydia was staring after him. The waiter was staring down at Lydia. She could always order a cup of tea. No, the waiter wouldn't stand for that. She could just order a meal and get off before it came. As long as she remained in the restaurant car, she'd be safe. All the gormless, sleepy diners in there would protect her, even if they didn't know they were doing it.

The corridor in the next carriage had a different carpet from the previous ones, which was somehow disorientating. Jim looked through the first window. They had just passed Garforth – a single lamp burning on the wall of the station house. The train was swinging about pretty wildly, but that was all right. The sooner they got to Leeds, the sooner something might be resolved. Jim was alongside a compartment that had the blind only half down and when he stooped to look in, he saw a youngish bloke smoking a pipe and reading a book. On seeing Jim's face, the bloke put the pipe down by his side. He was sitting in a non-smoker and so breaking a by-law, but he was more innocent than he knew.

The people in the next compartment along had the decency to show themselves completely: four people – two men and two women – all smiling in slightly different and silly ways. As Jim moved on, he was aware of a sudden dark movement to his left – a coat had slumped from the luggage rack onto one of the smiling people. On the other side, a black field that ought to have flown past in a second was persisting. The train was slowing, and they were stuck with this field . . . through which the thin man in the wide-brimmed hat was running.

With the Detective Special in his hand, Jim doubled back to the end of the corridor. He opened the carriage door as the train was stopping. The man who'd been running had now also stopped. He was about 70 yards off; Jim still couldn't be certain of his identity, but he couldn't imagine the Londoner Brooks splashing his way across a muddy field. The man had set down the carpet bag and was removing things – putting the stuff either into his coat pocket or the small doctor's bag. Then he ran on, leaving the bigger bag behind; he hadn't looked back. Jim jumped down – and it was a long way. He began to run after the man, as far as the mud and his crocked leg allowed. The running man was coming up to the boundary of the field – a straggling black hedge, maybe with a fence in it. He looked back – a flash of white face. It was Durrant, all right. He was through the hedge with a single stride.

Jim ran – while also limping – past the carpet bag slumped in the mud. There was a take-down rifle inside. Durrant wouldn't have left the rifle behind if he hadn't kept hold of the revolver. Jim came to the hedge, from where he surveyed another field, with Durrant already towards the far side of it. He'd stopped running again and was facing Jim. He held the revolver – in his right hand now. He must be weighing up another shot, and he was a far better marksman than Jim. One option for Jim was to throw himself face down in the mud, but he'd had enough of that carry-on for one lifetime. So he raised his own revolver. The two were motionless in the water-logged mud, and Jim nearly laughed. Their situation was the entire Fourteen-Eighteen show boiled down to the essence – and this was good. He must revisit the war in order to shake it off.

But Durrant lowered his revolver and turned away. He was running again. Jim removed the Detective Special from his pocket. As Jim pointed the Detective Special at Durrant's retreating form, he remembered the Cowboy Code. You don't shoot a man in the back. At this distance, Jim probably *couldn't* have shot Durrant in the back even if he'd tried. He fired, aiming above Durrant, who stopped and looked back – a look of reproach, maybe, or thanks for the deliberate miss. Then he was fighting his way through a second hedge and gone from sight. What would he do next? Probably walk to Leeds and try his luck with another Liverpool train. But he was being watched for at the ports.

Jim couldn't keep up the chase. He looked back at the train. Wisps of steam were drifting peacefully from the locomotive, like a man having a relaxed smoke. He couldn't see the footplate blokes. No doubt one of them had walked off to get hold of a signalman. Somebody was approaching from the train: the guard – the very chap Jim should have got hold of as soon as he boarded. Jim walked over to the abandoned bag. Cold rain and weak snow were landing on the barrel of the taken-down rifle. Otherwise the bag held mainly clothes – black ones. There was a lozenge tin, but the rattle was too hard for sweets. Jim had got it open when the train guard reached him. In the tin were cartridges, probably for a Colt revolver.

The guard said, 'What's going off?'

Jim fished in his pocket for his warrant card. He held it up.

The guard said, 'Did you pull the communication cord?'

Jim, who'd never heard that fancy term before, realized he had a lot of explaining to do. He embarked on it as he continued to riffle through the bag. There was another tin – no need to open this one. The words on the lid read, '50 No. 22 Rifle Cartridges'. There was a little blue velvety box like a jewellery box. It was the one Jim had seen in the room above Bassett's post office, and it still held Buffalo Bill's cartridge. So Durrant might have been back to Bassett's place since Jim's visit there in early October. Well, the police watch kept on the post office had never amounted to much.

Jim had finished his explanation, and the guard was frowning. 'So that fellow', he said, indicating the far field, 'is a murderer?'

Jim said, 'He's *wanted* for murder.'

'You don't think he did it?'

'I don't know.'

'But he shot at you.'

'I know.'

'Isn't that *attempted* murder?'

'Not necessarily.'

There were some handwritten papers in the bag, held together by a paper clip. There was just enough moon for Jim to make out that here was a Western story, written in the hand Jim recognized from the bedroom at Walter's place. Also in the bag was a tatty little book of photographs called *Impressions of California*. Jim flicked through it, seeing pictures of wide streets with big cars and traffic lights, but also palm trees. There were cars going along desert roads, and Jim could see this was a new sort of place, with everything up for grabs and beautiful weather. He showed it to the guard. 'He's a long way from California.'

'Come again?' said the train guard.

The bag also held a kind of brochure. On the cover was depicted a handsome black-and-white ship with a red train on the quayside next to it. Jim read, 'The world-famous steamers of the White Star Line will take you with comfort and expedition from Liverpool to Boston, New Orleans, Mexico and Central America.'

The picture seemed to have jogged the guard's memory. Tapping Jim on the shoulder, he said, 'We're the boat train, you know; we've got to get moving.'

They started back, with Jim lugging the carpet bag. After a few paces, he spotted an envelope lying in the mud. It must have fallen from the bag as Durrant ran. Jim picked it up. The envelope held three photographs.

On the train, a woman was leaning in the frame of an open carriage door. When he was still 50 yards off, Lydia put up a hand in salutation. It was impossible to read the expression on her face, but she seemed at ease, like somebody waiting on their doorstep for guests to arrive. When they reached the train, the guard turned to Jim and said with an unexpected smile, 'Going to take up a whole page in my log, this is.'

As Jim climbed up, Lydia, stepping aside to let him in, said, 'It was brave of you to chase a man with a gun, Jim. I won't say what *else* it was.'

'I have a gun of my own, remember.'

'It was Durrant, wasn't it?'

Jim nodded.

'I told you it was Durrant. Did *you* pull the stop chain or did he?'

'He did.'

'Well, everyone in the restaurant car thought it was *you*, and they kept saying, "Isn't that the man who was here with you a minute ago?" I feel like St Peter, Jim, because I disowned you three times in the restaurant car. Everyone was very annoyed, you see.'

'Yes. Well, let's go back there. I want a glass of beer.'

'I can't show my face there, Jim. Not with you.'

So they went back to their compartment, Jim carrying

the carpet bag. As they sat down, the train was moving. Lydia was still talking about the dining car. It seemed she *had* eaten – after she'd seen that Jim had given up his chase. The waiter had offered a 'snack'. 'It was a club sandwich,' she said. 'It's roughly four sandwiches, which sounds a lot, but they're very small and they're all on top of each other. They're held in place by a cocktail stick and they're toasted.'

'Was it nice?'

'No. Can I have a look in here?' She was indicating the carpet bag. She took Durrant's story out of the bag and turned up the dimmer switch on the reading light. 'The Other Battle of Wounded Knee,' she read. Then, laying it aside, she said, 'Will you accept once and for all that the man just now, Durrant, killed Cynthia Lorne?'

'It's not that simple.'

Beyond the window, a slow passing goods train was adding to the darkness of the night. Then Leeds was being heralded by railway lands and embankments of brick. Factories started appearing, some with lighted windows even on a Sunday evening, and Jim was looking down on them, because the train was on a viaduct. They ran through Marsh Lane Station – hardly anything ever stopped there – and then a long, blank wall intervened like a preview of death, but it was only a preview of Leeds New Station, where they would be alighting in two minutes' time.

Jim wasn't thinking of Leeds, however; he was thinking of London.

8

FLASHBACK TO
WEDNESDAY, 7 OCTOBER

Piccadilly Pictures

Jim went to London on Wednesday, 7 October, four days after his trip to Bolton Abbey. He had an appointment with Jerry Miller, who was either a film producer or a film director, but was certainly Brooks's business partner.

The trip had taken a while to arrange. Jim did not believe Miller was necessarily trying to avoid him. He was pally every time Jim got him on the phone, but the first two times Miller hadn't stayed long enough on the line to make an arrangement. 'Sorry, Jim – a call's come in on the other line and I have to take it.' (He'd called Jim 'Jim' from the off.)

Even the final arrangement was a bit up in the air. Jim was to give Miller 'a bell' when he 'got into town' – there being, of course, only one town. There was the equally vague prospect of 'a spot of lunch', so that when Jim was on the 9.25 ex-York semi-express, he didn't know whether to avail himself of the dining car. In the end, Jim remained in his compartment, where he took the *Police Gazette* from his topcoat pocket. It was that Monday's edition, and it featured Durrant. Jim had brought it along to show Jerry Miller.

Given that the alleged offence was murder, Jim was surprised to see that Superintendent Monk had not taken half a page for a PORTRAIT OF PERSONS WANTED. That was top billing in the *Police Gazette*. There *was* a portrait, but under the lesser heading, APPREHENSIONS SOUGHT, which commanded only a quarter page. Durrant was better-looking than the average 'Person Wanted' to a staggering degree, as even the *Police Gazette* had to admit. Instead of detailing such standard criminal features as 'eyes twitch', 'slouches', 'bald on top', it spoke of a 'well-set-up young man', 'tall and slender', 'high cheekbones'. The 'h' (which stood for 'hair') was 'thick and dark'. The 'e' (eyes) were stated to be 'piercing blue'. The description was more redolent of the fawning tones of *Picture Show* than the *Police Gazette*.

Durrant was 'Wanted for the murder of Mrs Cynthia Lorne at Bolton Abbey on 18 September. Absconded on that date. Mrs Lorne shot by revolver believed to have belonged to Durrant.' No wanted man in the *Police*

Gazette was ever 'Mr', and Jim believed that even if a peer or knight of the realm had featured in the *Gazette*, the title would be gleefully withheld. Professions were also described in the least flattering way possible. A constant stream of 'old metal dealers', for example, figured in the *Gazette*. Durrant was down as 'fairground performer', which was only moderately rude. It was mentioned that he had a 'prev. con' (previous conviction), but Monk had decided not to enlarge on that, possibly because the previous conviction was not for an offence of violence, and so might cloud the issue. It was stated that Durrant 'may endeavour to go abroad', which meant he was being 'watched for' at the ports, which in practice meant very little. Many a bad lad slipped through that net.

(The 'APPREHENSION SOUGHT' alongside Durrant was a certain Leslie Morpeth, wanted for 'stealing four briar pipes and a quantity of Player's cigarettes'. The 'e' were down as 'weak', and 'sandy moustache' and 'lump on top of head' were attested to by the photograph. So Morpeth really had no grounds for complaint against the *Gazette*.)

On arrival at King's Cross, Jim saw all the new public telephones – all of which were occupied. There was a queue, which he joined for a while, but on discovering that he did not have the required 2d he walked into the railway Police Office on Platform 1. After presenting his warrant card to a couple of sergeants and saying the words 'murder investigation' he was shown to a desk with a telephone on it – in fact, three telephones lying amid a tangle of wires, and it seemed he could take his pick. A woman at Piccadilly Pictures answered the call. She said Jerry Miller was on another call; he'd only be a minute.

'Jim!' said Miller, after about another five minutes. 'Lovely to hear from you. Where are you, old man?'

'King's Cross,' said Jim. 'The place we agreed I would call you from.'

'Perfect. Take the Tube to Piccadilly Circus. I'll see you in the Troc at about two.'

Jim had heard of the Troc. He had his guidebook – *London & Its Environs (1912)* – with him, and that would presumably give its location. But he wouldn't stand any more nonsense from Miller, so he said, 'What's that and where is it?'

'The Trocadero restaurant, old man – on the street that … can't recall the name, but it goes between Piccadilly Circus and Leicester Square. Everybody knows the Troc. Just ask when you come out of the Tube.'

'And how will I know *you*?' said Jim, but Jerry Miller had gone.

Jim went down into the Underground. On the escalator he stood alone, accompanied only by a cold, funnelling wind. He was subconsciously anticipating a platform of wood and a train with rattling gates along its length controlled by men in brown blazers with brass buttons. But the platform he stepped onto was of concrete, which was a shame. Boots had rumbled over the old wooden ones in a pleasant way, as when people walk along a pier. And the train that came in was of a type he hadn't seen before. With its clerestory roof it looked very American.

The carriage was long and luxurious, with yellow seats and sliding doors that opened and closed silently, whereas the old gatemen would give you a 'Take care,' or 'Mind how you go' if they liked the look of you. The message of these new doors was: 'Out you go into the streets of London. Don't blame us if everything goes wrong for you.'

Without the gatemen, you were stuck with your fellow silent passengers, and your own floating reflection in the window glass. There were two other people in the carriage – a haggard couple, clearly suffering the effects of London.

When Jim emerged at Piccadilly Circus, he saw that it had become a building site. Where Eros should have been, there was a big steam crane squatting next to a giant hole, and everything round about was being either knocked down or rebuilt. Some of the famous electric hoardings had survived, and one was already illuminated: 'Drink Schweppes Ginger Ale'. The motor buses still circulated, mostly advertising Sandeman's Port or films and plays that hadn't yet reached York. The steam crane was driving piles into the hole, so there was a great echoing clang every few seconds, as if the day were being timed by a gigantic, slow clock. Jim knew what was going on: the building of a new Piccadilly Circus Station. He'd read all about it in the *Railway Magazine*.

He crossed the Circus and was nearly run down by a horse and trap apparently being driven by a lunatic. He carried a load of jangling empty bottles. When Jim reached the pavement, he buttoned his topcoat right up, for a bitter grey wind was blowing. He took from his pocket *London & Its Environs* and turned to the maps at the back. He found the road as cursorily described by Jerry Miller, and began walking towards it, before realizing he was going in exactly the wrong direction, so he turned through 180 degrees and went the opposite way. London could really have done without this cold wind. The elegant umbrellas of the elegant men, carried rolled up, would be no use against it, and it played havoc with the light coats of the ladies – who were all powdered, even the bus conductresses leaning off the back of the buses.

Jim came to the Trocadero, but this was only the start of another mystery. The place was enormous, with a Lyons' Corner House stuck onto the side of it. Did the Corner House count as part of the Troc? No, because Corner Houses were only semi-smart, whereas the Troc was de-luxe. Jim entered a marble hall with numerous rooms leading off, and a wide staircase leading up, presumably to more of the same. There was a kind of reception, where several white-jacketed men waited, smiling patronizingly at Jim. One of them was a black chap. Jim stuffed *London & Its Environs* into his pocket. It wouldn't do to be seen carrying that in here: neither the Troc nor Jerry Miller had anything to do with 'environs' of London. Jim approached the black chap.

'Excuse me, I'm looking for Jerry Miller.'

Jim felt a tap on his shoulder. Turning about, he saw a small man with bent wire glasses and hair that was thin yet unruly.

'Are you Jerry Miller?'

'Aye,' he said, which was satirical – a comment on Jim's accent. But Jim didn't mind, since Miller looked a very jolly sort. Jim was not *surprised* to find Miller jolly (he'd been that on the telephone), but the smallness and scruffiness was unexpected. Jim had expected him to be a swell, like Brooks.

'Grill room or restaurant?' Miller asked, as they shook hands.

'Up to you,' said Jim. 'It's on me, either way.'

'I won't hear of it, Jim.'

'I can claim it as an expense,' said Jim as they headed off towards somewhere.

'So can I. You're my guest, Jim, and that's flat.'

They were approaching music – not quite the usual palm court affair: a strummed guitar was involved. But there were plenty of palms in the wide, chandelier-hung room they now entered, a place of soft, silvery light and loud conversation. They were shown to a quiet corner. Even so, a pretty woman immediately came up to Jerry Miller:

'Hello, baby,' she said, and they did a complicated double kiss. 'Any news on Tom?'

'Sadly no,' said Miller. 'His bank account's not been touched. In his apartment ... the dust is gathering.'

'And have they caught that horrible little cowboy man?'

'This gentleman is hot on his tail,' Miller said, indicating Jim, who embarked on a flustered explanation of who he was, and what he was about.

'Well,' said the woman, when Jim had faltered to a stop, 'I look forward to reading in my breakfast newspaper that the little shit has been hung from the neck until dead.'

She kissed Jerry Miller twice more, then departed. Then she came back. 'Oh, by the way, you missed Ivor just now.'

'Good!' said Miller, who was cleaning his glasses on his napkin.

'Now, now,' said the pretty woman. 'Naughty boy.' Then she went off again.

Miller said, 'You ever see a film called *The Good–Bad Girl*, Jim?'

Jim had not.

'Well, that's her. Lucy Delaware. It was a big smash in the States. I'm amazed she didn't tell you all about it.'

'Who's Ivor?'

'Ivor Novello. He's all right – bit much for a Wednesday lunchtime.'

Jim couldn't understand the menu, partly because it was

in French, partly because it was written in a fancy type supposed to represent handwriting.

'What it boils down to,' said Miller, 'is onion soup followed by plaice and fried potatoes, or—'

'That's fine,' said Jim. 'I'll have that.'

'Snap!' said Miller. He sat back, looking around the room and grinning at what he saw. Then he sat forward. 'You were probably expecting me to be in mourning for Cynthia and Tom.'

'Well,' said Jim, 'we don't know that Tom Brooks is dead.'

Miller blew out his cheeks and disarranged his hair, which was already disarranged. As the wine was being poured, he said, 'I *have* considered the possibility – that he shot Cynthia. But the thing is, Jim, he wouldn't run away.'

'You mean he'd face the music?'

'I mean he'd blame it on the other chap ... Cheers! I mean, Durrant's the suspect character, isn't he?'

'Was there anything suspect about Tom Brooks?'

'No ... I mean, I don't know ... A little maybe, yes ... Tom was a funny egg. We were in business together, but we weren't really friends, Jim. We're very different. He's a worrier, obsessive.'

'He was obsessed with Cynthia Lorne.'

'Yes. But then most men who met Cynthia were obsessed with her.'

Jim coloured up a bit at that.

'She was a movie star – that's what that means. And Tom was very committed to her success. I mean, he was always putting her in pictures.'

'Because that's what she wanted?'

'To some extent. I actually think he was wearing her out with all the work he put her way, but there was something else. It's as though ... if she were *not* in pictures, then it would just be him and her in the real world.'

'And what would happen then?'

'She might tell him to get lost.'

'Why?'

'Because he wasn't much fun, Jim.'

'Was he a producer or a director?'

Miller shrugged. 'We've both done a bit of camera-pointing in our time. He was a producer, chiefly. What do you think of this wine?'

'Nice,' said Jim, which of course was the wrong word.

'Good. What Tom eventually became was a kind of agent for Cynthia. All his projects had to have her in the lead role and he wanted to show the world she could act, which she couldn't do for toffee, really. Well, that's unkind. What I mean is she wasn't suited to the kind of melodramas he was always finding for her. I don't suppose you've heard of a picture called *The Black Circle*?'

'I've seen it.'

'You've *seen* it? That was above and beyond the call of duty, old man.'

'Was it Cynthia or Tom who wanted to put Durrant in films?'

'Cynthia.'

'Why?'

'There might have been a number of reasons. At first, I think, she wanted to find a project for Tom that would not involve her. Get him off her case, so to speak. Then I think she began to want to be in the film *with* Durrant. She fancied the idea of a bit of cowboy hokum after all that torrid stuff.'

'But do you think she *fancied* Durrant?'

Miller removed his glasses, mussed his hair up a bit more; put the glasses back on, waved at somebody across the room. Then he said, 'Yes.'

The food came.

Miller said, 'Durrant looked a bit like Tom, didn't he? That was her type: long and lean with blue eyes. And Durrant was twenty years younger than Tom. But were they having an *affair*? That I don't know.'

At the end of the meal, Miller said, 'I have to go off to a meeting, Jim. I don't *really* think Tom's a killer, you know.' He was summoning the bill. 'What time's your train back?'

'I can take any.'

'Can you kill a couple of hours in town, then pop round to the office? The meeting will be done by then, and I want to show you something.'

'What?'

'A reel of film.'

'All right, thanks.' The offer reminded Jim that he had something to show Miller, and he handed over the *Police Gazette*, pointing out the page with Durrant on it.

'So he's made big-time after all,' said Miller. 'You could walk through to the bar here. Have a post-prandial whatever.'

Jim said, 'Where *is* your office?'

'Oh, yes. Sorry. I tend to assume everybody knows where Piccadilly Pictures is. Egomania, Jim. We're just *off* Piccadilly. Air Street – number four.'

Armistead and Bannister

The Tube took Jim to Camden, where *London & Its Environs* guided him to Prowse Place, home of Armistead and Bannister, publishers – as Jim had discovered at Walter Bassett's place – of *Smoking Colts*, and presumably other cowboy tales. The grey, wind-blown streets reminded him of Waterloo, where he had lived after getting his 'start' as an engine cleaner on the London & South Western Railway. Camden and Waterloo were both criss-crossed by railway viaducts, and while the trains, riding imperiously on their high level, could get away from the houses, the houses couldn't get away from the trains.

Number 7(A) Prowse Place turned out to be partly underneath an arch of the North London Railway viaduct. There were no trains on the viaduct just then but, as Jim emerged from under the arch, he heard a telling thump. Glancing up, he saw a signal arm trembling, looking somehow guilty, as if trying to pretend nothing had happened. But there was no escaping the fact that it had just dropped from the upper to the lower quadrant.

There was no bell to push for 7(A), just a door to knock on. At length, a man smoking a cigarette opened the door. With a frowning nod, he beckoned Jim in, having possibly mistaken him for somebody else. Jim first thought the man was Scottish, on account of the thick guernsey he wore and the fact that he was surrounded by pasteboard boxes labelled Melrose Tea, which was Scottish tea. Also, he had the somewhat crumpled face Jim associated with the Scots.

It was a biggish room; then again, it seemed to be the only one at the disposal of Armistead and Bannister. The room held a truckle bed, an iron stove that was moaning because the wind had got into it and a small table that was evidently the man's desk. On the desk stood a typewriter of the portable kind and a Primus stove with an aluminium teapot balanced on top of *that*. But if the teapot held tea, the Melrose boxes did not: some contained books or magazines, others the personal belongings of the man. One box contained a quantity of boots.

The man was looking at Jim while smoking thoughtfully.

'Now, you aren't actually Scholey, are you?' the man asked. He had a soft accent – not Scots but Yorkshire.

'Stringer,' said Jim, handing over his warrant card for the man to inspect.

'I didn't think you could be Hubert Scholey, because he was going to bring me three manuscripts. I'm quite glad you're *not* him, to be perfectly honest. Fred Bannister,' he said, and they shook.

Jim said, 'I was wondering if I could have a word with you about one of your authors?'

'Don't tell me: Jack Durrant?'

'That's him.'

'I was debating whether I ought to mention to the police that Ned Keach was actually Jack Durrant, the famous murderer.'

'He's not necessarily a murderer.'

The train portended by the movement of the signal was thundering overhead.

'He is according to all the papers I've been reading,' said Bannister when the thunder had passed.

Jim was looking again at the Melrose boxes.

'No point looking here for art, Mr Stringer. We aim no higher than the station bookstalls.' Returning the warrant card, he said, 'You're from York. My dad lived all over the place, but mainly all over Yorkshire, and we did a stint in York – Scarcroft Road. You know it, right?'

Jim did.

'Have a seat, by the way,' said Bannister, by which he meant the bed. 'My old man sold insurance, and he had to keep moving, because there were only so many people in any one place who'd want to *buy* insurance. He was attracted to York because it was a railway centre. He found quite a ready market among signalmen, which is logical enough, I suppose. They were cautious men – safety first and all that. We would visit them in their signal boxes. Sometimes, they would let me pull the levers, or try to.'

Having come to the end of his cigarette, Bannister opened the door of the stove and chucked it in. He then took a packet of Capstans from his suit-coat pocket and offered one to Jim, who accepted. Jim saw that the kindling basket next to the fire held a dozen empty Capstan packets.

'Has the Ouse been in flood these past few weeks, Mr Stringer?'

'Call me Jim; and yes, it has a bit.'

'Whenever it rains here I think of the rain in York: how it makes the river flood in the middle of town. But I like the river flooding in York – the way the lamps on the New Walk are still lit, even though the water's halfway up them; and if it's a misty day, the old buildings on the edge of the river look like Venice. Not that I've ever been to Venice. I'm sure this all sounds a bit rum to you, Jim, especially if your house is near the river.'

'I do live near the river,' said Jim, 'but further out. Thorpe-on-Ouse.'

'Where in Thorpe?'

'On the Main Street, opposite the Marcia.'

'Know it well, Jim! Used to go on bike rides out there. Tell you what I liked particularly about Thorpe: that big house on the Main Street, The Orchards. I mean, it had orchards *plural* behind it ... and I hope it still does?'

'It only has one orchard now. Some of the land was sold off for house building.' (Lydia had tried to object to that – a memory Jim didn't care to revisit.)

'Well, now, tread softly, Jim, because you tread on my dreams. When I was about eleven, I was biking through Thorpe with my pal Phil Armistead, when the owner of The Orchards, a Mr Mackay, asked us if we'd like to come round the back and pick some apples. And not only were we allowed to pick them, we were allowed to climb the trees as well, so it was double the fun. I went away with so many apples in my saddle bag that the back wheel wouldn't turn – it was pressing down on the mudguard, do you see? All the time I've been stuck down here, I've been sustained by the idea that if this firm ever struck an author with the real golden touch – a Nat Gould, Jim, a Conan Doyle or a P. C. Wren – I'd buy myself a place like The Orchards. If not the actual place *itself.* I've often pictured myself knocking on the door and making a cash offer, but I don't suppose Mr Mackay would *want* to sell, would he?'

Jim gave a brief smile, hoping for a change of subject. But it was no use.

Bannister said, 'Mr Mackay is still there, I take it?'

'He became Major Mackay, and he was with the West Yorkshires at Passchendaele. He died of wounds in 1918.'

'Passchendaele,' said Bannister, shaking his head. 'It must have been even more hellish if you'd known The Orchards. There were so many red apples on those trees ... it was like Christmas in midsummer, the apples being akin to the red baubles. I recall it as a dream, Jim, like all the best memories.'

They'd talked about their own wars a little. Bannister brought this to an end, with 'Let's have some tea. We Yorkshiremen are supposed to drink tea, aren't we?'

They talked about Durrant. The story he'd submitted, 'One to Ten', had been accompanied by a letter Bannister had not retained, but he could recall that it had been from York. 'That's why I read it straight off. Normally, it would have gone under the bed.' Jim saw that the bed was held up on a mass of papers. Bannister said, 'If I could afford one employee, it would be a correspondence clerk.'

Jim, thinking of Old Man Wright, said, 'I've got one of those. I wouldn't recommend him. A letter might travel a hundred miles overnight to get to me; it might then take a week to travel the six feet from his desk to mine.'

'Got you,' said Bannister. 'I read the story straight off,

even though it was handwritten. That's usually not a good sign. But it was well done.'

'You paid him, I suppose?'

'Jim!' said Bannister, reproachful. 'Twelve bob – a postal order sent to the address on the letter.'

'Does Lawrence Street sound familiar?'

'Yes, Jim, it does.'

'Can you say when this correspondence occurred?'

'Summer. Because I was hot when I read the piece, yet I could imagine the weather of the setting – which is cold weather.'

'And that told you it was a good story?'

'Main thing was, it carried conviction; didn't read like a parody, which a lot of the stuff we get does. We deal in familiar genres, Jim: ghost stories, school stories, sporting stories, vampires, empire tales. As Cecily Cardew said, "You always need something sensational to read on a train."'

The teapot coming to boil on the Primus was commencing to shake – possibly not because of the heat coming from below so much as the train going by overhead.

Bannister said, 'The covering letter was signed Jack Durrant, but he said that if we saw fit to publish the piece, he'd like us to by-line it "Ned Keach".'

'Is that common?'

'Pretty common, yes. Hubert Scholey – that fellow who's threatening me with three manuscripts – writes ghost stories under the name Morton Lamont. He also writes equally terrible cricketing stories as G. W. L. Dunmore. But they all have to give me their real names.'

'Why?'

'The postal order, Jim.'

They finished their tea, and Jim thanked Bannister for his time. 'Incidentally,' he said, 'where's Armistead?'

'... Bit of a Scrooge-and-Marley situation. Late in 'fourteen, Phil went into the Navy. We have Joseph Conrad to thank for that. He made it to Jan 'fifteen, when he went down in the Channel with HMS *Formidable*. Five hundred and forty-six other blokes went down with him.'

'You'd met him in York?'

'Correct. Best pals as boys. We must be among the very few young lads led astray by a love of reading, Jim. We came down here in 1911, set up shop in the cheapest premises we could find. But neither of us could stand London. Phil used to say that his musician's ear – he played the cornet to concert standard – accounted for his dislike of the cockney accent. And we were both cyclists, Jim. People ride bikes down here, but they don't *cycle*. Still ... everyone in this game's in London. There are three station bookstalls on the North London viaduct alone. We always meant to go back to the real North – Leeds, most likely. There are – what – half a dozen stations there?'

'At least.'

'And lovely countryside in cycling distance. But

the move north is deferred, Jim. Other priorities just now, such as avoiding bankruptcy. But as you can see, everything here is temporary, conditional, ready to go.'

'I know that typewriter,' said Jim. 'It's a New Remington Portable – the machine for the man who travels.'

That's what the advertisements on the railway stations said, and Lydia, who owned a New Remington herself, was very indignant about them. ('What about the woman who travels?') A train was hammering over the viaduct; Fred Bannister was lighting another cigarette.

'The man who travels,' he said, blowing smoke. 'Here's hoping, Jim; here's hoping.'

'You'll let me know if you hear from Durrant again, won't you?'

'Will do.'

Powder Smoke

When Jim returned to Piccadilly Circus, the electric signs were pursuing their encouragement of bad behaviour. In the fading daylight, advertisements for Guinness and X Vermouth were coming into their own, while most of the buses were suggesting Gordon's Gin. With the aid of *London & Its Environs*, Jim found Air Street and Piccadilly Pictures, which occupied a plush floor of a marbled building. Everybody sat at big chrome desks.

They were all armed with telephones, and most had type-writers – not portable ones, either. Piccadilly Pictures was evidently a successful concern.

Jerry Miller himself was of course 'telephoning', one of the many women employees informed Jim, and he was doing so in some room off the main one. After a while, the woman apologized to Jim. Evidently, Miller was 'on the line to New York'.

It was about six o'clock when Miller walked up to Jim. He handed back the *Police Gazette*. 'Where can I buy this, Jim?' he said.

'I'm afraid you can't; it's not for sale to the public.'

'Pity. There are about a hundred film plots in this one alone. Come through to the screening room.'

This looked to Jim like a fancy modern living room, with squarish leather armchairs, a swirly pink carpet and big potted palms. There were no windows. A film pro-jector – somewhat reminiscent of a small upside-down bicycle – stood in the middle of the room on a special stand. It pointed at a white wall, and came with its own operator, a suspiciously good-looking young chap, most probably an out-of-work actor. There were a lot of those, as even Bernadette admitted.

Jerry Miller pointed to a few of the chairs. 'Have a seat, Jim. This'll only take ten minutes.' The operator (the word came to Jim – 'projectionist') corrected him with a smile: '*Four* minutes, Mr Miller.' He was American; Jim should have known because he looked like somebody in an advertisement. Americans were usually important, but Miller didn't feel the need to introduce this one to Jim. Having just sat down, Miller got up again and said, 'Glass of beer, Jim?'

Jim said no. He would be drinking beer on the train back to York – he'd been thinking about that ever since Camden. Miller turned out the lights and they went down gradually in a rather exciting way. Miller was back in his seat, having exchanged his wire glasses for a tortoiseshell pair. On the white wall, Jim watched the word, 'Presenting' shake about for a while. It was eventually replaced by *'Powder Smoke'*; then came 'Starring', then 'Kid Durrant', then ' ... And his six-shooter ... With A Special Guest Appearance by Miss Cynthia Lorne'. The screen then went black for a second or two.

'Shockingly edited, this,' said Miller.

The projectionist was grinning, so that might have been an in-joke.

New words appeared – 'The Kid doesn't just *shoot* his gun!' – and there was the upper half of Durrant.

He was dressed in black and standing in a field. He wore a cowboy hat and a gun belt and looked serious, but then he smiled his shy smile, as if someone standing off to the side had told him to do that. He performed a lightning action – just a kind of flick – and the gun was in his hand. He held it as though threatening to shoot the cameraman, but the smile lingered. Durrant began twirling the gun with his finger through the trigger guard. Another flick and the gun was re-holstered. Then the screen went black again. Eventually Durrant reappeared – perhaps elsewhere in the same field – and Cynthia Lorne walked into view. She wore a skimpy Western rig-out, looking somewhat like Miss Dorothy from the shooting show.

'She looks like a million dollars,' said the projectionist. Jim hadn't expected him to pipe up. It was perhaps a bit forward of him to do so, but that was the Americans for you. Miller didn't seem to mind, anyhow. The camera suddenly jumped backwards, and Durrant now began his sharpshooting, only with Cynthia Lorne instead of Miss Daisy chucking up the glass balls. After five hits, Durrant missed one. The camera jumped in close to Durrant's face and he frowned or scowled, which suited him better than smiling.

Miller said, 'Acting, you see, Jim.'

Another surtitle appeared, pointing out the obvious – 'Missed!' – followed by 'His Best Gal commiserates.' And Cynthia Lorne blew a kiss towards Durrant, as she had done in the shooting show.

Another close-up (that was the word, of course) showed Durrant smiling. Then Cynthia Lorne carried on throwing up the glass balls – with ever more extravagant gestures and a bit of sort of flapper-ish dancing in-between – and Durrant carried on smashing them, all of which business went on a bit too long. The screen eventually went black, and Jim was about to stand up, but Miller said, 'Not over yet, Jim.'

Another close-up of Durrant. He raised the tip of the revolver barrel to his lips and blew away a little wisp of smoke rising from it. Cynthia Lorne leant in and blew another kiss – from closer range than before.

'Hence the title, Jim,' said Miller, as the final words appeared: 'So long, folks!'

Miller turned up the lights. 'Tom was the director, Jim,' he said. 'Apparently it took forever to get that last shot. The modern guns don't give out as much smoke as the old ones.'

'They used to put the powder in directly,' said Jim. 'Now it's in the cartridge.'

'Yes,' said Miller, who'd put the wire specs back on, 'I daresay.'

'What was it in aid of?' said Jim.

'Little showreel for the talents – if any – of friend Durrant. Made at Cynthia's request, of course.'

'Or *demand*,' put in the projectionist, who was stowing the film back in a tin. 'I'd say that Cynthia enjoyed being around that fellah.'

'When was it done?' Jim asked.

'Early September, I think,' said Miller. 'Don't know for certain.'

'Do you know where?'

'I don't, Jim. The three of them were jaunting about up north quite a bit.'

'Looking for locations.'

'Well, that was the official reason.'

'And the unofficial?'

'Giving Cynthia an excuse to be with Durrant? But I really don't know, Jim. By the way, this is Kevin.' He finally introduced the projectionist. 'Kevin has a little story that might interest you.'

Jim had never met anyone called Kevin before.

'Well, sir,' said Kevin, who said 'sir' in that American way – not really meaning it – 'the fact is, I thought I saw Tom Brooks at a time when he was supposed to be dead. Cynthia was killed on – what?'

'September eighteenth.'

'And that was a Friday, right? I saw Brooks the next Friday. I mean, I *thought* I did, but now I don't believe it. Would you care to follow me, sir?'

'Call me Jim,' said Jim.

He and Jerry Miller trooped after Kevin into the main office. At the end of the room, windows looked down into Air Street, and a lonely illuminated gas lamp. 'I was working late on that Friday. I was tired, and – I'm going to level with you, Jim – I'd had a couple of glasses of vermouth. I was taking a break from an editing job. In years to come, I like to think film historians will distinguish between the films I edited while drinking coffee and those I edited drinking vermouth. I believe they'll find the vermouth edits superior.'

Miller was taking all this in his stride – looked rather bored, if anything.

'All the lights on Piccadilly are electric,' said Kevin. 'But down there in Air Street they're gas, which is more picturesque and more filmic, and on that Friday night I saw a beautifully composed scene: a man in a good suit and wide-brimmed hat tilted down. He was looking ... I would say elegant and enigmatic. He gave a kind of half-glance upwards. I couldn't make out his features, but perhaps he saw mine. If he did, he almost certainly didn't know my identity. At that point, I'd only been working here a matter of weeks – it was Jerry here who'd taken me on – and during most of that time Brooks had been away on his jaunts with Cynthia and Durrant. So I'd only formed a vague impression of him. I thought him polite but reserved, very English, and when I looked down on him – if it *was* him – he seemed to act true to form, by touching the brim of his hat before he walked away. Does that help you any, Jim?'

'I'm obliged to you, Kevin,' said Jim. 'On a scale from one to ten, how certain were you that it was Brooks?'

Kevin thought for a while.

'Five.'

9

CENTRAL LEEDS.
ABOUT HALF-PAST EIGHT ON
THE EVENING OF SUNDAY, 6 DECEMBER

The Other Battle of Wounded Knee

When Jim and Lydia stepped down from the train at
Leeds New Station, they found themselves alongside an
advertisement for the Queen's Hotel. It began modestly:
'Convenient for Station', then leapt to 'Sumptuous
Apartments', then 'Banquets'. Jim and Lydia looked at
each other. They knew they would be putting up there
tonight even though the Queen's was pricey. They'd stayed
there three or four times before, and they'd had sex every
time. Well, that was what deluxe railway hotels were
for, surely?

The station was bright and bustling. Sunday night in
Leeds was like Saturday night in York. Jim looked along

the platforms and saw a long line of new telephone booths, all occupied, so Jim did what he'd done at King's Cross back in October. He went to the Police Office to do his telephoning. Here, it was all go. There were five constables in the place and two detective sergeants, most of them 'on the phone'. The office was cleaner than the York equivalent – smelt of Jeyes fluid rather than anybody's acrid cigars – and lit by electric rather than gas. As Jim made his first call, Lydia appeared to be reading the tale by Durrant that Jim had found in the muddy field, 'The Other Battle of Wounded Knee'.

Jim was speaking to a detective chief inspector in the Leeds City Police Office. This fellow worked with Monk, who was not about just then. The DCI was evidently an efficient man, and he paid close attention to Jim's account of what had just occurred on the train. Then Jim got through to the York office, where Hemingway, the night sergeant, picked up. (Jim believed there was no night sergeant in the Leeds office: day and night was all the same to them, under their blaze of electric light.)

Hemingway said he had reason to believe the Chief was on the station somewhere, but he couldn't say where. Jim assumed this meant Platform 14 or the Parlour Bar, but then Hemingway said, 'I was looking for him just now, and he's not in the Parlour or Platform 14, so it's a bit of a mystery.'

Jim put Hemingway in the picture about everything

that had occurred, saying he could be contacted in the Queen's Hotel should the Chief turn up wanting to get hold of him. As he replaced the receiver, he did wonder what he'd achieved. Durrant was already being looked for. His name would now be cropping up in further bulletins as having been 'recently sighted' on the Leeds outskirts, but Leeds had a lot of outskirts and 'recent' was becoming not-so-recent by the minute.

Around the corner from the station was City Square, where the Queen's Hotel was located and a traffic block was occurring. Motor cars and buses added smoke but also light to the evening. There were no horses in City Square, except the gigantic stone one on which the Black Prince sat. Jim and Lydia looked up at the façade of the Queen's. It was black and Gothic, with orange light at all the windows.

When they entered the lobby, the din of the traffic was immediately gone. They might have been in the previous century; even the Christmas tree looked old-fashioned. The male staff dressed like footmen and the lobby was country house-like, with a great quantity of wood panelling and ornate fireplaces big enough to stand up in were it not for the mountains of coal burning away. (It was no doubt railway coal, but the Queen's was a cut above the adjacent station.)

Lydia handled the check-in. That was always her job, being the kind of socialist who loved big, expensive hotels.

Her argument was that it was a 'tonic' to stay in one, even for a single night. Jim didn't like hotel receptions or receptionists; he always felt he was not meeting the expectations of the staff, and he wouldn't be meeting them tonight, given the state of his boots and trouser legs. He sat down on a heavy leather armchair at a fireplace. He could hear most of Lydia's performance.

'I always have such lovely, long baths in your hotel,' she was saying to the desk clerk, an Italian-looking fellow. She was trying for a discount by suggesting that the Italian-looking fellow was the actual *owner* of the hotel and inviting him to picture her in the bath. It seemed to be working because, after a short discussion of – presumably – room rates, Lydia said, 'That's really very kind of you.' The man was torn between appreciating the compliment and frowning over at Jim, having clicked that this elegant woman was connected to the muddy little bloke by the fire. The man was indicating Jim and in particular the carpet bag. Would a porter be required? Lydia was shaking her head and saying something in a confidential and amusing tone, perhaps along the lines of, 'Yes, my husband is eccentric, but he's quite harmless, you know.'

Jim, using his un-shot left hand to lug the carpet bag with the rifle in it, followed Lydia up the wide stairs. There were no lifts in the Queen's Hotel, and their room was on the fourth floor.

The room – to Jim's mind – was unnecessarily big and

decorated with murky brown oil paintings of Yorkshire countryside. But there was a good blaze in the fire, as Lydia had predicted on the way upstairs, this because the room had been prepared for some fellow who'd cancelled at the last moment. Lydia sat on the bed, looking rather queenly and smiling.

'Proper furniture,' she said. 'No easy chairs.' Lydia hated easy chairs for some reason. 'And aren't those chrysanths lovely?' She was indicating some expensive-looking yellow flowers by the bed. 'We'd missed the last train back to York, hadn't we Jim?'

'There's a midnight train.'

'Oh.'

'But maybe not on a Sunday.'

'I should think it very unlikely there's one on a Sunday,' she said. 'So we *had* to stay in a hotel really, didn't we?'

'How much was it?' Jim asked, because the prices at the Queen's varied according to a lot of things.

'I'm jolly well not going to spoil your evening by telling you, Jim Stringer. You go off for your drink now. I'm going to have a bath.'

That went without saying. Lydia loved having baths, and she'd selected their cottage in Thorpe because she'd decided one of the upstairs bedrooms would be an ideal candidate for conversion to a bathroom. In deluxe hotels, she would dispatch Jim to the pub before they made love (reasoning, Jim presumed, that his performance was better in that department for a certain amount of alcohol) while she had an extremely long bath, and generally savoured her surroundings, perhaps by ordering a cup of tea from room service, or writing letters to her friends – the ones she wanted to impress – on the hotel notepaper, or just lolling about on the bed in her underwear.

Jim said, 'You should get the desk clerk to come and run the bath *for* you; I'm sure he'd be delighted.' Jim had found a clothes brush in a wardrobe and was trying to get the dried mud off his trouser legs.

'You go careful, Jim. Durrant might be anywhere, you know. You'd better take your equalizer.'

'Eh?'

'That's what the hero calls his gun in Durrant's story.'

Jim stopped brushing his trouser legs. 'Tell me what happens in that.'

'It's called "The Other Battle of Wounded Knee". There's this man who's a sheriff in a very bad town. Almost every man apart from him is a cattle thief.'

'Cattle *rustler.*'

' ... Or a bank robber; or both. And all the women, it goes without saying – and it is *not* actually said – are prostitutes.'

'Whores ... They generally have hearts of gold.'

'One day, one of the worst of the bad men robs the bank. He comes running out and he's just about to leap on his horse when the sheriff shoots him. But instead of aiming for his, you know, vital organs, which he would be within his rights to do, he shoots him in the leg.'

'That's called shooting to wing. I think it's what Durrant did to me.'

Jim looked down at his hand.

Lydia said, 'The bad man goes to jail.'

'The caboose.'

'Who's telling this story, Jim? After a few years, he comes back to the town, and he's got a very bad leg, so he's limping about the place and he hates the sheriff who did that to him. Then, one day, the bank is robbed again by some different men. The sheriff confronts them as they're escaping, and one of the robbers shoots the gun out of the sheriff's hand, so he's defenceless. The robber is just about to shoot him dead when he – the robber – is shot by the man with the limp, who then comes into the fight on the side of the sheriff.'

'Why?'

'Well, he'd been doing (and I quote) "some pretty hard thinking", and he's come to see that the sheriff had shown him mercy all those years ago; that it was quite nice of the sheriff, really, to shatter his kneecap instead of blasting his head off, and when he sees that this bank robber is not going to show the same mercy to the sheriff, he steps in. It's called "The Other Battle of Wounded Knee" because of course there was another, famous, battle of Wounded

Knee thirty years ago, which as far as I'm aware was no battle at all, but a terrible massacre of Indians.'

Jim stowed away the brush. He put the story in his top-coat pocket along with the gun and the three photographs. 'I'll have a look at it in the pub,' he said. 'I'll be back in about three-quarters of an hour.'

'I'll double that,' she said, 'but don't be any later than eleven if you want to . . . you know.'

There was a bootblack in the lobby, and Jim paid him a visit before stepping out into City Square again. The traffic had mainly gone, and Jim walked over to the little concrete island in the middle of the road. He stood beneath a black and white finger post, which looked rather lonely under the empty black sky as it indicated York, Harrogate, Selby. Over the road was the main post office, and the Majestic Cinema, the words appearing in glowing purple letters. Jim had once been inside the Majestic. It was beautifully decorated, with little white horses running all around the front of the Upper Circle. It was open on Sunday, of course, which the York cinemas were not, and the picture showing was *Go West*, which Jim had read about, and was a Buster Keaton film he intended seeing. Meanwhile Jim did not go west but east, to the pub called Whitelocks, well-known among the cognoscenti (Jim and the Chief) to be the best in Leeds.

Whitelocks was in a little yard off the central shopping street called Briggate. The pub was very electrified, and a searchlight flashing into Briggate from the yard advertised the fact. Whitelocks was long and thin like a railway carriage, and full of light and colour. It was full of people as well. There were at least four barmen, all constantly on the go and wearing smart white jackets. One of them served Jim a pint of brown with a good head on it – Jim downed it in one. A man was entitled to do that on a day when he'd been shot at. The glasses and bottles behind the bar were on shelves that were themselves glass with engraved mirrors behind them, and all the colours of the booze were beautiful under the clean electric light. Sometimes Whitelocks put Jim in mind of a warm pharmacy. A few of the bottles held bright green stuff (these had French labels); there was also yellow stuff, and bright pink stuff in triangular bottles. Jim stuck with the brown ale, though, and when he'd downed half of his second one (there was no doubt that he'd be having three) he was feeling pretty good. He was alive, for starters; he had – as they said in the kind of stories written by Jack Durrant – cheated death. But then again, had he? Only if Durrant had really tried to do him in, and Jim did not believe that was the case.

He took the story from his pocket, and even though it had been written by a man who had shot at him, and even though he was being continuously jostled at the bar, Jim found that he was enjoying 'The Other Battle of Wounded Knee', just as he had enjoyed Durrant's other effort, 'One to Ten'. When he got to the end, however, he realized he'd enjoyed the first part more, when the villain, named Chuck Seaton, was behaving appallingly – a 'one-man wild bunch' – and before he repented of his bad deeds. He had a habit of double-crossing his cronies: 'Maybe those mugs were thinking I'd back up their play. As if I couldn't raise another owlhoot gang at the drop of a hat!' Seaton lived in an unnamed town, residing in the Sun Hotel, which Jim liked the sound of, partly because it was next to a railroad depot. There was a 'golden haze of dust' in the town, which gradually turned pink in the evenings, when Seaton would always get 'liquored up' and start picking fights with his drinking cronies: 'After Seaton had said his piece, conversation became fractured.'

But when he teamed up with the sheriff, Seaton suddenly became worthy, and the final scene, where he limped up to the sheriff and shook his hand, saying, 'I just wanted to make things right or die trying,' was a bit nauseating, but it was also telling: in this story, as in 'One to Ten', the tale published by Armistead & Bannister, Durrant had proved himself a moralist.

Jim took out the photographs that had been dropped in the field. The first showed Durrant and Brooks standing in front of a wall of rock. Durrant held a six-shooter in his right hand; he was pointing it at the sky and might have been smiling. Brooks looked simply bored. There were two words on the back, in what Jim recognized as Durrant's hand. The ink had run, but Jim believed the words began with 'M' and 'C'. After a while, he figured out they said 'Malham Cove', that beauty spot in the Dales. The photographer, perhaps, had been Cynthia Lorne, who was herself in the second photograph. In this she was leaning towards Durrant, who was in full cowboy rig, with two holstered revolvers. Cynthia Lorne's lips were pursed, and about half an inch from Durrant's cheek. There had been the distant blown kisses of the shooting show, the nearer blown kisses of the short film, *Powder Smoke*, and now this. She was coming closer and closer all the time. Had Brooks taken this photograph? It seemed, like the first, to show in the blurry background some dramatic landscape suitable for filming. They were perhaps on a moor – rough country, anyhow – but the photograph also showed one end of a terrace of houses. So they must be on the outskirts of a village or town – and the house at the very end of the terrace seemed to have an additional, ugly chimney poking from the dead centre of its roof. This time, Jim could make out two of three words on the back: 'The ——— kiss!' Then it came to him: the missing word was 'first'. This, then, seemed to signify the first *proper* kiss – only on the cheek, but contact had finally been made, perhaps in the instant after the picture had been taken. If Brooks had taken the picture … how had he reacted to that? Well, these London types went in for a lot of cheek-kissing, so perhaps it had not meant as much to him in a negative way as it had meant positively to Durrant.

The next photograph showed Durrant sitting astride a merry-go-round horse. The merry-go-round did not seem to be moving, and Durrant was in mufti, so to speak – a plain black suit with no guns about his person (although he still looked like a cowboy). He was gazing at the camera through what might have been rain, and not smiling.

Jim fell to thinking about the few days in mid-October when, after reporting back to Monk about his London trip, he'd traipsed around some of the last of the year's fairs. This on the off chance that Durrant would be so brazen as to keep up his previous line of work.

They'd been cold, blue evenings when people stood near the naphtha flares for heat as well as light. Jim had learnt things in those little temporary towns: that every wooden horse on a typical galloper had a name; the prize fights weren't fixed; the arrival of a fair at a showground was called a 'pull-on', and the carnies really did circle their wagons, as in a Western story. He'd learnt that some of those 'living wagons' had wood panelling and stone fireplaces; that the sideshows – skittles, hoop-la, darts – were called 'joints'; that the 'hit' song of 1925 back-end was 'You Made Me Love You'; and that bumper cars, which the Americans called 'dodgems', were the big craze when it came to rides, although the ghost trains ran them close. (The ghost trains reminded Jim of his own war – that part spent with the Railway Operating Department. Yes, he'd been carrying munitions to forward positions, but there had been a fairground aspect to those little trains, with shocks laid on – like the occasional falling shell – to keep you interested. But it was nothing to being an infantryman.)

At the fairs, nobody had any knowledge of Durrant, even though his name was known to all.

Jim ordered a third pint, and a sixpenny cigar to go with it. The label on the cigar read 'Trump'. Jim was thinking of Lydia without any clothes on, or with nothing on but her stockings, and starting to feel rather 'hot'. They would sometimes – especially in hotels – do it twice in succession, and the second time, Lydia might suggest that Jim tie her hands with her stockings, 'Since I know you're a bit funny like that, Jim.' But really it was Lydia who was a bit funny like that.

The white-coated barman seemed a little distracted as he handed Jim his change. Then he lifted the bar flap and made his way to the far end of the bar, cleaving a smoky channel through the crowd. He was talking to some blokes who'd been making a row. Jim could hear the barman saying, 'It's just not Whitelocks behaviour, lads.'

Jim was thinking about his speech for the Chief's leaving do. The theme – it was always the theme on these occasions – would be, 'It's not goodbye, merely *au revoir*.' And no doubt the Chief would still be haunting the bars and billiard tables in the Insty after his retirement; still living in the little house on Jubilee Street, bang in the middle of the railway lands. In a leaving-do speech it was necessary to say what the departing officer would be 'devoting his energies to', and this was a bit of a problem where the Chief was concerned. The speaker ought to come up with something worthwhile like protecting the ancient monuments of York, or at least harmless, like golf. If the Chief had played golf, Jim would be able to say, 'He never landed in the rough ... his dealings with his men were always on the fairway.' But the Chief didn't play golf. His game was billiards, which he played against engine men for money, sometimes disguising his true ability until he'd talked the other bloke into a really high-stakes game.

Until recently, the Chief had conducted PT classes for the veterans, which showed how fit you could be on a diet of alcohol and cigars. Even so, the Chief was thinking about how he might be memorialized. While drunk, he'd said he was minded to fund a new cup in the Rifle Leagues, and Jim would be taking this as an accomplished fact, which would enable him to work into his speech a line about how he always found the Chief to be a 'straight shooter'.

There was another rising racket from the crowd at the far end. It wasn't the noise that told Jim this meant trouble: it was the rest of the pub falling quiet. The barman – Jim's barman – was going over again. 'You lot,' he said. 'Out!

My governor's been on to the police. They'll be round here mob-handed in a minute.'

Jim doubted that. Then it occurred to him that *he* was a policeman. If a punch was thrown, he'd have to step in. But amazingly enough, here were three hefty coppers now, trooping into Whitelocks with truncheons at the ready. After a bit of verbal back-and-forth, they escorted the bad lads out. The last one of the half dozen stared at Jim as he went past, and it was more than a stare – it was the evil eye. Jim believed he'd seen this customer before. He was a recidivist of some kind, all right: you could tell by the shape of his nose, and the particular way in which he was bald.

Jim was picturing scenes associated with the man. They'd been Leeds streets, unexpectedly near the centre. The cobbles had been shining darkly from late rain, and every street had included its own loitering thin man. When you came into view around a corner, he looked down the street towards you, as if to say, 'You sure you want to walk down here, pal? You really want to take it on?' Some of the houses had a double identity. Daubs of white paint advertised 'Livery', 'Good stabling', 'Saloon Bar'.

Jim finished his pint.

As he stepped into Briggate, a brightly lit tram rumbled past with almost everyone inside smoking, so it was like a cinema audience on the move. The tram gave two flashes, then disappeared around the corner into Boar Lane. Jim turned that corner half a minute later. As he did so, he heard a cry from the other part of Briggate, the bit that lay south of Boar Lane. It was darker down there, once you got past the big silvery jeweller's shop with the projecting clock inscribed '*Tempus Fugit*', which meant 'time flies', as Jack Durrant, the grammar school product, would undoubtedly know. Beyond the clock lay a railway viaduct and the Aire River, both of which were black and filthy, especially at night. The cry came again; Jim saw a bloke lying across the pavement.

Jim approached the man, who sat up. He looked spavined, but not especially ill. 'Thanks for coming over, mate,' he said. 'Just had a queer turn. Have you got a light?'

Jim had been given a book of Whitelocks matches with his cigar. He lit the man's cigarette for him.

'Where you off?' said the bloke, and Jim knew this wasn't right. Even so, he answered the question. 'Railway station,' he said, thinking it best to leave the Queen's Hotel out of account.

Then the bloke stood up, grinning, as another bloke – the bald one who'd eyed Jim in Whitelocks – came running over the empty road. 'No, you en't, pal,' he said. 'You're off to the infirmary, for a nice long stay.'

And now Jim placed this man – and the other – among the dark narrow streets where they lived, and where Jim and the Chief had gone to arrest their brother. They were called Green. Jim couldn't recall the first names of the present pair, but their brother had been John Green. In the garden of the station house at Church Fenton – that obscure spot Jim had rolled through just a couple of hours back – John Green had half-killed a woman called Procter. To do it, he'd used bits of the rockery the station master had carefully created in the garden for the amusement of the travelling public; he'd finished by trying to drown her in the ornamental pond the station master had also carefully created. But Green hadn't succeeded, and the Procter woman was alive today, to the best of Jim's knowledge. Green, however, had hung himself in York nick after the opening day of his trial for attempted murder.

'You did for our kid,' said bald Green. 'Now I'm going to do for you.'

'Your brother did for himself, as I recall. And before that, he'd beaten a poor woman half to death.'

'Right enough, and he'd good cause to do it.'

This Green had now taken up position so as to bar Jim from returning to the brighter part of Leeds. In the other direction stood the brother, who had the same face, Jim now realized, only with hair. Beyond him, some bad-tempered shunting of goods wagons was occurring on the viaduct.

'I en't going to kill you, Stringer,' said bald Green, 'but you might not be seeing straight for a while.'

Jim produced the Detective Special. Shame, really, that it was a double-action piece, because the cocking of the hammer would have made an impressive noise in the silence that had fallen.

'It's not loaded,' suggested bald Green.

Jim said, 'There's a quick way to find out, isn't there?' A nice phrase popped into his head. 'Cloud the dust.'

Bald Green said, 'Eh?'

'Piss off.'

And they did, after about half a minute of staring and thinking about it, and with bald Green walking backwards and continuing to address Jim. 'I'll get you, Stringer, and I'll tell you what, I've got a bigger gun indoors than yours. I've got a bigger fucking everything than you, Stringer.'

Jim took a roundabout way back to the hotel, going by the dirty river for a while with gun discreetly in hand.

The Chief

Lydia was on the bed, lying on her front and reading *Vogue*, which she must have borrowed, or stolen, from the hotel reading room. Being a progressive woman, she wore a wristwatch, and that was *all* she wore. Jim sat on the bed.

'You're not wearing any clothes,' he said.

'I know. It's too hot in here.' She turned over. 'I can't seem to turn down the radiators. Did you have a nice drink?'

'Yes,' he decided to say. 'What have you been up to?'

which was quite a lascivious question in the circumstances. There was a tray on the bedside with a silver tea set on it.

'I went downstairs for a scout about. That was while I had my clothes *on*, of course. Then I ordered a tea. It wasn't too expensive, Jim.'

Jim had walked through to the bathroom, which was all steamed-up after Lydia's bath. He began undressing, prior to having a bit of a sluice-down.

'There's a new option at breakfast,' Lydia was saying, with voice slightly raised.

'Oh, yes?' said Jim, also with voice slightly raised. He was wondering how he was going to get a shave in the morning, since he had no razor. But there must be a wash-and-brush-up room in the station.

He opened a cabinet under the sink and saw two towelling dressing gowns wrapped in tissue paper. Amazing that Lydia had missed those.

'It's a continental breakfast,' Lydia was saying. 'Half the price of the English.'

'What's in it?' said Jim, who was now examining himself in the mirror, which gave a flattering reflection, what with the rather golden light of this bathroom. But even here, he wasn't sure about the 'tache. Maybe the thing would be to suggest the wash-and-brush-up man shave it off, then see how he responded. Ideally, he'd say, 'Couldn't possibly do that, I'm afraid. It would be an act of pure vandalism.'

'Bread and jam, basically,' said Lydia.

Yes, that would be right, thought Jim, now standing up to wash himself in the bath, but not actually having a bath. (He might have a bath in the morning, so he was nice and clean for the wash-and-brush-up man.) He recalled from his days behind the front that the Frenchers didn't really go in for breakfast. Standard fare was a cup of coffee – at once too small and too strong – and a couple of cigarettes, of which you could say likewise.

He put on one of the towelling dressing gowns. There didn't seem anything to choose between them.

When he walked back into the dressing room, Lydia took in the dressing gown. 'Where did you get that?'

'In the bathroom.'

'But *where*?'

'In the cupboard.'

'You'd think they'd lay them out on the bed,' said Lydia, who was herself still laid out on the bed, now on her back with her hands behind her head. She didn't shave under her arms. None of the Co-Operative ladies did, apparently.

'It's very nice, anyway,' she said.

Jim removed the dressing gown. 'And that's very nice as well,' Lydia said, which of course she *had* to really.

Jim walked over to his suit coat and took out the envelope of photographs. He sat on the bed and handed them to Lydia.

'See what you make of these,' he said.

Jim put his hand on his wife's brown thigh – a very good example of one that had never got in the way of a 5.9 shell. It had bothered him that when they next made love, he'd be thinking of Cynthia Lorne, but on balance he didn't think that would be the case. She wasn't really sexy, he realized. There was another word for her: 'ethereal'.

As Jim lay down next to Lydia, she held up the photograph of Cynthia Lorne about to kiss Durrant. 'This looks familiar,' she said. 'The place.'

'Why?'

'I don't know ... think we went on a ramble there.'

They often went on weekend rambles, usually with do-gooding organizations that Lydia had signed up to.

'With who?' he said.

'With *whom*, Jim, with *whom*.'

(It was odd, Jim thought, to have your grammar corrected by a naked woman. But if anyone was going to correct your grammar, that was the ideal.)

'I can't think,' she said. 'I give up.'

Jim's hand had drifted over to another part of her that was functioning just as it should. She made a move to better accommodate his hand.

There came a loud knock on the door.

Jim and Lydia looked at each other; then they put into reverse their recent movements and Lydia pulled the bedclothes over her while Jim answered the door in the dressing gown.

'Detective Inspector Stringer?' said a hotel flunkey. 'I have a telephone message from a Sergeant Hemingway.' The message was on a bit of paper in his hand; it seemed he meant to read it rather than hand it over. 'Superintendent Weatherill has been taken to the York General Hospital.'

'Has he been shot?' said Jim.

'No,' said the flunkey, looking a bit outraged at the suggestion. 'He might have had a heart attack. But he's not in any immediate danger, and Sergeant Hemingway said there's no need to call back unless you particularly want to. But he thought you'd like to know.'

Jim thanked the man, who was lingering rather as the door closed on him. Surely he couldn't expect a tip for bringing news like that?

'Oh, Jim,' said Lydia, when he returned to the bed. 'I'm so sorry, but I'm sure he'll be fine. A heart attack needn't be fatal . . . I know he means a lot to you.'

This annoyed Jim as being sentimental. It was doubly annoying, since Lydia didn't usually talk like that – and they both knew very well that she couldn't stand the Chief. Jim was also annoyed with himself, because he was thinking *about* himself. One day, it'd be him keeling over, probably in the Parlour Bar, probably on a quiet Sunday evening when somehow death was in the air anyway – and *he* wouldn't be a superintendent, but a detective chief inspector at the very best.

Jim, as Lydia often pointed out, was quietly competent

at his job, and that wasn't enough. He did not 'play the game'; was not known beyond York. The Chief was known beyond York. Even in the days of the old North Eastern, he was known in *London*, on account of his connections with the military intelligence blokes, who seemed to like the Chief for all his uncouth manner. They tended to be long-haired blokes, quietly spoken and wearing slipper-like shoes that were also quiet – and they all had degrees from Oxford. The Chief had twice taken Jim to their offices in Whitehall (which, now that Jim came to think of it, somewhat resembled the Queen's Hotel), and those visits had been the prelude to his Baghdad and Calcutta stints. Now that the North Eastern had become the London & North Eastern Railway, it was even more important to 'play the game' – to have what Lydia called a career. But Jim hadn't had a career so much as a series of rather dazed adventures.

Lydia said, 'We don't have to do it if you don't want, Jim.'

But they did do it, and it was pretty good, but not one of their best, since Jim couldn't quite shake off thoughts of the Chief lying in hospital. Afterwards, they talked about other, pleasanter things for a while, like the bigger house in Thorpe, the one at the better end of the village that Lydia wanted to buy. It had *two* bathrooms, she had somehow discovered. Then Lydia removed the belt from the dressing gown Jim had been wearing earlier on. 'This is interesting,' she said. 'I'm sure you've probably got an idea about what you want to do with this.'

'Why don't you tell me what I want to do with it?' said Jim.

It was good fun the second time; in fact, they knocked the chrysanths over. When the wave had subsided, Lydia said, 'I love this hotel.'

Jim couldn't help thinking she ought to have said, 'I love *you*, Jim', but he believed she did, which he had always found not only very gratifying but also surprising.

He said, 'Do you think I should shave my moustache off?'

'Yes.'

10

MONDAY, 7 DECEMBER

Wash and Brush-Up

That night, in the Queen's Hotel, Jim had a bad dream that stopped short of being a nightmare. He was in a shattered town behind the lines and continually smoking a cigarette of a brand, Virginia Select, which he associated with his days of leave in Amiens. The war was continuing, but most of the blokes had cleared off out of it. There were only a few very determined customers left, all carrying revolvers, and they walked up and down sunny ramshackle streets (because the weather had changed as well), where only the fronts of the buildings survived. In the dream, Jim was observing all this from a hotel where he was waiting for the Chief. It might have been the Sun Hotel, as depicted in Durrant's story, because it appeared that Jim was also waiting for the villain of that piece, Chuck Seaton, although neither of these characters ever quite turned up.

It was the kind of dream that stuck around, anyway, and Jim was thinking of it as he climbed out of bed at six o'clock and walked quietly over to the window, so as not to disturb Lydia. He pulled the curtains apart a little way. In City Square, the traffic block was on again. In the sky above, a very reluctant dawn was breaking. His war dreams never involved the absolute horrors he had witnessed, as for example on the first day of the Somme battle, when he had been surrounded by thousands of men, as many dead as alive, and when, if you saw a dead body in one piece, you thought that man had been lucky. Instead, the dreams had the war in the background, or in the offing – something looming. Jim felt that he would only stop the dreams if he changed his own life. He was like a man whose automatic watch had stopped. He needed to shake the watch to start time going again, and it was going to have to be a pretty violent shake.

As he dressed, he wondered how the citizenry of Leeds had the will to go anywhere under that sky the colour of dirty iron. It struck him that heavy snow might be in prospect. He wrote a message for Lydia on hotel notepaper: 'See you at 9 in the breakfast room.'

Despite the early hour, it was all go in the lobby, with people queuing at the reception to check out, and heavy traffic into and out of the dining room where breakfast was being served.

A modern hotel would have a telephone in every room.

What the Queen's had was a single Post Office Room. Jim went into it, and came out again, sharpish. It was choc-a-bloc with angry, smoking 'businessmen'. The quaintly dressed flunkeys of the hotel were trying to assist them with making calls or sending wires, but they seemed a bit out of their depth.

Jim quit the hotel. After turning two cold corners he was in the railway station, where he headed for the Police Office. One of the constables from the night before was still there, and he certainly looked all-in, but that might have been the effect of the electric light. He showed Jim to a telephone, and Jim was put through to the York railway exchange, and the Police Office. It was Spencer, the bright constable, who picked up.

Jim said, 'How's the Chief?'

'Don't know, guv. We've had no further news. Apparently, you were at close quarters with friend Durrant last night?' This was rather pushing of Spencer, but then he was known to have a lot 'off'.

They talked about what had occurred on the Leeds train, with Jim feeling on the defensive. He didn't quite know why until Spencer said, 'Did you not think of pulling the communication cord?' And of course, he used the modern term. 'I'd probably have stopped the train before it left York,' he added.

'Would you now?'

Then Spencer seemed to remember that he was a

constable addressing a detective inspector: 'But of course, you'd just been shot at.'

'*Shot*, actually,' said Jim, but as he looked down at his hand he saw only an innocuous scab. 'And we'd had that memo from London, if you recall.'

'Oh, that,' said Spencer.

Among the annoying aspects of being patronized by this twenty-year-old was the fact he was right. Jim ought to have confronted Durrant at the first opportunity because Durrant would have had something to say to him.

'Speaking of London', said Spencer, 'have you heard the latest on the re-organization?'

There had been perpetual bloody re-organizations ever since the North Eastern Railway had become the London & North Eastern. Jim didn't want to think about them. He was not the kind of person likely to benefit from re-organizations.

Spencer said, 'The word is, York's going to stop being a region. It'll be a DO.'

'A what?'

'District Only.'

'Right.'

'Could be good for you, boss.'

Jim knew what he meant: that York might be in his grasp, since a detective chief inspector could run a district, and Jim might be made up. He was overdue for that promotion anyhow.

Spencer said, 'Of course, there's always Woolmer.'

'Who's he when he's at home?'

'DCI at Darlington.'

Yes, Jim had vaguely heard of Woolmer. 'How do you know all this?'

'It all came out yesterday, late afternoon, just after you'd quit the office. The Chief was in. He had a long telephone talk with London – with Colonel Maynard himself. The Chief had some good things to say to him about you, guv. Maynard's apparently very interested in the Cynthia Lorne case – he's keen on the flicks, turns out – and the Chief told him you were assisting. He let him in on your theory.'

'And what's my theory?' said Jim, who was not enjoying this in the least.

'That Leeds are going after the wrong man; that it's Brooks they want, not cowboy Durrant. I was wondering if what happened to you last night changed your opinion?'

Jim kept silence.

'Anyhow,' said Spencer. 'If anything comes up about the Chief, I'll let you know.'

'Right,' said Jim. 'I'll be in the Queen's for the next couple of hours.'

After putting the phone down, Jim sat motionless amid the bustle of the Leeds Station Police Office. He was thinking, in the first place, about Spencer. Was he genuinely enthusiastic about Jim's prospects of taking over at York? Seemed a bit unlikely. A more plausible explanation was that he was trying to rile Jim, because it did appear that his career (as Lydia called it) was now entirely dependent on Durrant being innocent of killing Cynthia Lorne.

Jim asked the worn-out-looking constable where he could find the wash-and-brush-up man, but he didn't know; didn't think, offhand, that there was such a person. So Jim wandered about the station, which was full of grey-faced people hurrying away to dirty, fuming trains. 'Commuters', they were known as these days. He kept seeing glimpses in grimy carriage windows of the 'tache. He would rather think about it than dwell on what Spencer had told him. Yes, the 'tache had to go; it was just a question of finding some amiable, white-jacketed war veteran in possession of a cut-throat razor.

But maybe George Wilson, York's washer-and-brusher-up, was one of a dying breed? He undoubtedly was *dying*, albeit slowly on account of having been gassed at the Ypres Salient. Famous for his cough was George Wilson. His own small premises had electricity laid on, and he wouldn't go anywhere in the station still gaslit – for example, the Parlour Bar of the Second-Class Waiting Room. All gas was poisonous gas to George, who was always liable to break off from shaving you in order to step out onto Platform 2 and cough his guts up. Then he'd return with a very polite and heartbreaking apology. He'd never mention the war, and if *you* did he'd gently change the subject. Otherwise, when he had enough breath to speak, George Wilson was quite a talkative fellow. But his Leeds equivalent – whom Jim eventually located on an out-of-the-way, apparently number-less platform – turned out to be a monosyllabic, miserable bugger, as he was perfectly entitled to be, given that his left leg was artificial below the knee. He inhabited a cold, white, dripping room with a single wooden chair aimed at a cracked mirror and a cracked sink.

Jim sat in the chair, and the bloke put a white towel around his neck.

'I want to lose the moustache,' said Jim.

The fellow was stropping his razor. 'Got you,' he said. He didn't try to talk Jim out of it, Jim noticed.

As the fellow set to with his razor, Jim eyed the fire-place, where the fire was not lit. Instead, there was a paraffin stove on the hearth, and that also was not lit. On the narrow white mantle shelf stood a collecting tin for the Leeds Old Comrades Association. There was a single Christmas card, and it was mainly white, like this little room: it showed a snowman lifting his hat, and saying, 'Hello, how are you?'

The fellow was slow about his work, but thorough, and Jim felt he wouldn't be needing another shave for a good week. The fellow would shift from Jim's left to his right side at regular intervals, shuffling around in a painful sort of way. Eventually, Jim – speaking for the first time in years as a clean-shaven man – felt honour-bound to ask, 'Where were you in the Big Show, then?'

'Somme, Arras, Ypres – places like that.'

So he'd gone through the whole second half, and of course the leg would have gone at Ypres, because there'd be no carrying on after that.

Jim said, 'I was in the Somme battle.'

No reply from the wash-and-brush-up man, who was now endeavouring to shut Jim up, with his very firm application of a rough white towel, which did cause Jim a slight flicker of alarm. The fellow might be one of those sent doolally by the War. About half the blokes taken in charge at York were veterans, almost all infantry men, and this wash-and-brush-up bloke would have been one too – a soldier of foot, somewhat ironically. When the job was done, Jim tipped the man sixpence (half as much again as the price of the shave) and put another bob in the Old Comrades tin, for which he was rewarded with a short speech from the wash-and-brush-up man.

Turned out he'd lost his lower leg when an NCO fired along a communication trench at one of his own officers and missed. 'A right pill, he was,' said the wash-and-brush-up man, by which he meant the officer, not the sergeant, which was pretty magnanimous of him, Jim thought.

'What became of the NCO?'

'What do you think?' said the wash-and-brush-up man,

and of course there was no *need* to think. 'Good luck, pal,' he said, when Jim quit the wash-and-brush-up room. As he walked back to the Queen's, Jim's right thigh began giving him gyp, which was probably ... what was the word? Psychological. The other word was 'nerves'. He was thinking it was a pretty poor look-out that he was now reliant on the innocence of Durrant, because if the war had taught him one lesson it was this: what you want, and need, to happen does not.

Harry

When Jim sat down opposite Lydia for breakfast at the Queen's, she said, 'I've just telephoned through to Harry at his work. He's very busy, of course. He has to bike up to Armley gaol for an interview with a chap on remand. I suggested a cup of tea in Lyons', and he's no time for that, but his way up to Armley takes him right past the door of this hotel. So he said that, if we're standing outside at half nine, he'll stop and say hello.'

She didn't appear to have noticed the disappearance of the 'tache, and neither did Harry when he rode into City Square half an hour later, although there was a slight frown of puzzlement when, after kissing his mother, he shook Jim's hand. But Jim noticed everything about Harry. For all this bicycling, he looked a bit heavier than the last time Jim had seen him. He wore an expensive bicycling cape – a blue alpaca job – and his bike was also new. It was an Ariel. They were advertised on railway stations as being 'light on ankling', whatever that meant; they were also expensive. Harry had a rack on the back, which might have been specially designed to hold his briefcase by three leather straps. That's what it *did*, anyhow.

Jim didn't like hanging about here next to his boy, just in case the Green brothers were looking on. They might think that doing for Jim's son would be as good as doing for Jim himself. In light of these thoughts, Harry looked a very innocent figure, and far too young to be tangling with the bad lads of Armley nick.

Lydia was saying, 'But how can you defend a man if you know he's guilty?'

She was fascinated by the profession of solicitor, and had been urging Jim to 're-train' as one for years. It was too late now, though. Harry's articled clerkship was a five-year touch, of which he'd done two so far. The next year would be an 'academic year' at Leeds University.

'If you know a chap's guilty,' Harry was saying, 'and I'm pretty sure this one today is, you can't call evidence to support what you're saying. You simply put the prosecution to proof, do you see?' But Harry didn't want to boast about himself for too long, so he said, 'How did Bernadette get on with her audition?'

He had battery lamps on the bike, Jim noticed, not the old-fashioned acetylene type that Jim still used. Maybe it was time Jim went over to batteries; trouble was, they ran down fast. But Harry's were not run-down: they were blazing brightly in an accumulating fog, which was a dirty Leeds fog with gold and black in it, not like the white fog that had covered York when Jim had gone to Bassett's post office. Jim realized he could hardly make out the giant stone horse of the Black Prince, and the traffic was ceasing to be a spectacle and becoming just a noise. But the focus on Harry increased. Even his bike clips were a bit fancy: silvery, instead of the usual dull black. They sort of gleamed in the fog.

'They're not silver, are they, Harry?' said Jim. 'I'd keep an eye on them in Armley nick if so.'

'Course not, Dad,' said Harry.

'What are they, then? They're not regular bike clips.'

'Jim,' said Lydia, 'will you leave off talking about bike clips, for heaven's sake?'

'They're nickel-plated,' said Harry, and he had the decency to look a bit embarrassed about it. After a couple more minutes he was off, with a 'Lovely seeing you folks,' as he faded into the fog – words that somehow made Jim feel extremely old.

Lydia, huddled up in her coat, turned to Jim with a brave smile. 'He has all the gear, doesn't he?'

It seemed their son was 'getting on' a bit too fast, even for Lydia.

In the hotel, Jim hung back a little way as Lydia asked for the bill. Handing it over, the Italian-looking fellow said, 'I trust you had a lovely bath, Mrs Stringer.' As Jim and Lydia moved away from the desk, Jim said, 'He's asking for a clout, that bloke. What's the damage?'

Lydia handed him the bill; it came to a pound exactly.

'You can get it on expenses,' said Lydia.

'I can put *in* for it.'

The Eyetie was calling over: 'Oh, Mr Stringer. There's been a telephone message for you. You're to call Mr Spencer.' He looked again at the chit in his hand. '*Constable* Spencer. You can call him from there.' He indicated a wooden alcove containing a single black telephone on a small shelf. The telephone was more like an exhibit than an instrument of communication, and Jim had the feeling it was reserved for the most important calls.

'Hello, boss,' said Spencer, in his confident and familiar way, when Jim got through.

'Is it concerning the Chief?' said Jim.

'What?' said Spencer. 'No, boss. Durrant's been spotted. It's either that, or someone who's the spitting image.'

'Who spotted him and where?'

'A woman who runs a tea shop at Knaresborough. She served him a cup of tea first thing this morning. She went and found a beat constable. He went back to the

Knaresborough cop shop, got on to Monk in Leeds, and one of Monk's men called through to us.'

'How did this tea woman know it was Durrant?'

'I was just coming to that. She'd seen him in a shooting show in the town.'

Durrant was too famous for his own good.

Jim said, 'Monk's men'll be sending someone up there, will they?'

'They asked if you'd rather go yourself. Monk's lot have got bigger fish to fry. Double murder in Leeds this morning. Regular war going on between the bad lads there.'

Jim wondered if somebody had murdered the Green brothers. He hoped so.

Spencer said, 'Do you want *me* to get up to Knaresborough, boss?'

'No,' said Jim. 'I'll go.'

'But I can get there faster than you.'

That was probably true, although there wasn't much in it. Knaresborough was about 20 miles from Leeds and York alike, but there were direct trains from York. From Leeds, you changed at Harrogate.

'I could meet you there,' said Spencer. He was pushing his luck, this boy.

Jim said, 'If it was Durrant, and he's still in the town, I don't want to go mob-handed. If I can get close to him, I think he might have something to tell me.'

Spencer clearly didn't think much of *that*.

'Any news on the Chief?' said Jim.

'No,' said Spencer, and it was a tit-for-tat 'no'.

'Can you give me the address of the tea place?'

Spencer was good enough to give the woman's name too: Mrs Ellis.

Jim hung up the call and turned to Lydia. 'I have to go to Knaresborough.'

'I gather they've spotted Durrant, and you want to go there alone so he can shoot you in person?'

'I have my Detective Special, remember?'

'That could be your epitaph, Jim.'

Hadn't the Chief said something similar?

Lydia was set on remaining in Leeds for the morning – wanted to look at the posh shops, have luncheon in Lyons. Jim thought about this. The Greens probably were still at large and looking for trouble in Leeds; then again, they didn't know Lydia, unless they'd seen the three members of the Stringer family having their conflab in City Square just now. But it had been foggy, and Leeds was a city of a quarter of a million people.

'All right,' he said.

'All right *what*?'

'About you staying in Leeds.'

'Well, thanks, I must say.'

'But go careful. There's a lot of crazies about.'

'Not in the County Arcade, Jim.'

Knaresborough

Jim quit the hotel before Lydia; he carried the black and blue carpet bag. In City Square, the trams swayed in the fog like lighted ships. In the station, he stood before the departure board for three minutes before he spotted a Harrogate train. Platform 12.

The train was short and, for some mysterious reason, packed. Jim found a seat in first class. His warrant card specified 'second', but any ticket inspector who fancied chucking him out would have an argument on his hands. It was an open carriage and, he as he sat down, various first-class statements were being made. For instance, by a man offering to a woman a small square basket with a white cloth on it: 'It comes from the delicatessen on Briggate. Will you take a chance on it?' The top of a half-bottle of wine poked from under the cloth on the basket being gracelessly received by the woman. The man liked her more than she liked him. Jim could do with a drink himself. It was – what – barely half-past ten?

He saw himself very clearly in the window as they rolled through the dim streets of Leeds. It had been a good move to lose the 'tache. He looked more first-class without it. The point at which a railway policeman received a first-class warrant card was, he believed, at the rank of detective chief inspector. He could see ever more benefits from being made up. He'd been out of sorts just now when he'd seen Harry in City Square. Harry was undoubtedly the star of the family, but Bernadette was coming up on the rails – or would be if she got into drama school – and Lydia was gradually taking over the York Women's Co-Operative Guild. It seemed to Jim as if everyone in the family but him was making good, and that was unfair on the others, since he might come to resent their achievements.

He thought of Harry. He'd be sitting in one of the interview rooms in Armley now. They were just prison cells, only with the door open and a screw sitting outside if the prisoner was likely to cause bother. Police business had taken Jim to Armley on a couple of occasions. You took the number 3 tram from Briggate. The gaol appeared suddenly over the brow of a hill, like a giant hazard in the road. Directly over opposite was a graveyard, and you imagined that everyone in it had somehow been killed by the gaol. The front gate of Armley had put Jim in mind of a raised drawbridge, but there was a small human-being-sized door set into it. The method of gaining admittance was surprisingly simple. You knocked on the little door. You felt a proper fool doing it, mind.

Jim was worried about Harry, who was now, for professional reasons, mixing with the dregs of Leeds society. Ought he to warn him about the Greens?

By now Lydia was probably browsing (he hoped not spending) in the County Arcade. There would be no fog in there: it'd be turned away at the entrance by those top-hatted blokes whose main job was to stop people riding (or even wheeling) their bikes through the arcades. Instead, there'd be golden electric light, and any number of Christmas trees. Lydia's favourite shop in there was a musical instrument shop, where she bought song sheets for Bernadette and where she'd bought Harry's briefcase on the day she and Jim had come to inspect his smart new digs out near Headingley. So Harry's briefcase was really a music manuscript case.

As a socialist, albeit one who frequented luxury hotels, Lydia ought to like a poor-boy-made-good like Durrant. But she had apparently preferred Brooks, a member of the privileged classes. It might come down to this: as far as Jim could recall, Durrant hadn't said a word to her on the day of the Gala.

Jim wondered how Durrant – if he was, or had been, in Knaresborough – had got there. By train? Jim had last seen Durrant in the vicinity of Garforth, which was about eight miles from the middle of Leeds. Had he been sufficiently brass-necked to walk into the middle of Leeds in order to take the last train of Sunday evening that would get him to Knaresborough? At a pinch, he could have walked overnight from Garforth to Knaresborough. Or he could have nicked a pushbike. But *why*? The little town of Knaresborough had featured in this matter before, of course. According to Walter Bassett, Brooks and Cynthia

Lorne had first met Durrant at a shooting show there; and Jim had gone over the viaduct that dominated the town on his way to meet Ibbotson at Bolton Abbey. But that, surely, was just an incidental detail.

Knaresborough Station was cosily enclosed by the nearby houses, one of which had been co-opted as a signal box; another was a pretty-looking pub, but Jim resisted the temptation. At one end of the station was a tunnel, at the other end the viaduct began.

The cop shop was on Castlegate, but Jim walked direct to the riverside tea room where Durrant had supposedly been spotted.

The tea room was in a prime spot for river-watching, and almost directly beneath the viaduct. It was one of a cluster of riverside buildings – cafés and the like – that resembled little cakes or gingerbread houses, and it was the only one that showed any sign of life. Just a few yards along lay the mooring for the pleasure boats, but they'd all been taken away. At first sight, the river was like black ice, but it was moving – and fast – towards the lethal weir. High above the water, a train was crossing the viaduct, all the carriage lights lit; the sky was so dark, you almost expected to see stars.

There was a small terrace with tables and chairs between the tea rooms and the river, but the tables and chairs were foldable, and they *were* folded and stacked. There were no customers in the tea shop; only Mrs Ellis at the counter.

The room was white, silver and green, with white cloths on the half-dozen empty tables, many green plants, and a row of silver teapots – like an exhibition – on the shelf behind Mrs Ellis. In spite of the redundancy of the teapots she looked cheerful enough as Jim introduced himself.

'Yes,' she said. 'They told me a detective would be calling. Would you like a cup of tea?'

Jim would, and when it was made they talked at a table; or rather, Mrs Ellis talked – and she was very good at it.

'He came in at about quarter to eight. I wouldn't normally be open at that time, but I was having a bit of a clear-out, and I just thought I'd serve anyone eccentric enough to pitch up in this weather, and at first I did think he was a bit loony, because he walked in with a grey muffler wrapped around his face. I mean, it was cold, but not that cold. He also had on a long black coat, and a hat with a big brim pulled low. I thought he was sinister. Of course, he had to take off the muffler to make his order, and as soon as he did that I was sort of reassured, and I thought, what a nice-looking and well-spoken young man. But then I was even more worried than before, because I'd recognized him as Kid Durrant, the sharpshooter, who I'd seen at the fair here in the Castle grounds, and who I'd read in the paper was wanted for murder. I must say, he didn't look like a murderer, but I suppose that was silly. As if all murderers *look* like murderers.' She smiled; Jim smiled back.

226

'Most of them do,' he said, 'in my experience. Did he carry a squarish leather bag, like a doctor's bag?'

'No bag, as far as I could make out. The moment I recognized him, I thought, "My life could be in danger here, so don't give him any reason to get angry." I thought, "Be polite," you know, so I was very polite, but then again so was he.'

'And did he *strike* you as eccentric – or troubled in any way?'

'No, except he looked pale – a bit worn-out. He asked for coffee, not tea, which is quite a rarity, but he said he'd have tea if it was too much trouble to make coffee. I said, "It's no problem. I prefer coffee in the morning as well; it sets you up for the day." His answer was a bit strange.'

'"You got that right?"'

'Exactly. That's *exactly* what he said. Is that known to be a pet phrase of his?'

'Yes,' said Jim. 'It is.'

'It made him sound a bit American, but of course he's not American, in spite of his cowboy act. He has a nice Yorkshire accent. He drank his coffee on the terrace, looking at the river – sort of wistful. Then he brought the cup and saucer back in. He thanked me – called me "Ma'am", which again is American-style, isn't it? Then he went off, heading for the steps.'

Jim said, 'Could you show me?' so they stepped out of the tea rooms.

A narrow road or walkway called Riverside ran behind the premises. Steep steps led up from here, winding through grey wintry trees to Kirkgate, a main street of the town. As Jim looked up at them another train was rattling over the viaduct; it seemed just then to be the only noise in the town.

'He was halfway up the steps,' said Mrs Ellis, 'when I decided to follow him.'

'That was brave of you.'

'Was he armed, do you think?'

'Almost certainly.'

'It wasn't really very brave. I was just curious. He was a long way ahead of me, and why shouldn't I be on those steps? If he turned around and challenged me – which I didn't think he would do, since he'd been so civil in the shop – I would just say I was off up to town for some supplies. I did think that, when I got to the top of the steps, I'd continue on to the police station, and let them know. Well, the steps bring you out at Kirkgate, and when I did get to the top, I ... couldn't see him. Then a car pulled away, and I think he was the driver. Can't be sure, but I think so.'

Jim had speculated on whether *Brooks* could drive a car, not Durrant. But it wasn't that hard, he believed. Lydia wanted to learn – reckoned you could pick it up in a couple of weeks. Of course, *she* would do it officially with a licence and paying the registration, but a lot of people didn't bother with that – especially if they'd nicked the motor.

'Now you're going to ask me what kind of car it was,' said Mrs Ellis. 'I can tell you it was red, and I thought it might have been an Austin 7. A friend of mine's got one of those. As it was driving off, I spotted a policeman walking down Kirkgate. I pointed to the car, and I said, "Is that an Austin 7?" but it was just disappearing at that point, and he said, "It might well have been, madam. Why do you ask?" So I told him all about it. Of course, by then the car was out of sight. They haven't found him, have they?'

'Not as far as I know.'

'Is it certain he did the murder?'

'Not quite,' said Jim.

'Well, do you know something? I hope he didn't.'

The Fiat that Goodall had sold at Bolton Abbey had been red. Jim would get on to that garage in Beverley where Goodall had worked. Then again, he trusted Mrs Ellis. She didn't seem the type to send you off on a false trail.

11

TUESDAY, 8 DECEMBER

The County Hospital

Durrant having got hold of a motor car, there seemed little point hanging about in Knaresborough on the off chance of bumping into him, so Jim went directly back to York. It was half past two when he got back to the Police Office. Wright was in, and a couple of constables – not Spencer. Wright was talking on the telephone as Jim walked through to the Chief's empty office, where he stowed the carpet bag and its taken-down rifle. The Chief's office was the place for guns, after all. Jim had retained in his pocket the photographs he picked up from the muddy field. As he emerged into the main room, he heard Wright saying, 'I en't a doctor, you know. We've no notion when he'll be back.'

'Has no-one been over to the hospital?' asked Jim, when Wright had replaced the receiver.

'You know the Chief,' said Wright. 'He wouldn't want any fuss made. And we've been hard at it, you know.'

'Doing what, Wrighty?'

'Well, now . . .' said Wright. He was peeling an orange while trying to think of an occurrence.

On Jim's desk was one of the big brown envelopes used for circulating documents. It was from 'The Office of the District Passenger Manager'.

'That's from Oughtred,' said Wright. 'Don't know what it's about.'

That meant he did know; that he'd unwound the string from the little stud that kept the envelope closed and had a read. Jim also knew what it was about. Oughtred would be asking the whereabouts of Jim's report on fare evasion. And so it proved.

'I'll tell you what's happened,' said Wright. 'You know those red buckets under the Christmas tree? Someone's had 'em away.'

'How much was in them?'

'How do I know? A fair bit, I should imagine. Meant for the Old Comrades Association, was that. Someone should tell the Chief – that'd get him up and out of his bed.'

'That's not a bad idea,' said Jim, more or less to himself.

'Come again?' said Wright.

'I think I'll go and see him,' said Jim.

'Well, you can try.'

'Which hospital's he in?'

'County.'

Under the beady eye of Wright, who was almost as nosy as he was bone idle, Jim telephoned through to the office of Monk in Leeds, but he was too busy to speak. It was hard to imagine Monk being busy; he would have to move about for that, and speak a bit. Cynthia Lorne's body had been discovered more than three months ago, and Jim believed Monk was losing interest in the case. That was liable to happen with intelligent coppers; they'd think, 'If I can't crack this, nobody can,' and move on.

At quarter past three, Jim collected his bike from the bike shed behind the lost luggage office and set off under a heavy sky for the County Hospital. On Lendal Bridge, a uniformed copper shouted out a reprimand – 'Lights!' – but this was Lowry, the desk sergeant at Lower Friargate, and the shout had been a joke, although it was perfectly true that Jim's back lamp was bust, and lighting-up time was imminent – although it had been lighting-up time all day, really. Jim slowed and looked back at Lowry, to see if he had any news on the movements of Walter Bassett. He'd had nothing out of the way to report since Jim had first asked that the City beat constables keep an eye out – save for the fact that Bassett would make frequent trips on his motorbike; and it appeared there was nothing new now, because Lowry simply made his jokey salute, which Jim returned while cycling on. Should Jim stop and tell him about the latest developments? No, he had to see about the Chief. He pedalled on.

Was the cheerfulness of Lowry a good omen? Jim was interested in omens. The smallest thing – a simple gesture – could herald a good or bad event, a tipping of the balance, and so many things were *in* the balance just then. What had become of Brooks? Was he in London . . . the States . . . dissolving in the Strid? Had he or Durrant done for Cynthia Lorne? Would Bernadette get into the drama school, and what was the condition of the Chief? On the river there was a great concentration of smoking boats and the water looked like oil, but there was nothing to be read into that. It was life going on as normal despite the darkness of the day – creditable bravery, if anything.

Jim's route took him past the Minster, which was a fulcrum of the town, after all. In the adjacent Deanery Gardens, he observed what he first took to be a large-scale outdoor funeral. The participants – apparently all men – wore expensive-looking black coats and suits – and the Deanery Gardens just then would have suited a funeral, what with the Roman ruin (which, ever since the war, to Jim's mind, had taken on the appearance of a shelled house), the bare trees, and the lonely gas lamps giving a feeble blue light. But the men seemed too spread out for a funeral party. Jim dismounted from his bike for a better look. His next thought was that the men in black were erecting a marquee or inspecting a collapsed one. But then it came to him that this was Mary Ainsworth's balloon spread out on the grass, although by gaslight the colours looked wrong.

Standing in the gateway to the gardens, Jim called over one of the men in black to ask what was going on. 'What you see here,' said the man, 'are the members of York Balloon Club.'

'I thought it was a funeral,' said Jim, but he had noted that the man's tie – and all the men's ties – were bow-ties.

The man said, 'You might say we're giving the last rights to Miss Ainsworth's balloon.'

'How do you mean?'

'Some of the more technically-minded members have been giving it the once-over – see if it can be patched up for another summer.'

'And can it?'

'No. It's completely worn out.'

'Is Mary Ainsworth all right?' asked Jim, and with some urgency, because the omens were mustering, and he couldn't dislodge from his mind the idea of a funeral.

'She's absolutely fine. She's our honorary president, you know?' the man said, as if that were a guarantee of immortality. He pointed at the one woman in the party.

Mary Ainsworth was standing beneath a gas lamp and looking towards the top of the Minster tower, as though unable to bear the sight of her balloon prostrate on the grass. She did not look herself – because she was on the ground, was not smiling, and was dressed with such conventional smartness in a blue coat with fur collar.

'Will she get another balloon?'

'Probably, but it wouldn't do to ask her just now. She was very attached to this one.'

Half a dozen of the men were rolling up the balloon. Mary Ainsworth still looked towards the top of the Minster. To think she had once – in fact, many times – looked *down* on the Minster.

'We're all off to the Station Hotel,' said the man. 'It's our annual dinner. I'm sure Miss Ainsworth will perk up after a couple of glasses of champagne.'

Jim rode on, thinking of mixed omens. Mary Ainsworth's balloon might be dead, but she wasn't; and she might be back in the sky next summer.

He cycled automatically – along Bootham, turning left into Gillygate, right along Lord Mayor's Walk, left into Monkgate, where the hospital loomed.

Of all the York hospitals, the County was the most depressing, which was saying something. It looked like a workhouse, and was set back from Monkgate along a little avenue of dead-looking trees imprisoned behind railings. In the sky over the hospital, heaviness and greyness seemed folded over too many times; Jim wished it would get on and bloody snow. He leant his bike against the railings, glad to be rid of it. The three-speed kept slipping;

it was ridiculous for a detective inspector to be riding such a decrepit push-rod, and it would be quite inconceivable for a detective chief inspector to do so.

Jim knew he had pitched up outside visiting hours, and he suspected his mission would be a dead loss as soon as he entered the hospital lobby. A couple of nurses crossed in front of him, cutting him dead; the place smelt of cooking and carbolic. Here, as in York Station, the Christmas tree was surrounded by collecting tins, and these were in aid of hospital expansion. Propped-up placards read, 'BUILDING FUND. £10,000 STILL URGENTLY NEEDED. HAVE YOU HELPED?' Jim was not sure that was quite in the Christmas spirit.

Off the silent lobby was a silent corridor of closed doors. The first of them read 'Enquiries', so he knocked on that and somebody eventually said, 'Come in.' He knew from the look of the bloke behind the desk – old, with a closed face – that any enquiries were not likely to be answered.

'I'd like to ask about a patient, a Mr Saul Weatherill.' Then he upped the ante: 'Actually it's *Superintendent* Saul Weatherill of the railway police.'

The fellow made no response, didn't even blink, which might be a good thing. If the Chief had died today and this fellow had heard of it, he probably *would* have blinked.

'Are you the next of kin?'

Bloody hell. It sounded like the Chief *had* pegged out. Jim shook his head. He hadn't the faintest notion who *might* be the Chief's next of kin. Was it possible not to have one?

'You can't visit him just at the moment,' the fellow said, standing up. 'If that's what you want to know.'

So the Chief must not be dead after all; you couldn't visit a dead man. Jim decided he'd have a pint on the way home to celebrate – call in at the Swan on Bishopgate Street. He hadn't been there for a while. He could have two pints of Brown – and there was a bottle shop so he could take half a pint of mild home with him in the saddle bag.

The old man had disappeared through a door in the back of the office.

... Or maybe the best option for a drink would be the Reindeer on Penley's Grove Street. Jim always thought of that place in the run-up to Christmas, and not just on account of the name. It always had a really good fire. It wasn't exactly on the way home, though.

The man returned and looked Jim up and down. He held a little card. 'Mr Weatherill has requested no visitors.'

'How is he?'

'Very poorly, I should imagine.'

'Well, thanks for all your help,' said Jim, but sarcasm was lost on the bloke.

12

WEDNESDAY, 9 DECEMBER

Monk Again

The next morning Jim was in the Police Office at nine. He was feeling pretty cheap, having had four pints of brown in the Swan on Bishopgate Street, and half a bottle of mild when he got home. Spencer, who didn't seem to drink at all, was stirring up the fire. 'Any luck in Knaresborough, boss?'

There was no obvious resentment in his tone. Spencer was too canny for prolonged sulking. Jim told him what had occurred.

'If he's come by a motor,' said Spencer, 'he could be anywhere by now.'

Jim didn't quite agree, but he decided to change the subject. He asked Spencer, 'What do you make of the Christmas tree business?'

'It's serious,' he said. 'There could have been thirty quid in those buckets.'

Wright's phone rang, and Jim beat Spencer to it. It was Wright on the line, calling in sick, which he very often did on a Wednesday for some reason Jim had not yet figured out.

'About the collection buckets,' said Jim, replacing the receiver, 'it's going to be one of the regulars: Turnbull or Burdekin or someone like that.' Those two were among the crew of what were known in the Police Office as station loungers. 'They'll have got wind the Chief's off.'

'That's what I thought,' said Spencer. 'I was scouting about for them yesterday, and I'll be off over to Scawin's again later on.'

Scawin's was a pub frequented by the loungers. It was on Tanner Row, a short walk from the station. It had once been Scawin's Railway Hotel, but then half of it had been taken over for railway offices and some of it, Jim believed, had fallen down. It had never been much bigger than a coaching inn, and now there were only a couple of bedrooms, usually taken up by blokes who'd drunk themselves to a standstill.

'Right you are,' said Jim.

So there was a degree of harmony between them as both set about some paperwork. By half past one, Jim had finished his report on Fare Evasion – fifteen pages' worth. He signed it and drew a big double underline for good measure, and with no smudging this time. He put it in a circulating envelope, marked it for Oughtred and put that in the tray for the messenger to collect. He then commenced writing a letter to Harry in Leeds, care of his office. He said how nice it had been to see him; that he was looking forward to seeing him again at Christmas; that there was no news as yet about Bernadette's application to drama school. He then said that, since Harry must to some extent be mixing with 'bad lads' (which he crossed out and changed to 'criminal elements'), he should watch out for two brothers called Green, and had he considered investing in a pocket revolver? Of course, he would need a certificate, but that – as he would know – was little more than a formality unless he were believed to be of 'unsound mind'. Jim gave details of the Detective Special. He wanted to add something along the lines of, 'It's helped me out of many a tight spot', but that seemed like over-egging it, so he concluded by urging Harry not to mention this letter to his mother, or to ever let on about owning a gun, should he buy one.

Jim found a stamp in his pocketbook. He quit the office and walked over to the post box next to the book stall. When he returned to the Police Office, Wright's phone was ringing just as Jim happened to be passing.

It was Monk.

'Morning, sir,' said Jim, as Spencer looked on. 'Stringer here. I was trying to get hold of you yesterday. I wanted to let you know about the Durrant sighting.'

'Yes,' said Monk. 'Well, he's been sighted again.'

'Where?'

'Pickering.'

Jim felt the beating of his heart because, for some reason he couldn't quite put his finger on, Pickering made sense.

Evidently, the fellow who'd sighted Durrant was a certain Miles Howell, the one railway copper of the town, the Ibbotson-equivalent.

'When did he see him?'

'Just now, more or less. He got straight on to us.'

'Do you want to know about Knaresborough?'

'Not overly. The thing is to get up to Pickering.'

'I'll get up there right away.'

Jim told Spencer, 'If anybody asks, I'm off to Pickering.'

Obviously, the boy wanted to be in on the action, but he knew better than to ask a second time, and Jim had no intention of offering. This was all between him and Durrant.

Pickering

Jim put on his topcoat, which on that day was – strictly speaking – a long pale angling coat made of waxed canvas or similar and bought for him by Lydia, who thought that, since he lived in a village with a river, he ought to look like he went fishing even if he didn't. The coat had many pockets; the Detective Special was in one of them.

Jim walked fast to Scarborough Corner. A train was in, and all the Scarborough trains called at Malton, from where you changed for Pickering. It was an old loco, a Class A Tank, one of the late Mr Wordsell's engines, and not long for this world, judging by the way it was leaking steam. The stock was old, too, and liveried in faded North Eastern Railway maroon. But when Jim took a seat in an empty second-class carriage, there was a notice in the panel above his head, reading, 'Our new name – LNER. Our aim – to serve you.' Jim resented that notice.

Looking through the window, he saw that the day was already dark. He fished about in the pockets of the fishing coat, where he found a back number of the *LNER Magazine* (living up to its boast of being 'pocket-sized') and a packet of ten Gold Flake (which contained *one* Gold Flake) and a box of matches.

He lit the cigarette as the train rattled over Scarborough railway bridge. The water below was black, which made a lonely, drifting swan appear very white. Jim closed his eyes and must have dropped asleep, because he seemed – but only seemed – to wake up and see the words *Défense de Fumer* above the seat opposite, indicating that he was approaching the Western Front. Then he really woke up.

At Malton, he waited for the Pickering train next to a poster showing a fat little boy skipping along a sunny beach above the legend, 'Scarborough Braces You Up. It's the Air That Does It.' But in Malton, the grey air was spotted with snowflakes, like a defective reel of film.

As the train rolled through Pickering, the town was already giving up on the day. People were going into buildings rather than coming out of them; in the Market Place, stalls were being packed up.

Jim found Howell in the little room marked 'POLICE' on Platform 1. He was a studious-looking young bloke with floppy blond hair, and he was evidently no Ibbotson. He seemed bright, in other words. There wasn't much more in his office than a single desk, but it was an impressive desk with, from left to right, a neat pile of *Police Gazettes*, a Remington Portable typewriter, a telegraph instrument and a telephone.

After the introductions, Howell said, 'I'll show you the sights, sir,' and Jim told him to leave off with the 'sir'-ing.

Jim knew Pickering, of course. It was something of a holiday ground, and he'd come for days out with Lydia. Also, he'd got his railway start as a lad porter three stops further up the Whitby branch at Grosmont, but Howell meant the sights in relation to Durrant.

As they came out of the station, the light sagged again, and the snow was increasing. They walked into the deserted Market Place and stood in front of a wide shop called Chadwick's General Stores. Among the goods being snowed on outside were brooms, shovels, wheelbarrows and bathtubs, so it seemed more like a hardware store than 'general'. Howell said, 'He was coming out of here when I saw him. He walked up the road a bit and got into a car – an Austin. At this point, I wasn't sure of his identity. He had his hat down low, but he did look familiar.' As he spoke, he referred to his notebook, like a policeman in court. 'By the time I'd clicked on to who he was, he had the car started. It had taken a bit of time to do that; I don't think he started it by the regular method, but then he was off.'

'What direction?'

'Impossible to say. He turned right at the top of Market Place, and that would have taken him to the junction on Hungate. From there, the world was his oyster. He could have gone north to Whitby, east to Seamer and Scarborough, south to Malton, west to Kirby. Anyhow, there was no point chasing the car, so I went back to the office and telephoned straight through to one of Monk's men. Then I started asking around, to see if he'd been to other shops.'

'And had he?'

'Yes. But let's start by having a word with old man Chadwick, shall we?'

'Old man Chadwick' turned out to be only ten or so years older than Jim. He inhabited a wide, wooden room with goods arranged on shelves as neatly as books in a library, and all the shelves were labelled even when labelling surely wasn't necessary, as in 'Buckets', 'Jugs', 'Plates'.

Chadwick had already been interviewed by Howell, so he was well-practised when he spoke to Jim.

'The fellow came in about half eleven; a quietly spoken chap. First thing he bought was an oil lamp with a glass protection – we call 'em storm lanterns.' Chadwick pointed to the label on a shelf where plenty of storm lanterns remained. 'He picked out a small tin of paraffin to go with it.'

'Only a small one,' said Jim, 'when he could have bought a big one?'

'He could. But he went for half a pint. Pratt's Royal Daylight Paraffin, which, by the way, he called kerosene.'

'What does that signify?' asked Jim.

'You tell me,' said Chadwick. 'It's what the Yanks call it. He seemed to like saying the word. He also bought a little stove.' He indicated the label for those. 'And two blankets.'

Jim said, 'So the paraffin was for the stove and the lamp?'

'Expect so ... Then he bought an enamel cup, a notebook and three pencils.'

'Why three pencils, do you think?'

'Daresay in case one went blunt. We don't run to sharpeners.'

'And that was it?'

'That was it.'

Jim looked around the shop, taking in all the items

Durrant could have bought but didn't. Chadwick ran to basic food, for example – oatmeal, flour, bacon, pickles, tea. Chadwick could see where Jim was looking. 'Could be that he bought the stove for heat, rather than cooking,' he said.

Before the Durrant trail resumed, Jim made a detour to the Post Office, where he wired Lydia: 'SCOUTABOUT IN PICKERING RE DURRANT. BACK TOMORROW.' He always used 'scoutabout' to suggest work that carried no danger, but since Lydia knew he only used it when there might *be* danger, he really ought to come up with another word.

The tour of Pickering resumed, under snow coming down with more determination.

Howell, notebook in hand, indicated the premises next door but one to Chadwick's, a crude building somewhat reminiscent of a warehouse. The words 'Scarborough & Whitby Breweries' were painted on the bricks over an archway. To the side was a smaller entrance, and the words 'Off Licence' were painted there.

'He bought a bottle of whisky from the off sales,' said Howell.

'A big bottle?' said Jim; it was a drinker's question.

'Smallest one going,' said Howell. 'Half a pint.'

'Can we go in?'

'Aye.'

But Jim went in alone, because just then a laughing

man on a horse approached, wanting a word with Howell.

The Off Licence was just a long, battered counter with no drink visible, and nothing on the counter but a brass bell. Jim rang it, and it was a woman, somewhat unexpectedly, who appeared. Being small, worried-looking, and bespectacled, she looked more like a schoolmistress than an assistant in a bottle shop. Jim explained what he was about, and the woman said, 'I'm glad you came in. Mr Barraclough – that's the manager here – spoke to the constable earlier on. Mr Barraclough told the constable that the man who came in bought a small bottle of Bell's whisky.'

'Is that not correct?'

'It *is* correct, but it wasn't Mr Barraclough who served the man, it was me, and he didn't just buy whisky. He also bought a bottle of Moët & Chandon.'

'That's champagne, isn't it?'

'I can see you live the high life, sir,' said the woman, who suddenly gave the most amazing smile that undermined all Jim's assumptions about her.

'A full-sized bottle?'

'Full-sized. Fourteen and six. The most expensive single item we sell, apart from one or two special malts.'

Jim said, 'How come Mr Barraclough didn't tell Constable Howell about the champagne?'

'Well, it's a bit involved. Constable Howell came in by the other door. He asked Mr Barraclough about the man. Mr Barraclough came round here and asked me if I'd served a man of that description. I told him I had. Mr Barraclough asked what he'd bought, and I showed Mr Barraclough the ledger.' She stooped down and effortfully picked up a heavy black book that had been on a shelf under the counter. She dropped it with a thud onto the counter. 'That's the ledger,' she said. 'As you've probably already guessed.'

She opened it and showed Jim two entries under that day's date: one for whisky, one for champagne. 'I pointed them both out to Mr Barraclough, but it seems he only clocked the whisky. That came out when I was talking to him a few minutes ago. He said he wouldn't have believed a fellow like that would have bought champagne. He's busy just now, but he was meaning to go around the station to see the constable and tell him about the champagne.'

'Well, you can tell him he needn't bother now.'

'I will do,' said the woman. 'He'll be pleased about that; not very keen on walking through snowstorms is Mr Barraclough.'

'Why didn't Barraclough refer Howell to *you*?'

'Mr Barraclough thought *he* should speak to the constable.'

'Why?'

'The constable being a policeman.'

After a second, Jim laughed, and so did the woman.

'Policemen are important, you see?' she said.

'What did you make of the man? He's called Durrant, by the way.'

'Good-looking. Polite. He called me "Ma'am". He was also sad, as I suppose he *would* be.'

'Yet he bought champagne?'

'Maybe that's why.'

'I'm obliged to you,' said Jim.

Back on Market Place, the laughing horseman was riding at a canter towards the station – something ghostly about him now, his coat turning white, and the horse's hooves muffled by snow. He had left Howell with a dazed sort of smile on his face, and this was all quite uncharacteristic. Howell was a serious young bloke, and punctilious. Jim was surprised he hadn't followed him into the brewery premises.

'Sorry about that,' said Howell. 'That was Henry Barley, one of the local squires. He wanted to tell me a funny story.'

'And was it?'

'Not overly,' said Howell, and his smile accordingly fell away. He jerked his head towards the brewery. 'Learn anything new in there?'

Jim told him about the champagne, and Howell made a note.

'Suggests he was going to meet someone,' he said, completing the note with a very emphatic full stop.

That had occurred to Jim, too. But it wasn't the first thing that had occurred to him.

Howell took Jim around a couple of corners to a grocer's shop. The grocer couldn't be *sure* he'd served Durrant, but he'd served someone very like him who'd bought a small loaf, a few slices of ham, a bit of cheese, a bottle of mineral water, a slab of chocolate and two ounces of ground coffee: the smallest quantities available in most cases.

The last call was at Horseshoe Garage on Smiddy Hill, which had lately been a blacksmith's and – despite the petrol pump standing outside, like a smart soldier on guard duty – it still was to some extent, so it was difficult to know whether the black stuff that clarted the big hands of the owner was coal dust or oil. This fellow, it turned out, had not had sight of Durrant's car. Durrant had turned up with a petrol can, which he asked to be half filled. The bloke knew that much, but nothing more of the matter. 'You need to speak to the car bloke,' he said, and he turned and shouted 'Sidney!'

A smaller man emerged from the workshop, and Jim saw that the blackness on his hands was definitely oil. This Sidney fettled the cars; the boss fettled the horses.

Sidney said, 'It was a one-gallon can; he wanted half a gallon in.'

Jim said, 'Why do you think he brought the can rather than the car?'

'Maybe the car had run out of petrol, or he didn't want me to see it; or he didn't want me to see how he started it.'

'If he'd stolen the car, how *would* he have started it?'

The snow was streaming down like silent rain. The governor had retreated into the workshop. Sidney said, 'Well he wouldn't have had the key – unless he'd nicked that as well. So he'd have torn the switch out of the dashboard. That way, he could twist the wires together and press the self-starter at the same time. Bit of a palaver, and of course a dead giveaway that the car was nicked.'

'How far would half a gallon get you in an Austin 7?'

'About ten miles. It en't much. Maybe he was short of funds. Sixpence, it cost him, plus a penny tax.'

Another car that seemed to be missing was the one indicated by a sign propped outside the workshop: 'Car for Hire.'

In Market Place, the sky had turned violet. The man on the horse was there again, cantering away from the station this time. His brown bowler and his long riding coat looked a bit worn, but they had once been expensive, and the horse had the looks of a thoroughbred. The fellow saluted Howell: 'See you on the nineteenth, Miles!'

'You will that, sir,' said Howell. 'Looking forward to it.'

When the horseman was gone from sight, Howell said to Jim, 'I know what you're thinking – that I'm sucking up to him.'

'Not a bit of it,' said Jim (which was a lie).

'I have to, really,' said Howell. 'My mother has a cottage on Barley's estate. He could turn her off at any moment.'

'What's happening on the nineteenth?'

'He's having a party.'

'And he's invited you?' Jim was surprised; it wouldn't do to say why.

'After a fashion. Some of the railway blokes have got together a small orchestra. I'm second violin. Mike Thompson at Kirby is first violin. Pat Bulmer at Grosmont is cello. Well, I won't give you the whole line-up. We play at concerts at Easter and Christmas, and this year we're booked at Barley's house on the nineteenth. Of course, "house" isn't quite the right word.'

'He's paying you, I hope?'

'He offered but I waived the fee. The other chaps weren't too pleased about that.'

'Does he always go on horseback?'

'It's how he gets about in the snow.'

On Platform 1 of Pickering Station, the station master himself (going by the high collar) was chalking on a board 'No More Trains Today.' It was quarter to five.

Jim wondered about the morning trains. The ones heading south would be the first to resume, in all likelihood. The weather was better in that direction. The lines west and east would be next: they skirted the south of the Moors. But the line to Whitby – that went *over* the moors, and a snowfall could close it for days on end. Jim considered the motor road to Whitby, picturing its high banks. It was unlikely to be passable, but Jim didn't believe Durrant was heading there in any case. Whitby was twenty miles off, and he might not have enough petrol. Yes, the odd passenger boat sailed from Whitby, but not for the Shangri-la of America. Whitby was on the wrong side of the country for that.

Miles Howell had nipped into his little office to offload his snowy coat; the plan was to have tea in the refreshment room. Meanwhile, Jim went into the Gentlemen's, from where, as he pissed, he could hear the SM responding to a lady passenger who wasn't having this cancellation business – 'But I absolutely *must* be back home tonight!'

Jim buttoned up his fly and walked over to the sink.

'It's drifting, you see, madam,' the SM was telling her. 'The cuttings are blocked. Where are you for, again?'

'Kirby; I've just told you.'

Jim stopped washing his hands. He looked at his face in the mirror over the sink. It was an old sink, but a new mirror, with the letters LNER engraved into it, but Jim was mentally back in the past. It was 1907 or so – a good few years before the war, anyhow – and a Sunday morning. Lydia had booked them to go on a ramble with an outfit called the Labour Church, and they were to meet up with the party at Kirbymoorside Station, which was about seven miles west of Pickering, on the line to Gilling.

The locals called it Kirby, as the woman on the platform had just done.

You could get to Kirby from York either via Pickering or (if you knew nothing about railways) via Gilling. For some reason Lydia had been campaigning to go via Gilling, but Jim had told her it took about half the time via Pickering, and they'd had a row about it. Well, it had been that sort of a day.

The station at Kirby was on the south of the town, and the town was on the south of the moors. Jim had quite liked the look of Kirby's station; it had a really enormous cattle dock and four waiting rooms – one very old and made entirely of wood. He hadn't liked the look of the Labour Churchers though. They were not an overly humorous bunch, and the ramble had started with a bloody prayer in the station yard. Under light rain and greyness they had walked about seven miles north to the village of Rosedale Abbey, which was in the great valley called Rosedale.

There was a decent pub in Rosedale Abbey, and Jim had ducked in for a half of brown ale, but the other ramblers (including Lydia) just rambled on, being teetotallers twice over, so to speak: once on account of socialism, and again on account of Christianity. When he came out of the pub, Jim had the humiliation of having to ask about what direction the troop of do-gooders had gone in. Turned out, they'd headed north-east, and Jim had caught up with them half an hour later, when they were all sitting on a grassy bank eating their sandwiches and drinking their pop. Lydia had handed Jim a salmon paste sandwich without a word, and in fact nobody much had talked to him after that. He was in disgrace for having taken a drink.

What was important about the recollection was where the ramble had ended up: a handful of houses called Rosedale East, a couple of miles beyond Rosedale Abbey and a sort of satellite to it. Ironstone miners lived at Rosedale East, and they worked in what were known as the East Mines.

Jim had read about these workings in the *Railway Magazine*, but they had remained in the distance on the day of the ramble. Jim had wanted to walk up to the mines, but the Labour Churchers wouldn't have it. The sites were too dangerous. Rosedale East, Jim recalled, was little more than a couple of rows of terraced houses and some sort of reading room; it had no pub. A pub would have been fatal to the mining enterprise, with the amount of booze the miners would get through.

Jim dried his hands and took the three photographs from his inside pocket. The ramble he had recalled, he believed, was the one Lydia had been thinking of when she saw the photograph inscribed 'The First Kiss'. Jim was now sure that it showed Rosedale East, and the tall chimney on the terraced house in the background was not *on* the house at all, or indeed any building. It arose directly from the hill behind and was part of the ventilation system of the mine. Jim recalled Cynthia Lorne's mention, in the Station Hotel, of a 'gold mine scenario'. That might have been what took her and the Kid, and presumably Brooks, to Rosedale.

As far as Jim knew, the ironstone mines had lately closed, or were in the process of closing. It wasn't worth the cost of getting the stuff away from such a remote location. So the mines would make a good place to hole up. There were miles of tunnels underground, and they were drift mines: you could walk into them and you could walk out again – or you might not want to walk out again. For someone with a sentimental attachment to the location, they might be just the spot to do yourself in, having eaten a last supper, so to speak, and drunk a bottle of champagne for Dutch courage, supplemented by whisky if the champagne didn't do the job.

Jim came out of the Gentlemen's as the lady passenger departed.

'Evening,' said the SM, and he seemed to half-recognize Jim. Well, they might have coincided on the Whitby branch twenty years before, only this bloke had stuck at it.

Jim said, 'What are the chances of getting to Kirby tomorrow?'

'About even money. I suppose we might get the first train away.'

'What time's that?'

'Seven-ten. The stopper for Gilling.'

Jim was sure he was on the nail when it came to Durrant. He had bought small quantities of everything save booze, but not because he was short of funds. The purchase of the champagne proved that. It was because he was short of *time*.

The SM shifted to the left, and Jim saw that Howell was on the platform, or at any rate *half* on it and half in the doorway of his little police office. He was looking a question at Jim: *Why do you want to go to Kirby?* He wouldn't ask directly, because he had two much respect for a senior man who'd been through the war. But Jim didn't deserve that respect unless he played straight, so he would share his theory with the boy. If Howell had been the first and not the second violin, and if he hadn't had a sick mother being tyrannized by some sod on a high horse, Jim might have resolved differently, but he felt sorry for the boy.

They went into the refreshment room, which was like somebody's front parlour, with a good fire and Christmas cards on the mantlepiece. The woman serving looked about right for the room – like a farmer's wife. Howell, at the counter, ordered a pot of tea. 'Sorry, dear,' he said. 'I know you want to get off home.' But she shook her head, dismissing any such notion.

As that pair talked, Jim was sketching a crude map in his pocketbook.

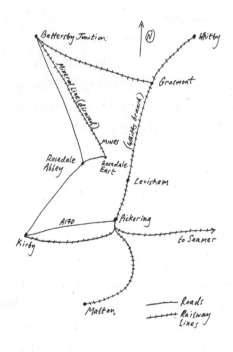

It showed Pickering at the centre of a railway network. The line to Seamer (and eventually Scarborough) ran east; the line to Malton ran south. The line to Kirby ran away to the west. The line to Grosmont (with Whitby beyond) ran north. From Grosmont, a line ran west to Battersby Junction. The East Mines of Rosedale lay between Kirby and Battersby Junction, in other words to the north and west of Pickering. There was no railway line running north from Kirby towards them. There *was* a steeply undulating line running south from Battersby Junction towards them, but it was a mineral line, and

Jim believed now abandoned, owing to the closure of the mines. There was a one-in-five incline on that line, which was bloody ridiculous.

Battersby Junction was only half a dozen stops west of Grosmont, where Jim had worked. Once or twice he'd been *through* Battersby – it was on the Middlesbrough line – and he'd been interested to see the sorting lines for the Rosedale traffic, but he'd never alighted there.

It occurred to Jim that if Durrant had wanted to lay in supplies for a night on the moors, he might have done it at Kirby. He would have reached Kirby before Malton if driving from Knaresborough, but Jim recollected that there was a big cop shop in Kirby. That Durrant had favoured Pickering might also suggest that he had called at York, since York was on the way between Knaresborough and Pickering.

When Howell brought over the tea, Jim said, 'I reckon he might have gone out to Rosedale – to the mines out there.'

'Really? Why?'

'Because he'd been there before – with Cynthia Lorne.'

'The woman he did in?'

'That's everybody's working assumption.'

'But not yours?'

'I don't know.'

'Why would he go there?'

'Sentimental attachment.'

'Funny spot to be sentimental about. They took a lovely

bit of country and ruined it. They have spoil heaps and all sorts.'

Jim handed Howell the photograph. 'On the back, he's written "The First Kiss".'

Howell looked at both sides of the picture and returned it without comment.

Jim said, 'That was taken at the mines, I think. Kirby would be the nearest railhead, wouldn't it?'

'It's still a good way off.'

'Then there's the mineral line from Battersby.'

'But that's out of commission.'

'Have they lifted the track?'

'As good as.'

They drained their cups. Howell said, 'I don't see why he'd go there, just because he'd been kissed there.'

Jim said, 'Because he's a romantic.'

But in spite of his violin playing, Howell evidently was not. 'Well, there's no hope of getting there tonight,' he said, 'short of in an aeroplane.'

'Is there a place I can put up for the night?'

'We have a lodge for Whitby crews on a late goods turn. Or there's the station hotel.'

Jim had forgotten that Pickering ran to one of those. It was thirty seconds away from where they were sitting, and not much bigger than Scawin's in York. It would presumably be cleaner than Scawin's, and there'd be no difficulty about claiming the expense.

'That'll suit,' said Jim. 'I think Durrant might be fixing to do himself in.'

Howell was nodding, but he didn't seem to take this point either and, even though his trusty notebook was ready on the table, he hadn't made a note.

They agreed to convene at the station at seven in the morning.

A Shout From a Doorway

At the Station Hotel, which was on Station Road, Jim was provided with a room overlooking a long snowy garden. There was a golden gleam in the air above. In the fireplace, a mass of kindling and best Yorkshire engine coal awaited the touch of a match, but Jim knew he'd be in the pub this evening ... unless Durrant turned up – or maybe even then. Jim's feeling was that they were fated to have a conversation, a lot having gone unsaid in their brief encounters.

The hotel laid on a good tea, which it called 'evening meal': Welsh rarebit, fruit cake, cocoa. Jim was the only guest at dinner, which is to say that he ate his meal alongside three empty tables. All the photographs on the dining room walls showed the prizewinning garden of Pickering Station.

Jim returned to the Market Place as the church was

striking seven. Otherwise, the snowbound town was silent. There were many pubs to choose from, including a Black Swan and a White Swan, but Jim determined on a little walk first, otherwise he'd be dead drunk by half nine.

He heard a shout. 'Stringer!'

Ten yards to his left, a thin man was leaning in the doorway of Chadwick's General Stores.

Jim put his hand into the Detective Special pocket.

'I thought it was you,' the man said. 'You've not changed.'

Vernon Bibby had. They'd been lad porters together on the Whitby branch – Jim at Grosmont, Bibby at Pickering. He'd been a jolly, fat little bloke, always getting into scrapes; now he was a tormented-looking thin one. Handshake and preliminaries completed, Bibby muttered that he'd been with 'the Yorks', which was about the shortest way of saying 'the Yorkshire Regiment'. Infantry, of course, so he was the genuine article.

'Came home in 'sixteen,' Bibby said. 'Wounds. You don't want to know, Jim.'

'Are you still on the railway?'

Bibby shook his head. 'Don't do owt much these days. Odd jobs, you might say; help out on a couple of farms.'

Jim said, 'But you were a passed cleaner, weren't you?' He recalled being jealous, back in 1902, having heard that Bibby had got his foot on the ladder to footplate work.

'I did a lot of firing on the branch,' said Bibby, 'but

I never really took to it. I could get by, but I never had the rhythm. Then one day I was rostered with Clive Merriman. Do you remember him?'

Jim didn't.

'Well, I'll tell you this: he wasn't very fucking merry. He was a good driver, though – been a top link man in his day. Anyway, I was in the shed here, watching him as he looked at the worksheet, and when he saw that I was down to be firing for him, he said to his mate, "Oh, no, not him. I've drawn bloody Bibby as a mate." Sort of knocked me flat, that did. I lost heart for the job from that moment. Then the war came along.'

Jim nodded. 'Do you fancy a pint, Vern? I'm just off to the White Swan.'

'No ta. Beer en't good for me. Anyhow, I'm barred in there.'

Jim nodded again.

Bibby said, 'You got your start down in London, didn't you?'

'I did,' said Jim, and, not wanting to appear too fortunate, he said, 'The one bright spot about that was that I met my missus down there.'

'So what are you now? Driver down south, I expect?'

'Policeman,' said Jim.

'Christ,' said Bibby. 'But you were so keen on the railways.'

'Well,' said Jim. 'I'm a *railway* policeman.'

'What rank?'

'Detective inspector.'

'You're on velvet, Jim.'

'It's only a middling sort of rank.'

Of course, compared to Bibby, Jim had been lucky. Only, he didn't *feel* lucky.

'What are you doing here, Jim? You're not investigating *me*, I hope?'

Jim shook his head, smiling.

'Well, must be off,' said Bibby. 'It's about my bedtime,' which was a somewhat unbelievable statement, but Bibby had certainly had the stuffing knocked out of him.

Jim, feeling down, walked directly into the White Swan, which had many rooms, mostly wood-panelled and empty. In the smallest room, he ordered a pint of brown and ten Gold Flake. There was a good fire – too good. It was crackling – making the noise of snipers in the night on the Western Front. Fires would tend to do that when Jim was feeling out of sorts. It was guilt at having survived, and that old feeling: *You came through the war, but for what?*

The snow on his trousers began to steam. He took off his topcoat and ordered another pint of brown. It was decent beer, but it tasted like stewed tea in his mouth. He was being left behind by his own family, and by the bloody London & North Eastern Railway. He was the Chief's favourite, but the Chief was about to die. Nobody else would look out for him; he might as well be dying himself.

He'd be talked about behind his back – by Spencer in particular: *'Never mind about the old boy. Leave him to his brown beer.'*

Chuck Seaton, in Durrant's story, resided in the Sun Hotel. Jim felt that he himself resided in the *Sunset* Hotel. Cynthia Lorne, whom he secretly loved, was dead. He wanted to believe Brooks had killed her, rather than Durrant. Why? It was true that Durrant was an arrogant young bloke, but Brooks had been Cynthia Lorne's husband, so there was even more cause to be jealous of him than of Durrant. All these emotions were wrong, undignified in a man of Jim's age. *Everything* was wrong, and Jim felt sympathy with Chuck Seaton, who had wanted to make things right or die trying.

Behind the raggedy curtains at the window, snow was floating down more slowly than before. The landlord of the White Swan was standing behind the bar gazing into the little room. When Jim had ordered his two pints of brown he'd had to shout for the man, the bar – like the whole pub – being somewhat of a wooden labyrinth. But here he was now, smiling at Jim and waiting to be asked a question.

'I don't suppose there's any way of getting over to Kirby tonight?'

The landlord had a better moustache than Jim had ever managed: positively silky, it was. 'What's the weather up to?' he said. Jim pulled back the curtain. 'Slowing down,' said the landlord. He took his watch out of his apron pocket. 'You might be in luck with a fellow called Ezra Clifton.'

'Who's he?'

'A railway carter. Unofficial, like.'

Jim wondered what that meant. Carters were either licensed by the railway company or they were not.

'Where can I find him?'

'He's in the other pub, the rotten sod.'

Jim imagined this must mean the Black Swan, and that its name was not to be spoken in the *White* Swan, just as you were not supposed to mention the House of Lords when you were in the House of Commons. But it turned out the landlord meant the Rose Inn, which was on Bridge Street.

Ezra Clifton

The bridge of Bridge Street went over Pickering Beck, whose black waters flowed on past white banks. The man Jim took to be Ezra Clifton was standing on a wagon outside the front of the Rose Inn with a heavy white horse hitched up. He was a tall, thin man, hatless with long white hair and a long grey coat. He might have been in his seventies. He was lugging a sack from one end of the wagon to the other. Jim said, 'Any chance of a lift to Kirbymoorside?'

Having shifted one sack, Ezra Clifton was now shifting another. By the light spilling from the pub windows, Jim could make out the word 'Meal' on both sacks. Ezra Clifton didn't appear to have either seen or heard Jim.

Jim said, 'Hello there!' very loud in the silence of the town. Still no reaction from Ezra Clifton, but the horse gave an impatient whinny, and that made Clifton look down at Jim. He pointed with his two black-gloved hands to his two ears. He was deaf; he mimed writing.

Jim took his pocketbook and wrote, 'Are you for Kirby or thereabouts? Will pay for a ride.' It seemed too much bother to spell out the precise location he was after. If he could get to Kirby, that would be a start.

Ezra Clifton read the note, then sat down in the driving seat. He shouted something – some blurred word like 'Haribup!' – to still the horse and took out a pen from a leather pouch he wore under his topcoat. He began to write. The wagon was the type known in Yorkshire as a rulley: four wheels with low sides. There were several mysterious objects on it, and one not so mysterious: an oil barrel. The wheels were big, which might be useful in the snow. They were also colourful. One of the two on Jim's side had 'London & North Eastern Railway' painted around the rim in gold against a green and red background, none of which had anything to do with any official livery or design of the company. Jim also suspected that 'London &' had been painted in front of 'North

Eastern Railway' at a later date, since it was in a different shade of gold. The other wheel had 'E. Clifton' painted over and over again in multi-coloured letters.

Ezra Clifton handed down his reply. In perfect copper-plate, he'd written, 'Ten bob', which was coming it a bit (a lot, in fact), but Jim nodded and Clifton held out his hand. Jim didn't have the money in coin, so he handed over a quid, and got four half-crowns in return. Jim climbed up, using the wheel as a step, and, since there was no seat for him, he sat on a pile of sacks behind Ezra Clifton.

They rolled out of Market Place, heading south and passing the completely snow-covered gas works. They crossed the sleeping railway line at a level crossing; then they were heading west on a biggish road. The snow in the road was perhaps a foot deep, with no wheel or tyre tracks that Jim could see. The snow in the fields on either side was deeper. They came to a junction, and Ezra Clifton called something like 'Dubbelup!' to his horse, which stopped – not for any on-coming motor or wagon, but so that Ezra Clifton could jam a wide-brimmed, off-white hat on his head. Another incomprehensible shout, and they were rolling again, in a direction indicated by a sign that had read A170. Jim realized he had been able to read the sign because the snow had stopped. He was cold but not yet shivering. He lit a Gold Flake, reasoning that a cigarette does offer a little warmth. There was no moon, a greyness to the sky and snow.

Alongside 'Meal' on the sacks, he read 'Cotton Cake', which made him none the wiser. There was a small can of petrol next to the oil barrel. Jim knew it was petrol because the word 'Esso' appeared in jolly letters. The road was undulating but Ezra Clifton's horse made steady progress, like the ticking of a clock. Jim began to feel tired, and it might be that Ezra Clifton himself was asleep on the driving seat, but Jim could only see the back of his hat, which was low and nodding in time with the horse.

Then the world began to be ablaze with yellow light. Ezra Clifton looked up; Jim stood up. He and Ezra were staring into a fast, flying sun: a motor car. Jim had forgotten about motor cars. It went past in a spray of snow. As the engine sound faded away Ezra Clifton was talking, apparently to his horse, in quite an even tone. Jim sat back down and after a little while he dropped asleep.

He awoke because he was shivering, or because the wagon had stopped. He seemed to be back in snowy Pickering Market Place, except that some buildings had been moved around and some new pubs brought in. The wagon was next to one called the Black Horse, which was closed, of course, like everything in the town. It was gone midnight. No smoke rose from any chimney. No snow fell from the sky. On the other side of the wagon was a signpost pointing in many directions, including 'Pickering', so they obviously weren't *in* Pickering; they were in Kirbymoorside. Ezra Clifton had been as good as his word, and now he was standing on the wagon and looking down at Jim.

Jim stood up. Looking directly into Ezra Clifton's white face so he would be able to see the words, Jim said, 'I want to carry on – to Rosedale Abbey.'

Ezra Clifton set his hat down on the oil barrel and pointed to his ears again. Jim climbed down from the wagon and walked over to the road sign. Reaching up, he indicated 'Rosedale Abbey'.

Ezra Clifton nodded, then signalled to Jim to come up and sit next to him on the driving seat – and there was just about room. It was quite an honour to be sitting next to Ezra Clifton on that torn leather cushion, although he did smell peculiar – he smelt of petrol, Jim realized, in spite of being horse-drawn. On his pad, he had written: 'We need two horses for Rosedale.'

Jim took the pad and wrote, 'For the wagon?'

Ezra Clifton wrote, 'For riding.'

And the exchange went on like this:

'Why?' (That was Jim.)

'The roads and weather – no good for wagons.'

'Where will we get the horses?'

'I know where. But we won't have them until half four or 5 o'clock.'

'Why not til then?'

'People sleeping.'

'All right.'

'Will be ten bob on top.'

Jim handed over the money. Ezra Clifton had now cleaned him out.

He said something to the horse which meant turn right. At any rate, that's what it did, and they were rolling over snowy cobbles, apparently heading for the railway station. A rake of empty carriages stood on the 'Down'. Jim saw the red lamp glowing gently from the rearmost one, but there was nobody about. Jim touched Ezra Clifton's arm and said, as distinctly as possible, 'No trains.'

But that didn't stop Ezra Clifton climbing down and walking into the station through a side gate. The horse was stirring again. Jim shouted any old thing, but it didn't have the desired effect, and the horse started walking. Jim gave a yank on the reins, wondering what Ezra Clifton was playing at. But here he was, coming out of the station, and he held two bars of chocolate. He threw one up to Jim. It was Nestle's chocolate – a 1d bar of the kind sold in machines on railway platforms, and it seemed to be given gratis. Jim and Ezra Clifton were eating their chocolate as they rolled out of Kirby. After about a mile, they came upon a dead and abandoned car, snow-loaded. It wasn't an Austin 7, but it did make Jim wonder whether Durrant might have got marooned in the snow.

They came to the village of Hutton-le-Hole, which slept in its hollow. The river that ran through it was frozen solid, so the whole *village* was frozen solid. Jim felt that he and

Ezra Clifton were travelling through a Christmas card. After Hutton-le-Hole they began to be on the moors. Jim had thought they'd been on the moors already, but now things were different. They might have been on the Moon. Jim wrote on his chocolate wrapper: 'I actually want to go to Rosedale East. That all right?'

Ezra Clifton read it and nodded without looking at Jim.

Every so often they passed distinctive little cones of snow – buried mileposts. Then they were at a broken stone barn. Ezra Clifton climbed down and made the sleeping mime to Jim, who mimed being cold in return, but Ezra didn't seem to see that. He was busying himself on the rulley. The oil barrel, Jim realized, held no oil at all but had been adapted for storage, and he looked on as Ezra Clifton produced a variety of articles from it including kettle, spirit stove, hurricane lantern, enamel cups.

The barn had no roof; only some charred beams, and it smelt of past burning. Ezra Clifton set about building a fire in it with old newspapers from the wagon and some snow-coated twigs and heather. It'll never take, Jim thought, on account of the wet snow, but Ezra Clifton seemed confident of a blaze because he piled some timber on it that he'd found around the back of the barn. He'd been here before, all right. He brought the petrol can from the wagon and splashed what seemed like a good pint onto the wood. He motioned Jim to stand back, then threw a match on the wood. The fire exploded into life, and it was possible that Ezra Clifton gave a small smile. He'd enjoyed doing that, no question.

He made tea by putting some leaves from a tobacco tin in two twists of greaseproof paper. This he served up with two bonus bars of chocolate, which came free of charge like the first. When they'd drunk the tea, Jim offered Ezra Clifton a Gold Flake. He indicated that he would prefer to have three, and Jim could hardly refuse, in light of the free chocolate and warming blaze. He watched as Ezra Clifton filleted the smokes, decanting the tobacco into the bowl of a clay pipe. In the next little while, Ezra Clifton smoked his pipe and Jim got through a couple of Gold Flakes.

Then Ezra Clifton went out. Jim stood in the doorway to see what he was doing. He was feeding the horse. When he came back, he fettled the fire before going to sleep in a sitting position with his back to the wall of the barn – although Jim couldn't be quite sure he *was* asleep. Either way, he began to feel a bit lonely. He took from his pocket the *LNER Magazine* and read the most interesting-looking article, namely, 'The Railway Motor Bus Service Between Ballater and Braemar' by W. M. G. Grigor, station master at Portgordon. It was not that interesting, in fact.

Then he read an article called 'A Day in a Running Shed'. An hour later, having read every article, he started on the advertisements: 'For Better Cleaning. Grym-Off

Gets the Grime Off.' 'The Most Distinctive Waiting Rooms are Decorated with Walpamur Water Paint.' When the lamp oil ran out, he chucked the magazine on the fire, which was burning low. Ezra Clifton slept on. Jim believed that a man's hair might still grow after he'd died and, if so, it would look like Ezra Clifton's hair. Or perhaps he was a kind of elderly angel, taking Jim towards his death.

13

THURSDAY, 10 DECEMBER

The Mines

Presently, Jim too went to sleep, and when he woke up, Ezra Clifton was standing over him. It was the second time this had occurred. Whether or not he ever slept himself, Ezra Clifton was very considerate of people who did. Jim had been having a complicated war dream which involved Cynthia Lorne singing in an estaminet behind the lines. What had mainly been complicated about the dream was the light, which was always on the point of changing. You had to be very careful of the light: if it became the wrong kind, everybody would die.

'We off, then?' Jim said, rising to his feet, but of course Ezra Clifton was deaf. This time, however, he pointed to only one of his ears, so maybe he'd half heard. He nodded, anyhow.

Jim sat in the back of the wagon as they approached the edge of an enormous white valley. The sky had changed;

morning was coming on but taking its time, the valley being so big. Jim resumed his sleep but not his dream, and when he woke up, they were in the yard of a grand, stone farmhouse. The farmer stood in his doorway: a grizzled, unshaven fellow wearing denim trousers and a thick guernsey. But he somehow looked rich. He held a surprisingly small teacup, from which he was taking surprisingly small sips as Ezra Clifton wrote something in his notepad. When the farmer had read it, he glanced over to Jim on the wagon. He saluted Jim with a raised hand. He then admitted Ezra Clifton, but not Jim, to his house.

When Jim saw them again, they were coming around the side of the house, Ezra Clifton leading a saddled white horse, the farmer leading a black one, and he was addressing Jim. 'You'll like these lads,' he said. 'Great friends, they are. Ez'll take you up to Rosedale East, then he'll bring the lads back.' He was talking about the horses. Jim, climbing up onto the black horse, was beginning to think the extra ten bob not too unreasonable, since it must include the hire of the horses. Then again, they might have come free of charge to Ezra Clifton. He did seem on excellent terms with the farmer, who was stroking the neck of the now-redundant carthorse in the yard.

'Remember, Ez,' the farmer called out, 'we want fish!'

The farmer gave a humorous shrug, since Ezra Clifton had paid no attention to the shout. He was talking to his horse. 'Pass away,' he seemed to be saying, ' ... pass away' – somewhat unsettling words, but obviously meant kindly.

They began a really steep descent. Sometimes, a wall seemed to have been built across the road, but it was only that the road had turned a corner and the snow had concealed the fact. When they came to some level ground, Ezra Clifton said something like 'Bardit!' to his horse, which fell into a canter. Jim's did likewise, which was fine by Jim.

He was a fairly competent rider. In late 1916, when the Light Railway Operating Company had created the railhead at Aveluy Wood, the little Baldwin locomotives had been the last items of equipment to arrive, so Jim and his mates had taken some of the stuff forward (barbed wire, fence posts and other fixings), using wagons drawn over the prefab lines by heavy horses. And they would ride those horses in the wood during quiet times, for exercise and fun.

Sometimes he and Ezra Clifton were passing trees, and in these little woods the morning would become quieter still. Soon they were skirting the village of Rosedale Abbey, where a yellow light showed at the occasional window and wisps of chimney smoke dirtied the white sky, like somebody sketching with a fine pencil. Whereas there was an abbey at Bolton Abbey, it was a curious fact that there was none at Rosedale Abbey; it was just a dreamy sort of name for a place.

They came to the little settlement of Rosedale East – a matter of two rows of ugly terraces that might have looked more at home in Leeds. None of the window lights glowed or seemed likely to. Ezra Clifton must be wondering why Jim had wanted to come here, but the only thing certain was that he had climbed down from his horse and was stroking its head. Jim also dismounted and walked over. Should he explain, in writing, that he was seeking out a dangerous customer and could use some back-up? He was sure assistance would have been forthcoming, at a price. Looking directly at Ezra Clifton, Jim said, 'Thank you.' He also handed over the packet of Gold Flake, in which there were four left. Ezra Clifton removed two before handing the pack back to Jim, and a smile might have been involved – very hard to say.

Ezra Clifton trotted off on the white horse, talking to it as the black one followed behind.

Jim turned to face the two terraces and, by stepping a little way to one side and aiming his gaze, he made the black chimney on the hill align with the roof of a dark end house. He was standing on the very spot where Cynthia Lorne had kissed Durrant. He walked on, around the houses. He was on the track to the mines, walking on loose stones beneath snow. A little way ahead was another abandoned car. Not an Austin 7 – too big – but was it the Fiat Tom Brooks might have purchased at Bolton Abbey? Jim didn't believe it was a foreign car. There was something rather pompous and British about it. Brushing away snow, he read the maker's badge: 'Crossley'. The roof was up, but snow had got in from the sides and was piled up on the red leather seats. Whoever had brought the car here must have been meaning to go to the mines. The track didn't lead anywhere else.

Walking on, he came to a more spectacular abandonment. As though from a sense of decency, the snow had attempted to conceal the extent of it, but the disaster was clear enough. The remnants of a railway line ran along a ledge. About a hundred yards to the left – in the direction of north – the line ran in front of a weird embankment made of brick arches, like giant mouseholes in a giant skirting board. The arches projected about ten feet from the hillside. You'd have thought they were the beginnings of tunnels into the hill, but they were ovens – kilns – and Jim knew that if he had been able to look down on them from the slope rising behind, he would see they were open at the top. Another shattered railway – this one narrow-gauge – ran along above the kilns, and a few frozen ironstone tubs on wheels remained, as though for historical interest, to show what had stopped happening about a year before. The ironstone would have been dropped from these tubs into the kilns where it was roasted. That way, it was cheaper to shift – by means of the line on the lower ledge – to Battersby Junction. Even so, the business was too expensive. Battersby was about a dozen miles off – too far.

Some of the kilns had iron doors on them; some of the doors were lying on the track. Steel cylinders were also lying about: big ones for oxygen, smaller ones for acetylene. There'd no doubt be brass blow pipes amid the clutter, and then you had all the ingredients of a metal burner.

Jim gained the lower track. It was important to keep moving, otherwise he might seize up like the Rosedale Railway. He would make a little tour of the dereliction. He took the Detective Special from his pocket and looked along the line in the direction of north. There was an abandoned loco, evidently a big tank engine with snow piled around it like white rubble. As he set off toward it, Jim heard a shot.

It came from somewhere in the lower whiteness, perhaps from Rosedale East. Jim did not believe it was meant for himself, but he stepped inside the nearest kiln. Had Durrant killed himself at the very spot where the kiss had occurred?

After ten seconds or so, Jim heard another shot. So this couldn't be the suicide of Durrant. He wouldn't need two shots to do it, any more than he would have needed two to kill Cynthia Lorne. But if it was an exchange of fire, it was somewhat leisurely, and now it seemed to have stopped.

Then Jim began to hear the scuffling of bootsteps. They were coming from above the kiln. His particular kiln was half open to the sky and half covered with a rusted iron grate. The bootsteps were approaching, and now here were the boots – the boots of a thin man – clanging over the grating. He was making for the forward edge of the kiln, as though wanting to look down into the valley. Whatever happened, he must not look *directly* down. Evidently, he did not; the boots retreated.

Jim had set down the Detective Special in order to try and warm his gun hand by blowing on it. He picked the piece up again and stepped onto the track. He knew he was vulnerable to a shot from above. Now something drew his eye to the abandoned engine – only a crow flying up from the chimney as though in place of black smoke. Jim walked that way, glancing down now and then into the valley, where the white haze was clearing, revealing the harder whiteness of the snow on the fields. He saw two clusters of houses. They stood boldly grey, with interior lights no longer needed. Things were happening down there amid what seemed like low white smoke, the remnants of the haze. A slow avalanche turned out to be sheep entering a field on the lower hills. There was a road – must be, since a car was going along it. But you could only see bits of the road because of the way the hills folded.

Jim came to the engine. Might its cab make a hiding place for a fugitive? He'd known men on stricken engines to sleep inside the firebox. Surely the tunnels of the mine itself would be a better bet, but Jim had been unable to see any sign of a drift entrance. He stood beside the engine: a long-boilered o-6-o, built to last and in reasonable nick; it would be a shame if some bloke came at it with a metal burner. The engine had an all-over cab for protection from the weather. Jim stood back and shied a lump of track ballast at the cab side. It seemed that nothing stirred within, but he climbed up to double-check. The controls were black with muck, but the great regulator handle seemed clean and was painted bright red, as if conveying the message: don't bother about these fiddly little levers – this is the one you really want. The regulator made the engine go, and Jim believed this one *would* go, given a couple of tons of coal and five hours to fettle the fire.

Jim climbed down and followed the track beyond the engine. The track curved on its white ledge around the hillside; Jim curved with it. About fifty yards off lay another set of kilns. On the track in front of them was another motor car, but this one was upside down. Jim approached it – an ordinary workaday car, looking as helpless as a beetle on its back. It was a red Austin 7, and surely it was *the* Austin 7. There was nobody inside, unless they'd been crushed very small indeed.

Jim couldn't grip the Detective Special any longer. He lowered it, and his right hand, into one of his many pockets. Flexing his fingers to move the blood, he set off back the way he'd come. Twenty yards short of the first set of kilns, he came to a stand, looking down and right towards Rosedale East. Then he looked sharply back left. A ribbon of smoke was flowing from the chimney on the hill. It signified a small fire burning in the mine. It was possible the fire had been lit hours before – that the smoke had been streaming all along into the white fog.

A figure stepped onto the track from beyond the kilns.

'I know you're packing; let's see it.'

It was Durrant, late of the mine. He had on the wide hat and long coat, somehow hitched back on the right side, where the holster hung. He said, 'Take out the piece, nice and slow.' The dialogue came courtesy of *Wild West Weekly*. Durrant, after all, must keep up the right tone for his or Jim's final moments.

Jim took the small gun from his pocket, showed it to Durrant.

'What is it?'

'A thirty-eight.'

Jim had thought Durrant would ask him to pitch the gun into the snow, but he did not. Instead, he muttered something along the lines of 'That'll do.'

Jim shouted into the wind, 'What happened to the motor?'

'Rolled it over the edge. I wasn't fixing on leaving here.'

Jim wondered whether Durrant had drunk the champagne. How many times in the night had the moment of truth come and gone? He said, 'You came here to do away with yourself.'

Durrant nodded slowly. 'It's not as easy as ... Maybe you'd like to step in – do something useful for once.'

'I won't shoot you. I don't think you did it.'

'Yes, you do.'

'Why would *you* shoot her? You loved her.'

After a while, Durrant said, 'You got that right.'

'I found the photograph,' said Jim. '"The First Kiss".'

Durrant nodded. 'When I'm lying in Boot Hill— '

'Come again?'

'When I'm *dead*, I want that in the casket with me.'

Jim shook his head. 'She wasn't shot cleanly; there were two bullets in her. You wouldn't have needed two. Brooks might have done. His body's never turned up. I believe he got hold of a car and drove away from Bolton Abbey. And it might be that he was in London afterwards.'

'I don't buy it, Stringer. It's all soft soap.'

Silence again; only the sound of the wind on the moor, which was itself a kind of silence.

'Here's the lay,' said Durrant. 'I'm going to pull on you. I'm going to shoot you dead unless you shoot me dead first. That should be pretty easy for you, seeing as how you already have your piece in your hand.'

Jim said, 'I don't believe you'll shoot me.'

'I have every reason to do it.'

'What reason?'

'In the first place, I'm tired of not killing you, Stringer. This time, I'm going to aim square. In the second place, you're a cop, and it's you cops that have put me in this fix to start with.'

'How?'

'By coming after me for a crime I didn't commit. But if I'm going to be marked down for all time as a killer, I might as well do a killing.'

Jim thought he could hear a distant, thin motor starting up.

'I can't dangle about here all day, Stringer. I'm going to count to five, then I'll draw. If you're even half a man, you'll shoot me down before I get to three. In the Old West, they'd call it frontier justice. Here, it'll be self-defence. They'll find me with a six-shooter in my hand and bullet in my brain pan – that's if you shoot straight, which I hope to God you can. They'll probably give you a fucking medal.'

Or a promotion, Jim thought.

'One,' said Durrant. His hands were easy by his side, but with just a flicker of movement, like a mistake in a film, the piece would be in his gun hand.

'Two,' said Durrant.

'On York Station,' said Jim, 'you fired with your left hand.'

'That was to throw you off. Make you think I was Brooks. I'm quicker with either hand than anybody in this God-forsaken country. Four.'

And there came a shot – from elsewhere.

285

A hatless man was descending the hillside towards them, rifle in hand. The Chief. He was covering Durrant, but also glancing down into the valley. Of the dozen or so strands of hair on his head, about five were wavering about in the wind. As he walked on, he shouted to Durrant, 'I want you to put your hands in the air.'

'Why should I?' said Durrant. 'I pull on Stringer, you shoot me down, which suits me just fine. Or I pull on you, and *he* shoots me.'

'But I don't think you're going to do any shooting,' said the Chief. He stood now on top of the kilns in the place Jim had been maybe half an hour before.

Durrant said, 'What makes you so sure?'

'Because you're talking about it.'

The Chief's boots clanged as he walked to the front of the grating over the kiln. From there, he could drill a bullet hole down through the top of Durrant's hat.

There came again the motorized noise from down in the valley. The Chief nodded at Durrant and said to Jim, 'Keep him covered.' He was trying to peer down into the valley.

'Why aren't you in the hospital?' Jim asked him.

'It's some other bugger who's going to be in the fucking hospital.'

The Chief was aiming his rifle, moving the barrel from left to right, tracking something in the valley. Jim risked a glance that way, seeing a small object moving along the road. A motorbike, but it wasn't moving easily – something straining about it. The rider's long coat was not flying out behind as it ought to have been. It might be that he carried something on his back: a rifle or shotgun. The Chief fired. 'Bastard!' he roared, so he had obviously missed. But the motorcyclist had been way out of range all along.

'Was that Walter Bassett?' Jim asked the Chief.

'Aye. The fucking flying postman.' The Chief turned to Durrant. 'Unbuckle your gun belt, kid.'

Durrant said, 'I'd rather be shot than hung.'

'If you don't look sharp, it'll be both,' said the Chief.

This was not the right approach, thought Jim. He said, 'There's a way out of this for you, Jack.'

'You're saying I can beat the charge?'

'That's it.'

Durrant looked at the Chief: 'What do *you* reckon?'

'Course you can, you daft sod.'

'And will you help me?' For the first time, Durrant sounded like a young man out of his depth.

'I give you my word I'll help you get out of this,' said the Chief, somewhat unexpectedly.

Durrant unhitched the belt and let it fall.

The Chief came down from the top of the kiln; he picked up Durrant's gunbelt and fastened it beneath his own coat. He flashed a nasty little smile Jim's way. Two figures were coming up behind the Chief. They approached from different directions but were converging on the top of the kiln.

'It's the fucking posse,' said Durrant, and Jim supposed he was right in a way. They were the Chief's hastily assembled team, recruited no doubt during the small hours at Pickering. The first was Constable Miles Howell; the other was Sidney, the little bloke in charge of the cars at the Pickering garage. He wore the slightly ashamed look of somebody who's just come out of hiding, but Howell held a revolver, probably supplied by the Chief. He'd been covering Jim and the Chief from some oblique angle on the hill.

Jim turned to Durrant. 'We do have to take you in charge,' he said, and Durrant looked blank as Jim formally arrested him for the murder of Cynthia Lorne.

14

FOUR TRAINS

The First Train

Sidney was so annoyed about the snow piled up inside the car near Rosedale East that Jim concluded that he must be the owner of it, as well as the driver made available to anyone who hired it. The car had not in fact been abandoned, but driven as far as possible towards the mines until the weather barred the way.

They had walked at a lick back to the car, with the Chief forcing the pace as he formulated his plan – which was a plan of revenge. With Durrant in the bag (and being remarkably quiet about it), he wanted to go after Walter Bassett, who'd had the nerve to fire on him from some hidden location in the mine workings. That shot had been fired after the Chief had put a bullet in the back tyre of Bassett's motorbike – an act Bassett had observed from a distance. Jim had told the Chief about Bassett's bike back at the start of October. But it was not clear to Jim now whether the Chief had known the bike for what it was when he saw it near the mines, or whether he'd just put a bullet in the tyre on the off chance that it belonged to some bad lad.

A few other things, however, had become clear during the fast march back to the car.

The Chief had discharged himself from hospital at teatime that day. ('There was nowt bloody wrong with me and I wanted a drink'). In the early evening he'd pitched up at the Police Office (no doubt somewhat canned), where Spencer had told him Jim had left in a hurry for Pickering. The Chief had got hold of a car and driver from the garage over the road from the Station Hotel.

Because of the state of the roads, the Chief and the driver had not got to Pickering until about midnight. Once in Pickering, the driver had wanted to head directly back to York, for fear of becoming stranded. He must have got a right rating from the Chief over that. Anyhow, once Howell (whom the Chief had knocked up at one in the morning) had let on that Jim's likely destination was the mines, the Chief had got hold of Sidney to take him. The three had reached the mines when Jim had been snoozing in the barn with Ezra Clifton. They'd taken a different route from Jim and Ezra Clifton, turning right off the A170 before Kirby. Otherwise, Jim might have seen the tyre tracks of the Crossley.

Once at the mines, Sidney had been told to lie low while Howell and the Chief had scouted about. They'd failed to find Durrant, but the Chief had had his encounter with Walter Bassett.

The only time Durrant piped up on the march back to the car was to explain how Bassett had come to be at the mines. 'He'd worked out I was going there. I'd told him I wanted to do a spot of hard thinking, and he pitched up on his bike to save me from myself, I suppose. I sent him away. His motives were honourable, and I'd appreciate it if you'd go easy on him'.

To which the Chief said, 'Stow it, son.' He said exactly the same when Jim asked him why he didn't put a bullet in both the front *and* back tyres of the bike.

Durrant professed to have no notion of where Bassett was headed. It had been Miles Howell, in his practical way, who had said, 'He's heading north, and I don't think he'll turn around. Going back to York's out of the question. Also, he's far too conspicuous on the bike.'

Sidney had agreed with that. 'There won't be more than a couple of Harleys in the whole county.'

'Odds on he'll try to get on a train,' Howell had continued, 'and they'll be running again by now. My money would be on Battersby.'

So the plan was to drive to Battersby Junction. Jim had counselled against. To his mind, Walter Bassett was a red herring. Jim wanted to get down to cases with Durrant – hear his version of the occurrences at the Strid. But you couldn't deflect the Chief when his blood was up.

Sidney was pushing the snow off the car seats, while the others waited about in the road. 'No side panels in these bloody things,' Sidney was saying.

'What are you going to do if you find Walter?' Jim asked the Chief.

'You'll see.' The Chief was reloading his rifle.

Durrant's face, Jim noticed, was dead white.

Sidney was making adjustments at the dashboard. He went round and started the car with the crank, and they all got in. The Chief sat in the front passenger seat. He specified that Durrant must sit between Jim and Howell. Durrant was not handcuffed. Howell had suggested putting the cuffs on, but the Chief did not generally go in for handcuffing prisoners. It was as if he liked to give them a sporting chance of an escape. There might be a bit of a roughhouse, and he always enjoyed those. Sidney reversed the car out of the roadside rut and Jim found himself going faster backwards in a car than he'd ever gone forwards. Sidney was a good driver, and probably wanted to show he was up to the mark, having been rather spare during the events at the mine.

They went back into Rosedale Abbey, then north following the road Bassett had taken. Whereas he'd been rattling along it with one tyre burst, they were fairly flying. It was cold, mind.

'My arse is fucking freezing,' said the Chief.

In point of fact, all their arses were freezing, owing to

the dampness of the seats. There'd been a fur rug in the car, but Sidney had stowed that in the boot out of harm's way.

It was an ashy, grey morning on the Moors. Sidney drove with the lamps switched on. The light held none of the magic a snowfall can bring. Yes, when they passed a tree it generally *was* a conifer and generally did look like a Christmas tree, but a very undecorated one. It was a hangover type of morning, Jim thought, even though he'd had less to drink the night before than for months. It just showed there was no point giving up. Jim believed it was his life that was the problem, not the beer.

It was necessary to bring off some bold stroke. If Durrant had not killed Cynthia Lorne, then Jim must go all out to find Brooks. He had half hoped to find him at the mine, involved perhaps in some sort of negotiation with Durrant. So far, however, Jim had made no progress on the matter of the Fiat motor car, having been unable to turn up any Paul Goodall in connection with any garage in the town of Beverley.

They'd just flashed through a village when the Chief turned to Sidney. 'Can you not go a bit faster?'

'We're pushing sixty miles an hour, you know,' said Sidney. 'If there's any motorist in Yorkshire driving faster than me at the present time, I'd be amazed.' He was very keen on county-wide comparisons, this fellow.

Howell was looking at his watch. 'It's nearly ten,' he said. 'If we can get to Battersby for ten past, I reckon—'

But Sidney cut him off. 'We'll get there when we get there.'

The Chief was continuously looking to left and right, presumably hoping Bassett might have come off his bike, preferably sustaining an injury. But empty fields were all they saw.

They did get to Battersby at ten. Sidney parked the Crossley in the station yard. As they walked away from it Jim saw that it was yellow. He hadn't noticed that before; there'd been too much snow on it.

For a junction, Battersby was very quiet. The infection that had killed the mines seemed to be seeping into the station. One siding held a dozen crippled ironstone wagons. A fence made of vertical sleepers, meant to stop the snow sweeping in from the moors, looked like a row of wonky gravestones. The whole place was black and white: white where snow remained, black everywhere else. A stopping train for Whitby Town was due at five past ten. Three people waited for it on the 'Down', and none of them was Walter Bassett. Only when the train rolled in did the Chief make a further plan. He, Jim and Durrant would board the train. They'd change at Grosmont for Malton, then at Malton for York, where Durrant would be taken into custody.

Howell and Sidney would continue on the trail of Walter Bassett. They'd visit two country garages that Sidney had mentioned as being likely suppliers of motorcycle parts.

Sidney reckoned Bassett would be needing a whole new wheel by now. He didn't seem to mind being roped into the investigation – not after the Chief told him he could apply to the York Railway Police Office for a week's worth of car hire money. By way of a goodbye to Howell, the Chief said, 'If you see an excuse to put a bullet in the fat sod, then take it.'

Jim believed the Chief had given up the search for Bassett as a dead loss, but there was an outside chance of him being on the Whitby train. He might have got on at Ingleby, a couple of miles west of Battersby, so, on boarding the train, Jim walked the length of it, with his hand resting on the Detective Special. There was open seating throughout, and no sign of Bassett in any of the five carriages. This stood to reason. If Bassett *had* got to Ingleby, he'd be more likely to have taken an 'Up' train. Most of England lay in that direction, whereas Whitby was a dead end, unless you wanted to jump into the sea.

When he re-joined the Chief and Durrant, Jim realized the open seating in the carriage would militate against Durrant's making any sort of statement. The elderly couple over opposite were staring at the Chief's rifle, which he held across his lap. Every so often they'd switch their stares to Jim or Durrant in apparent hopes of some explanation. What we need, thought Jim, is a compartment. They would have one between Grosmont and Malton, he believed. Meanwhile, Durrant appeared to be asleep. The Chief was shifting the position of his rifle so he could light one of his Babies. The carriage was a non-smoker, but Jim didn't believe the pair sitting opposite would raise any objection.

After forty minutes, they came to Grosmont. When Jim had worked there it had been oil-lit. Now it had gas, and the lamps were burning against the gloom of the morning. You could see almost the whole of Grosmont from the station platforms. It was a mucky kind of village, what with the brickworks and many smoking chimneys. In Jim's day, the station had been painted cream and red-brown; now it was cream and *light* brown. It had been cosier before. The station master of 1925, however, was a big improvement on the pill who'd run the place twenty years ago. As they awaited the Malton train, he took them into his office for a cup of good strong railway tea. It seemed to revive Durrant somewhat, and there was a bit of the old flash in his eyes as he said, 'You know what this reminds me of? *The Five-Ten to Durango* – a pretty good Western tale. A marshal and his deputy are escorting a prisoner under sentence of death.'

'What happens in it?' Jim asked.

But Durrant only smiled, and the question was lost amid the loud ringing of the bell to announce the arrival of the Malton train. The motive power, Jim believed, was provided by a smart G5, nicely polished up – brasses and everything. This was a good omen, and on boarding they found an empty first-class compartment, which was likely to stay empty, what with the Chief's guns and cigars.

The Second Train

Jim took out his pocketbook and pen. He would make a brief note of Durrant's account. Durrant would then make a formal statement, either in the York Station Police Office or at the City cop shop, and he would sign that this was voluntary and true.

'Spill,' the Chief said to Durrant, who gave a grin. He liked that word.

'Well,' he said, 'you fellows know we were at Bolton Abbey: Cyn, Brooks and me. We went there on the train. The day before, we'd been at Malham Cove. We were scouting locations, as they call it in the picture business. Brooks wanted a river, or fast water at any rate. He had a cowboy scenario – that's another of his favourite words – that involved a hat floating fast down a river. A woman would see it and assume that somebody who was dead wasn't really dead.'

Here he fell silent and looked out of the window, at a steep forest of snow-dusted pines. On the Whitby branch, sometimes, you might have been in Switzerland. Jim took out the last two Gold Flakes. He offered one to Durrant, who shook his head.

'We were on a sort of working holiday,' said Durrant. 'A tour of the Yorkshire rivers. It was Cyn's idea.'

'Was it really about a film,' said Jim, 'or just an excuse for her to be with you?'

'Both. She *did* want to be with me, I reckon. We'd fallen in love, you see.'

'Oh, bloody hell,' said the Chief.

'I don't see why Brooks would go along with it,' said Jim. 'On the day of the Gala, you were barely on speaking terms with him.'

'That's true. But he's a weak character, so he always did what Cyn wanted. The way he figured it he had no choice in the matter. He reckoned she'd walk out on him otherwise. And he blamed her for the situation, not me, so me and him ... we rubbed along pretty well most of the time, except when Cyn was up to her little games.'

'What sort of games?'

'I'm sure you can imagine. I told you I loved her; I didn't say I considered her a perfect person.'

'Why *didn't* she walk out on him?'

'Money?'

'Did you ever see their place in London?'

'Nope. I was never in London with them.'

'Did you try to persuade her to leave him?'

After a pause, Durrant said, 'She knew I wanted that.'

The train had stopped. Out of sight on the platform, a lad porter called out, 'Levisham! This is Levisham!' But there didn't appear to be any takers.

'At Bolton Abbey,' said Durrant when the train was moving again, 'we walked along to the fast river: the Strid.

298

Brooks took a few photographs with his box camera, and Cyn took one of me holding my revolver.'

'What became of those photos?' Jim asked.

'Search me. We had a picnic. Wine was the main ingredient – well, it was for me and Cyn. Brooks barely drinks. We were a bit merry, the two of us, and Cyn was larking about, singing and dancing. It's how the drink would take her.'

Jim said, 'Was it just the drink?'

'She used cocaine as well.'

'Did *you*?' the Chief put in.

'No, sir, I did not. We had a guidebook with us. That's how we found the hotel, and it was that guidebook that did for Cyn. There was an entry about the river – about how the River Wharfe becomes the Strid at that particular narrow point. She read out some jokey thing about how the test of a true Yorkshireman is that he's jumped the Strid. Then she said, "Right, I'm going to jump it."'

It seemed unnecessary to point out the two reasons why Cynthia Lorne could never be considered a true Yorkshireman.

Durrant said, 'Mind if I have that cigarette after all?'

Jim gave him the last Gold Flake.

'She was standing on a slippery rock, looking at a slippery rock on the other side. It was odds-on she would crack her head open. Brooks was a little way off. When I realized she was really set on doing it I tried to grab her, but she made the leap, and she landed OK on the other side. She said, "Right – now I'm going to jump back." Well, I couldn't have that. She wouldn't get lucky twice in a row, so I jumped the river as well, thinking to walk her around to the nearest bridge that would bring us back to Brooks. When I landed safely, she gave me a kiss – on the lips, mind you – and maybe that's what did it for Brooks. But I think it was more than that. The river was sort of symbolic. Our party of three was always going to boil down to two, and Brooks and I were biding our time to see whether it was going to be him or me with Cyn. But now it might have seemed clear to him how things would pan out, because he was on one side of the water and me and Cyn were on the other. Anyhow, when I looked at him he was holding the Colt.'

'Your Colt?'

'Yup. It was lying on the riverbank. I'd left it there after doing the cowboy poses for Cyn's camera. I hadn't thought to pick it up before I jumped. He fired – hit Cyn in the shoulder blade or thereabouts. I don't know ... maybe he was aiming for me. Anyway, she didn't go down. She'd have survived that shot. I grabbed her hand and told her to run. If we could make ourselves a moving target and get into the trees we might be safe, because Brooks wasn't man enough to jump the Strid, and he was an indifferent shot. He fired again – missed entirely. But his third shot ... I believe that got Cyn through the heart.'

Durrant had finished his cigarette. He put it out carefully and slowly in the ashtray set into the arm of the chair. 'Brooks turned and ran off into the woods on his side. I put Cynthia into the river. I presume you don't need me to say why.'

'You might as well,' said Jim.

'Of course it was a mistake, but I panicked. I was the well-known gun hand, the shootist with a criminal record. I'm known to carry a forty-five. If her body turned up, a forty-five would have been shown to have killed her. It was quite well known that Brooks carried a piece, but it was a Webley short-barrel, thirty-eight calibre. So what chance would I have in a court of law?'

Jim said, 'The bullets found in her were distorted,' and the Chief shot him a look. It was quite a nasty look, but it could have been worse. As coppers, he and Jim were basically prosecutors. They'd arrested Durrant because there was a reasonable suspicion he'd killed Cynthia Lorne, and that was that. Everything else was for the lawyers to sort out. Then again, the Chief had said he would give Durrant some assistance.

The train was slowing. Pickering Station came and went. As they rolled on through the town, Jim saw that the snow in Market Place was melting. He believed he caught sight of Chadwick standing outside his hardware shop. Chadwick's customer of the day before, Durrant, was not looking in that or any direction. He had closed his eyes. He opened them after a minute or so to continue his statement. 'I don't want to say too much about how I got through the next – what was it? – ten weeks.'

Jim said, 'Because you had help from Walter Bassett?'

'I've already said too much about Walter. He can account for himself.'

It seemed Durrant wasn't quite done with Walter Bassett, however. 'If he took a pot shot at you,' he said, pointing at the Chief in a way not advisable, 'it was to frighten you away from his bike.'

The Chief made no reply. He was being surprisingly reticent. The train rocked on, passing fields made to look untidy by melting snow.

'On Sunday,' said Durrant, 'I decided to take the boat train for Liverpool. Of course, the idea was to sail for the States. I knew I must be on all the watch and wanted lists, so it was desperation stakes, really. I just wasn't thinking straight. If I had been, I wouldn't have tried boarding at York. When that scheme collapsed there was only one left.'

The train was slowing for the next station.

Durrant sighed and folded his arms: ' . . . And ain't that the doggonedest story you ever heard?'

The Third Train

They reached Malton at ten to twelve. Here, they must wait for the York train. The station was all but deserted, the only sound the tuneless whistling of a platform guard on the 'Up'. Jim asked him, 'What time's the York train?'

'Twenty-two minutes past,' he said.

'Is it a stopper?'

'Aye.'

In that case it would get in to York just after one o'clock. The porter did not resume his whistling, and the only sound now was that of melting snow dripping off the platform ends. Jim said to the Chief, 'Shall I phone through to Wright? He can have a car waiting.' The car would take Durrant to the city copper shop at Lower Friargate, but no need to spell that out.

The Chief nodded, so Jim walked over to the Station Master's Office, knocked, was promptly admitted, and used the SM's phone to call through to York. He was glad Wright picked up. He didn't fancy talking to Spencer, who would pounce on any ringing telephone. Spencer would have congratulated Jim on finding Durrant, and Jim, not knowing whether it was genuine, would have had difficulty gauging his response.

When Jim returned to the Chief and Durrant, the Chief kept glancing over to the SM's office that Jim had just left. It seemed the Chief wanted *his* turn in there as well. 'Hold on a minute,' he said, and went over and knocked. As he closed the door behind him, Jim heard the Chief say, 'You don't have such a thing as a timetable, do you?'

Why did he need a timetable? The time of the York

train had been established. Jim glanced sidelong at Durrant, who was probably thinking the same but, having said his piece on the train, had gone silent again – silent and white in the face.

When the Chief came out of the SM's office, he said, 'I reckon we've just time for a pint.' Whatever he'd done in the office seemed to have perked him up a bit, Jim thought, as the three of them trooped along to the Refreshment Room. This had lately been redecorated. Previously, it had been a homely spot with a green-painted fireplace of the kind you might find in a country cottage and wallpaper depicting pink roses. Now it was all bare and white with electric light, and the fireplace had gone. The counter was chrome and there wasn't much on it, apart from a great, complicated silver urn and a glass display case that was both illuminated and heated by an electric bulb, and contained what Jim believed were called Cornish Pasties, which were the in-thing in railway food, even here in Yorkshire. The advantage of a Cornish pasty, apparently, was that it could be carried onto a train.

The old Malton Refreshment Room had been decorated with pictures of Scarborough, Malton being the principal stop on the line to it from York. But these had been replaced by only two framed posters. One showed London – Piccadilly Circus at night, an ideal version of the scene Jim had observed on that bleak day back in October. All the lights of the Circus glowed warmly under a dark velvety sky and the slogan read, 'Why not visit London? Travel LNER.' The second poster showed a red oval with a black star in it. Around the edge of the oval, letters read 'Wm. Younger. Brown Ale', which was promising, even though Younger was a London brewery whose products were unfamiliar to Jim. But no beer, brown or otherwise, was currently available, as was explained by the pretty young woman standing at the counter, who looked unreal somehow, as if she'd come as part of a job lot with the white paint, electric light and London poster. Jim and the Chief had a cup of tea and a Cornish pasty; Durrant drank half a cup of coffee. Didn't feel up to eating, apparently. He kept looking at the London poster, which must have made a depressing sight. His association with the film world had never taken him as far as London, let alone America.

Jim wondered how things might go for Durrant when they reached York. He'd be taken to Low Friargate, where he'd be charged by Lowry, or perhaps an inspector since it would be a murder charge. Of course, Durrant had also – most likely – stolen the Austin 7 as well, but that matter would be deferred.

When he came before the magistrates, Durrant would give his account, and his solicitor would ask for any assize court trial to be put off and the case adjourned until a special investigation had been held into Durrant's central claim: that Tom Brooks had shot Cynthia Lorne. As the arresting officers, neither Jim nor the Chief would be involved in that investigation, and it was by no means certain it would ever take place. If it did take place, the results would be considered at a special hearing. Jim was a bit hazy about the form it would take, but in any event Durrant would be needing a really good brief. The best ones were in Leeds, and it occurred to Jim that he might have a quiet word with Harry, who'd talked to him about a KC called Blezzard, who'd take on a case gratis if he found it interesting or likely to get him into the national newspapers. Jim had once seen Mr Blezzard in action. He was a big, completely bald man (no eyelashes, even), which you wouldn't know in court, thanks to his horsehair wig.

The Chief said to Jim, 'You've lost your tea strainer.'

'Eh?'

'The moustache.'

'What do you think?'

'I'm saying nowt.'

'How *are* you, Chief? You look pretty well.'

'I'm all right. Apparently, my heart attacked me; so I attacked it back.'

The platform bell was ringing, announcing an arrival.

The three rode the drowsy little train to York. It stopped at every signal going, and every time Jim wondered whether it would have the energy to re-start. Durrant still didn't speak; the Chief smoked, contentedly enough. He had something up his sleeve, all right.

The Fourth Train

When the train got to York, Jim was surprised to see Lydia waiting on the platform. Jim excused himself to the Chief and went up to her. She handed him a biggish envelope that had been torn open. 'I thought you'd better see this; it came this morning.' At first Jim thought it must be from the Royal Academy of Dramatic Art, in which case – going by Lydia's expression – Bernadette had evidently been turned down, and Lydia wouldn't stand for that: some sort of protest or appeal would be on the cards. But the address on the envelope did not have an official look. It read, 'Mr Jim Stringer, Main Street (Opposite The Marcia), Thorpe-on-Ouse, Nr. York, Yorkshire.' Papers were inside – a handwritten manuscript of not more than ten pages, with a typed covering letter. The address was 'Armistead & Bannister Limited, Publishers, 7A Prowse Place, Camden, London NW.'

Lydia said, 'I opened it because the address was weird.' But she would quite often open Jim's mail when the address was not weird. Jim watched the Chief taking Durrant in the direction of the Police Office.

Then he looked down at the letter, which carried yesterday's date.

Dear Jim,
   I thought you'd better see this, and in light of what you said about the inefficiency of your 'correspondence

clerk', I'm sending it to your home address. It arrived here by post this morning, with a Knaresborough postmark – can't make out the date. The covering letter was undated with no address; it was signed 'Rowdy Hardin', and that's also how the story is by-lined. Aside from the usual formalities, the letter read:

'Please find enclosed "What the Eagle Saw", a cowboy story with a somewhat psychological angle. I hope you will find that it fits the bill for inclusion in a forthcoming edition of Smoking Colts. I am keen to see this story in print, and money is of no concern. In fact, you need not trouble about any payment.'

Both letter and story were written in a hand that seemed familiar, and it turned out that the protagonist in the story was called Ned Keach – the pen name, you will recall, of the author of 'One to Ten', aka our friend, Jack 'Kid' Durrant. I checked, and the handwriting is certainly that of Durrant/Keach. Make what you will of the tale; it might be of some use in your investigation.

Here's hoping our paths will cross again, Jim – in God's Own County!

Regards,

Fred

PS: No telephone here, but a wire will reach me on Armbanner, London.

308

Jim sat down on a baggage trolley to read; Lydia sat on the other side of the trolley. Jim noticed that the Chief had not in fact taken Durrant into the Police Office; they were walking on. The Chief must be taking him directly to the car, which would be waiting on the carriage drive. Or there was an outside chance he was taking Durrant for a pint in the Parlour Bar, to make up for the absence of beer at Malton. Jim turned his attention to the story.

WHAT THE EAGLE SAW
by Rowdy Hardin

Arthur and Belle Rutherford and Ned Keach were the only people in the Zion canyon. Their horses were also present, and there was an eagle, circling between the walls of rock, looking down on the scene. The eagle was interested, perhaps, to see what would happen next.

The kaleidoscope of colours was turning to evening shades. If a painter had made an accurate depiction of Zion Canyon under the setting sun, you simply wouldn't have believed the result. You'd have thought he was way too heavy on the orange. The sunset was orange; the rock walls were orange; the rocks in the Virgin river were orange. You'd also have thought that water racing over those rocks was far too blue, and surely the greenness of the riverside trees should be toned down somewhat? You'd have thought it the work of a madman.

Arthur Rutherford was the closest to the river of the three. One shove in the back and he'd be gone from sight; even the eagle wouldn't be able to keep up, as his dandified form, rolling in the cold blue water, gradually became a corpse. It was Ned Keach who'd harboured this thought, and he wondered whether Belle, sitting cross-legged on an orange rock and sipping whisky from a coffee cup (and didn't mind who knew it), might not be thinking the same. Ned was tortured at all times by wondering what Belle was thinking, and it seemed to him that it suited her down to the ground to keep him so. It was not enough that he should keep looking at her, she must occupy every corner of his mind and star in all his dreams.

Whether her husband, Arthur, was party to the game she was playing ... that was another mystery Ned was forced to grapple with. Did his wife's flirtation towards Ned give him some secret pleasure? He never seemed to discourage it. But Arthur didn't give much away. He had been staring at the racing water for five minutes. Maybe he would jump, having been driven crazy by his wild, whisky-drinking wife?

Like many superior types who ended up in the west, Arthur Rutherford was from the east, but from further east than most, being an Englishman; an English gentleman, in fact, and how Ned hated those words. You couldn't say them without making a pinched and prissy face. The one time Ned had tried shortening Arthur to Art, he'd been smartly corrected, and the fellow never wore a plaid shirt, always a white one. He also said 'curse', not 'cuss', and he never did it.

'Fancy a swim, darling?' Belle asked her husband.

Arthur half turned to his wife. 'I don't have a costume.'

'A costume!' echoed Belle. Her husband's English phraseology never ceased to amuse her, and she seemed to want Ned to be amused by it too. She turned and flashed her conspiratorial smile – and had she given a wink? She might as well have done.

'He'd probably rather go rowing, wouldn't you, darling?'

'Hardly.'

'He did rowing at university you know, Ned. Sorry, I mean The University. Oxford. He has a blue, you know.'

'A blue what?' said Ned, with great weariness. He was like an actor trapped in a bad script.

'Now that would be telling!' The echo of Belle's laughter bounced between the walls of the canyon, lingering long after the joke had died. Ned didn't care for Belle's laugh; it was one of many things about her he didn't care for – which made for another tormenting mystery. He didn't know why he was in love with her, apart from the fact of her blonde beauty, of course. Maybe that was enough.

Arthur, at the edge of the water, was examining his pocket watch. He replaced it in his waistcoat pocket, making sure – over the course of a clear ten seconds (Ned counted them) – that the gold chain hung just so.

'Seven-fifteen,' he announced, seemingly to the river, whereas any normal man – any man full stop – would have said 'Quarter after seven', or would not have bothered with the watch, but just made an estimation from the colour of the sky. 'We really ought to be making a start back.'

Why can't you just say, 'We best be heading back'? thought Ned. But what he said was, 'Reckon so, Arthur.'

Nobody moved, however. The two men never did anything until Belle gave her orders, and she was still sipping her whisky. What Ned wanted to do was to start loving her in the proper way – at close quarters – in order to see how long it took before he could shake his mind loose of her. Get her out of his system – that was the expression – and the impediment to this necessary process was Arthur Rutherford.

If only he would wear a gun belt. A man with a shooter to hand could be called out in the heat of an argument. But Arthur more often held a book than a gun, and he went in for some pretty stiff reading: novels, the longer the better, and once or twice in French. His Colt six-shooter was more or less permanently stowed in the fine leathern bag that was part of his expensive assemblage of luggage. Ned had seen it on the single occasion in their month's tour when he'd been obliged to room with Arthur, or when Arthur had been obliged to room with Ned. (His distaste had been pretty clear.) The piece was nickel-plated and ivory-handled, more ornament than killing machine. It might even have been deactivated. A gentleman didn't want a gun accidentally going off in his saddlebag and singeing his silk smalls.

Belle, of course, admired the way Ned threw his gun, and perhaps Arthur did likewise. He would give a kind of sly smile when Ned hit a spinning silver dollar tossed up by a giggling Belle. 'This is a skill all right,' that smile seemed to say, 'but of a pretty lowly kind, and something only a young cow prod would think of boasting about.'

*

Rutherford had come east via New York, where another 'gentleman' had introduced him to Belle. That fateful meeting took place in a theatre, for Belle was an actress, famous enough to have excited the interest of newspaper correspondents wherever she had travelled out West. And she had travelled a good deal, for Rutherford was looking to acquire a ranch. Did he have the makings of a ranch boss? Not as far as Ned could see. He would be more at home in a Gentlemen's Outfitters than a ranching outfit.

Ned had been riding the range of the Lightning 5 spread in Grand Junction, Colorado when Rutherford and Belle had pitched up. It seemed they were thinking of acquiring the Lightning 5 from Ned's boss, Lou Tarbert, who was certainly looking to sell. But after Ned had spent a day showing them over the somewhat dusty acreage, Belle had given her verdict: 'The place isn't pretty enough.' Then she had turned to Ned: 'You are, though. I think we'll have you instead.' And so Ned was on their payroll at three times the rate he was on as swingman on the Lightning 5. He had been retained as bagman or gunhand on their search to find a spread that met the artistic requirements of Belle.

Arthur remained on the brink of the bluff; the water still raced.

Belle, her voice thickened with liquor, called to him: 'What's the quaint expression of yours, darling? Penny for your thoughts?'

He turned about and smiled at her in such a way that Ned lowered his right hand towards his holstered Colt.

In the barrel, four bullets remained. One had been accounted for by a little demonstration of sharpshooting that Belle had required on their arrival at the river, another by the shooting of a rattlesnake that morning. It had caused Arthur's horse to rear. Accordingly, you'd have thought thanks were in order. But Arthur had merely said, 'Yes, do keep an eye out, Ned', as if the spotting and killing of the creature had been the very least thing Ned could have done.

Arthur turned away from the river and walked towards his wife. He sat down on the rock beside her. It was big enough for two, but no more than two. Ned stood at about twenty yards' distance from them, but he might have been a mile away for all the attention the all-of-a-sudden happy couple paid to him.

Arthur said, 'I was just thinking of some lines of verse.'

Ned's hand settled on the handle of the Colt.

A faraway expression came into Arthur's eyes. He began to slowly orate:

The river water carries light
And so it takes the days away
It rolls them down into the sea
Where memories churn
Eternally

Arthur continued to look into the distance, or at any rate the orange rock wall opposite, heedless of his wife's apparently loving gaze.

'But that's absolutely beautiful, Arthur. Who wrote those lines?'

'Nobody's written them down as yet.'

'You mean . . . they're yours?'

He nodded, and Ned was surprised – not that Arthur had come up with that bunkum, but that he had admitted to having done so. Ned knew what to expect now. Another instalment of the double-game. Belle reached out and turned her husband's face towards her. She kissed him fully on the lips, and as she drew away, she flashed the flickering smile Ned's way, so as to suggest what? That this was all a joke? That her real affection was for Ned? That it would be his turn next to be properly kissed, as against the kisses on the cheek (which had become progressively more lingering) she would bestow in hotel lobbies, before the three turned – the married pair to their double room, Ned to his single – after another day's drifting?

Ned's trigger finger was now engaged. He saw how convenient the river might be. Here, in the narrows of the Zion Canyon, he realized the time had come.

*

The eagle responded minimally to the three shots, lifting itself a little higher into the reddening sky, but it never stopped observing. It would have seen the young man shooting and killing the older man with a single bullet. It would have seen the young man doing the same to the woman. And when the woman was dead – and even though she was dead – the eagle saw the man shoot her again, which must surely have seemed a great waste of energy and time to the eagle, a creature for whom a kill is a quick, clean thing, and when it's done, it's done. The eagle must have been equally puzzled, and possibly disgusted, by the sight it next beheld: that of the young man sitting on a rock for a long time, his head in his hands.

*

Presently, Ned Keach stirred himself to the act of dragging the Dude over the bluff and into the water; he did the same with Belle. He tried to tell himself that he had put the second bullet into her for a considered and practical reason: to make it look as though somebody other than a skilled shootist – in particular, Arthur – had been responsible for her killing. But he knew it had been done from pure rage, all of which had now faded away. Ned Keach loosed and unsaddled their two horses and sent them away with shouts. The third horse (his own), Ned Keach mounted.

But he did not ride away, for the simple reason that he didn't know where to go. The hotel at Springdale was out. He and Belle and Arthur were checked into there for one further night. Then again, perhaps it would be a clever play to return there alone, cheerfully asking after his companions.

But even pretending to be cheerful was way beyond Ned Keach, and he recalled that Belle had told the desk clerk where they were headed that morning. The sheriff and his men would be here in the Zion Valley in a matter of hours. The bodies would not float far; they would have been located and lassoed by this time tomorrow. Ned climbed down from his horse and walked over to the rock where Belle had sat. He saw blood on the rock, a little residue of whisky in the upended cup, and he thought of the time, in the hotel before last, when she was sipping whisky on the porch an hour before supper. Then as now the slanting rays of the sun had made the sky red, the world an infernal place. For once, she had not been in a talking humour. 'Is something wrong?' Ned had said.

'Of course it is.'

He ought then to have caught her up in his arms and taken her away, or at least attempted to do so. Matters between them would have been resolved one way or another. But he hadn't dared; he was not even half a man. Ned Keach climbed down from his horse and sent the animal away. He took out his revolver in order to make what he considered the best possible use of the last bullet.

*

The eagle circled indifferently above the body of Ned Keach. It had no use for human remains, and the entertainment seemed to be concluded. The eagle quit the Zion Valley some five minutes later, its mind, we might assume, having already turned to more important things.

Jim put the story back in the envelope. It was a confession of sorts to the double murder, and meant to be traceable to Durrant, albeit by a roundabout route. The manner of the confession accorded with Durrant's romantic temperament – and Jim was a romantic too, which is why he had wanted to believe the Code of the West would have prevented Durrant from killing Cynthia Lorne. Jim had not, after all, learnt the lesson of the war. Besides being a romantic, Durrant was also imaginative and, having been encouraged by Jim to think he might beat the charge, he had dreamed up the story of the Strid jump. But Durrant must have known all along it was hopeless, and of course the 'confession' in Jim's hands was always going to come to light and would surely be seen for what it was.

Jim and Lydia began walking towards the Police Office. Beyond the end of the station, in the direction of 'up', Jim saw a long train heading 'down'. It was drawn by a Pacific-type locomotive coming on like a giant bullet and with such violence in its momentum that it was hard to believe that people in the carriages would have been taking anything as genteel as 'luncheon'. But this was the London-to-Edinburgh Restaurant Car Express, and the people inside were insulated from the rain or snow, and life in general. The Express would have called at Doncaster about twenty-five minutes beforehand, but was not scheduled to stop at York ... for which York would have its revenge, by directing it away from the main station canopy, and as Jim looked on, the train was swerving to the left.

He was running up the footbridge steps, over the bridge, down the other side. His right leg hurt, and he could barely breathe when he came to Platform 14, where the Express went roaring by, showing Jim a flickering film of repeated dining car scenes; and then the brake was applied with a kind of bang, and the engine was no longer pulling the train; instead the train was pushing the engine, which was moving even though its wheels were not, and they were screaming out their protest. Soon there began to be human screams as well, because for once there were other people on Platform 14 as well as the Chief, and some of them were women. The Chief himself was walking quite slowly in the direction of the engine, which had stopped a little way beyond the end of the platform.

Lydia had caught up with Jim and, as the platform began to be crowded with officials, he told her what had happened. Some Permanent Way men were looking under the train, and with real urgency, as if expecting to find Durrant alive down there. The Chief was saying the same thing over and over to anyone who asked: 'I was taking him to the waiting room for a private conflab. He got away from me for a second, and that's all he needed.' To Jim, he spoke at slightly greater length, albeit not looking him directly in the face: 'It's hard on the driver, but he was doing the boy a favour. It was all over in a flash. He didn't want to live with himself after what he'd done – not even for the few weeks he'd have left before he swung.' And that was another confession, really. The Chief would have worked out, from the timetable he'd consulted at Malton, roughly when the Express would be going by York. You could make the calculation from the Doncaster departure time. On Platform 14, he'd have said to Durrant, 'I don't believe your story', and then indicated the onrushing train. The plan must have been in the Chief's mind all along. It was what he'd meant when he'd promised at the mines to help Durrant.

The Chief was walking away again, lighting one of his cigars. Lydia was nearby. Jim said, 'I'm off for a pint of brown ale in the Parlour Bar. As a matter of fact, I'll probably have two.'

'You do that, Jim,' she said.

THE END

Acknowledgements

For the purposes of the story, I have adjusted some historical facts. For example, the iron mines at Rosedale weren't closed until 1929. I have also simplified the administrative structure of the LNER police. For giving me the *correct* facts on the LNER police I am grateful to Steve Beamon of the British Transport Police history group, and for the true history of the mines I am grateful to Malcolm Bisby and the Land of Iron project. I would like to thank David Cormack for information about how a car might have been stolen in the 1920s, and Matthew Neill, of the National Fairground Archive at Sheffield University, for facilitating my visit to the Archive, where I read about the travelling fairs of the inter-war period, which often included Wild West acts. Thanks also to Mark Mason, author of *Mail Obsession*, for information about London postcodes. Lastly, I am grateful to the North Yorkshire Moors Railway for giving me a free ticket to ride on their beautiful line, referred to in this book as 'the Whitby branch'.

Andrew Martin